HAMMERED IN IRON

BOOK THREE OF CRAFTING HUMANITY

For Meghan and Denis

PART I

Chapter 1

Starless skies added depth to the inky black air. Crickets and birds rustled in the trees while animals moved swiftly through the darkness finding their way using instinct rather than sight.

A branch shifted, unnoticeable to the human eye, but enough for James's sensors to detect in the opaque stillness. James crouched closer to the ground. His knees tensed while he waited.

Four.

Three.

Two.

One.

"Down." Deck's voice crackled over his earpiece.

James responded by lifting a thumb in the air, knowing Deck would see it with his night vision.

Night's blanket, along with the pines and leafy deciduous trees, hid him as James walked over the forest ground. A layer of dense pine needles was underfoot, and the scent of dried sap clung to the air. If it had been any other night James would have taken the time to enjoy his surroundings, watch his breath in the dark cool air and relax.

But it was not any other night. It was another night in the woods where his actions would shape the future.

Focus, James thought, shaking his head and pushing the sweet thoughts of a fall without war from his mind. *Time for that some other day.*

Within minutes he was perched with full visibility of the camp. He caught sight of Kevin, a hundred and fifty yards away in his position signing at James:

Jon and Deck in position. Sentinels housed. Four minutes with cover.

Four minutes felt like a lifetime at this point. James took a deep breath and went over the motions in his head. His job was to take out the guards on the north and west sides of the camp. Jon and Kevin would follow to clear the middle while Deck took care of the south and east boundaries.

Simple.

James took a final deep breath and, before he could back out, started his move. In stride, James swiped the dial on the watch hidden under his wrist, setting his timer. They were on the clock.

Four guards with goggles on their foreheads wandered the grounds, keeping half an eye on the darkness. One walked towards the tree line near James who slipped behind a knobbed trunk and waited. His hand dipped to the ion knife sheathed on his belt. He thumbed the worn switch that would send a charge coursing through the weapon while he took deep breaths, controlling his heartbeat. The sound of a zipper being pulled down was followed by a splatter of liquid.

The guard hummed while he relieved himself against a pine tree. James ran his ion knife swiftly under the man's chin. He held the guard's mouth shut, avoiding the teeth hidden by the prickly beard that scratched his palm. The body went slack. James laid the dead guard against the tree, wiped the blade on his pant leg, and returned the weapon to its place on his hip. With a glance at the other guards to ensure a safe approach James sprinted to the camp and posted behind an outcrop of shrubs.

Two of the remaining guards bunched together on the far side of the encampment talking and chuckling in voices too low for James to understand.

Placing the lone guard by the northwest pole in his sights, he timed his shots with their laughter. Two in the chest. One in the head.

Speed was of the essence as James left his cover and dispatched the other two guards while they were still distracted.

"Halfway down the hill," Kevin's voice floated through his earpiece.

"North side cleared," James replied. "Headed west."

"East side cleared. Headed south," Deck announced.

Right on time, James thought exchanging his magazine and reentering the shadows of the compound's lights.

The five guards on the west side had more discipline. They were spread across the defensive front, keeping a keen eye on the horizon. James waited ten seconds deciding on his angle of attack before making his move. He stole silently behind the men, slipping along the edge of camp. James waited patiently in the darkness for his opportunity.

It came. Three heads turned in one direction, and with two quick shots, the first guards were down.

The third's head burst into a display of liquid illuminated by the halogen lights while the fourth turned to make a noise. James stifled the alarm by lodging a bullet in the man's frontal lobe. The fifth and final guard knew what was happening. James watched as the man's arm went up and panicked at the thought of an alerted camp—sirens screaming, floodlights glaring, and a swarm of battle-ready Sentinels flowing from their holding cells waiting to be unleashed. Familiar nightmares of a clandestine attack. Instead, black liquid pooled in the guard's mouth, and he fell forward as Kevin's knife glinted in the dim overhead lights while he wiped the blade on his sleeve.

James nodded at his friend. *Too close.*

James's heartbeat returned to normal, and they made their way further into the camp.

Jon and Kevin floated past James in the darkness towards their mark. Deck emerged from the shadows pointing in the direction of his and James's target. They walked, listening intently for the peppering sound of silenced gunfire over the hum of batteries and thermal extractors purring outside tents. They found the tent they needed and, after a sweep with their sensors, entered through the flaps.

Racks of Sentinels stood in long rows. Extractors pulled from a source deep under the Earth's crust to power the weapons, and humid air from the heated steel was captured in the dense canvas room.

James inspected the walls, shaking his head. The magnitude of violence he had witnessed these devices create and the number of friends he had lost to such simple-looking machines was absurd. But Sentinels were the one thing the BZ could count on more than anything: perfect implements of war.

Mostly perfect, James thought, glad to strike back when he could. They had been lucky to catch a camp on the move. More established camps always kept a few of their pets floating around the boundaries. The power load for one Sentinel could charge an entire camp for weeks, and unless they were traveling with full battery complements, it was impossible for the BZ to keep the Sentinels running in transit. *All the better for us*, James reasoned, looking at the soft glow emitting from the racks.

A tap on his shoulder told him Deck's job was complete, and they exited the way they had entered, fastening the tent as they left.

The two made their way in silence to the meeting point. James checked the timer on his watch.

Thirty seconds to go.

He counted breaths waiting for Jon and Kevin.

Ten, breathe in, nine, breathe out, eight, breathe in, seven, breathe out. Two shadowy figures skulked around the edge of the building, and James stopped his count.

Kevin's thumbs-up told him everything he needed to know. With a final glance around their surroundings, the team retreated with Kevin and Jon following Deck through the tents in a quick, but controlled gait. James covered their rear, counting his breaths.

He let out a whoosh of air when they reached the tree line. They made their way into the forest, blending in with the night, becoming invisible again.

Regardless of the years and number of times he had gone on these missions, James's mind always spun to the worst possible scenarios, imagining hordes of Sentinels swooping in on them, always having to convince himself everything was fine. He looked at his watch.

+3:30

He tapped Kevin on the shoulder who tapped Deck.

Deck nodded and turned uphill. They continued west, traveling deep into the dense pine forest. James kept an eye on his watch until they reached +10:00.

James stopped the team with another tap on Kevin's shoulder, and they turned to look onto a blank abyss over a sheer cliff rising dramatically from nothing.

The team was silent. Jon handed James an emitter and a HOLO screen popped up illuminating his camouflage-streaked face in its soft blue glow.

Fourteen minutes ago, the forest had been a blanket of comfort. Hiding them from the dangers of an enemy sleeping at the base of the mountain, unaware of the recent dose of lethal force delivered in the span of four minutes. Unaware of the charges set in the Sentinel operators' tent. Unaware of the explosives tucked around and underneath the tents of their barracks. Unaware their lives hinged on the tap of a finger and numerals counting down on a digital clock.

James searched the darkness, unable to discern the camp he was about to incinerate, only able to sense its existence. He tapped the screen without a second thought. The long strands of hair hanging across his forehead swept back as the blast tore through the air.

Fire burned in the distance sending black columns of smoke into the air. Animals in the area fled for cover as the explosion destroyed their lives of peace and solitude.

James watched with an unwavering sense of calm. He knew what this was. He had been doing these things for too long to ignore it. This was war.

Chapter 2

Fingers of terror circled his eyes brushing jagged nails across his skin. His breath quickened and he found himself in a jungle clearing. Dozens of bodies lay scattered across the ground, their blood-soaked wounds glistened in the sunlight. Their arms and legs were splayed unnaturally, twisted and torn.

James's body moved as if pulled by an invisible mechanism, inspecting each one. Wounds to the faces, necks, and bodies. Eyes open. Lips parted in a whisper.

His stomach recoiled, and he was on his knees staring at the ground, his hands gripping the dirt, begging the moment to stop. He was underground in a cavern. His breath left him in waves, ebbing and flowing without control. He gasped for air when it escaped him and clung to the wind when it rushed back into his lungs.

Panic swelled. It became tangible. Solid. Eternal.

Darkness and heavy breathing greeted him. James pawed at his chest heaving with exhausted fear.

He stared at the roof of his tent, raw anxiety gnawed at his stomach. He hoped he wouldn't revisit his tortured dreams the next time his body let him sleep.

Hours later, James knelt alongside a trickling stream as he splashed cold water on his face and the nape of his neck, sending a bitter chill down his forearms. Goosebumps prickled his skin while he dried his face, and he draped the towel over his shoulder.

Spreading his arms out, he stood and looked at the spotless sky. An azure backdrop broken by the speck of an odd bird greeted him. Fresh mountain air, tainted by a hint of woodsmoke, filled his lungs with a pine scent.

"Any more biscuits left?" Deck inquired, breaking James's momentary solitude.

"Last one," Kevin replied.

"Gracias, mi amor," Deck replied.

James turned to the camp where Deck munched on the last of the biscuits while Kevin stirred the fire with a stick, poking at the remaining embers under a cast iron skillet suspended by wire above the heated rocks.

"I can't wait for a real oven again," the large chef grumbled. "These sausages would take half as long and taste twice as good if I could finish them the right way. Not to mention how much better I could make the biscuits."

Deck flipped an ion knife in his free hand alternating the power on and off with each toss.

"You know what they say, Kev, a poor carpenter blames his tools," Deck chided between bites. "But if these are the last of the biscuits, I've gotta agree. What're you seeing over there, Jon? Can we head back to Doll and my lady yet?"

"I think that was the last of them," Jon replied. Their techy sat on the hard dirt ground leaning against a tree examining a 3D map hovering in the air. He manipulated the vast swath of land nimbly with his fingertips inspecting every angle. In a separate box, a set of coordinates hung loosely in a list with two columns of seven paired latitudes and longitudes. Most had strikethroughs with two pairs boxed and one circled.

Jon dragged the circled set to the map, placing it in a spot designated with a star. "I'm about done here, needed to show the work buuut…" Jon released the title of the circled set of coordinates and the screen changed, actively flipping the coordinates to strikethroughs.

"Got it!"

James let out a sigh. *Finally*.

"You sure? I really need to get back," Deck asked, standing and walking closer to Jon to peer over his shoulder. "I have a lady to see if you catch my drift." Deck nudged Jon on the shoulder, who ignored the hint, but flicked the ionic blade's power off.

"We all know what you're talking about, and I don't understand Cristina for putting up with you in the first place. Also, I'd like to go back to NOLA with two ears intact, so watch the knife. But that's beside the point. These last coordinates and the ones that I erased were all at the same place and tied to the camp we took last night. I thought it was weird when they sent us the extra coordinates, so I backtracked them and found they all originated from the same camp. Somehow the sats must have picked them up as separate groups. Either way, we're done, gentleman."

"Fuck yes! Jon, I could kiss you." Deck slapped the curly-haired tech master on the back.

"Please don't."

"Okay, fine. I'll buy you a drink!"

"I own the same bar you do."

"Well, how the hell can I pay you back?"

"Just get us home."

"Right! Can you rig me up a map there, Jonny boy?"

"Always me," Jon grumbled, pulling up a new 3D display for their scout.

James grinned. He was as excited as Deck. The four of them had been isolated in the field for three months chasing five different Sentinel camps. It was stressful and they needed to get back home. Deck clearly missed his wife, Jon probably missed Rich, Kevin needed a good oven to make him happy, and James wanted to confirm the rest of the team had returned from their trip.

"You're sure, Jon?" James asked optimistically walking over to take a closer look. They had to be one hundred percent positive. No mistakes. Otherwise, the next group leaving HQ would get torn to pieces because of their error. James pushed the visions of limbless torsos and gore-drenched body parts from his mind. The BZ's violence knew no bounds. *Neither does ours*, he thought grimly, as the harsh scent of oily smoke assaulted his senses for a brief second.

"I'm sure. These three groups moved to the same coordinates through the valley here," Jon pointed between the mountain ridges on the eastern edge of the map, "They came inland and made a break north."

North? Too many of the Sentinel camps and raider teams were headed north. It made him nervous about the rest of the team traveling back to NOLA. *They'll be fine*, James rationalized. *Stacie's got it under control, and they're pure recon. We're on the more dangerous missions here.*

As if reading his mind, Kevin clapped him on the shoulder. "Don't sweat it, man. They're fine."

"All right, enough of this, what's the word boss man?" Deck asked. His eyes pleaded and James took a glance at the other two team members. The sentiment was palpable, they needed a break.

"Let's head home."

"Thank God!" Deck exclaimed. "I'll get the truck. Back in a few."

Deck threw his water on the fire and left without waiting for a reply.

"He's a unique boy, isn't he?" James said. The stones in the fire hissed as their scout walked away and hopped in the air, clicking his heels together.

"That must be what Cristina thinks, too," Jon replied.

"Poor girl," Kevin said, taking a deep swig of water.

An hour later James drove down the mountain, crossed a final stream at the bottom, and was on the road.

Jon had installed live-action radar on their truck that confirmed no Sentinels were in the area. They had learned that lesson the hard way, James thought, recalling unpleasant memories of testing the truck's radar system in the wild for the first time. A mass of Sentinels pouring from the edge of a nearby woods flashed across James's mind, and he gritted his teeth to rid himself of the vision.

"Hey, boss, mind if I get some shut-eye?" Deck asked. His bucket hat was already pulled over his eyes.

"Go for it."

"That sounds good," Jon added, leaning back in the passenger seat.

"Kevin gave me the idea," Deck chimed in. James glanced in the rearview mirror and saw their explosives expert fast asleep with his head against the window.

"I've got this trip. You all get some rest."

Silent agreement answered James, and he settled in for a long drive.

He followed the pine bordered roads along the mountain high above long flat valleys where trees blazed in the early fall.

Battle strategy had changed since the beginning of the war. Missions were standardized now. Dolly and the rest of NOLA HQ identified the Sentinel outfits traveling anywhere in the country and James led the elimination team. They had done the job often over the last few years.

Midway, Lima, Rio, San Diego, Portland, LA, Seattle—the list of cities that had experienced the early wrath of the BZ ships preying on the coastal towns went on and on. Fire and brimstone attacks resulted in total annihilation and millions dead within hours. Cities transformed into husks of charred concrete and lakes of molten steel.

The motherships, as Deck named them, remained as a constant presence skirting the coasts like man-powered mountains waiting for their next target. They followed a rotation, but no one had figured out the rationale yet, not even Jon and Stacie. No one could get close enough to try. The BZ had built its strongholds in the Northern Federation along the West Coast with the ships reinforcing their bases and anchoring solely in the Pacific. The invaders continuously expanded their reach in the Southern Federation, spreading like weeds across the continent. Unfettered growth and zero resistance allowed the BZ to dominate the land,

and after almost nine years of war, they were the lone power in the former Southern Federation.

Since their first attempt at taking the East Coast in the Northern Federation, the BZ had never tried again. Their failure at Midway focused their attacks on the West. Besides, James was sure the BZ understood that the motherships would have been useless there. Populations had fled the coast for inland fortresses leaving only outposts and small villages tangentially connected to NOLA and the Federation as coastal centers. The formerly peaceful gulf wasn't an option either. Federation militia filled the basin with an underwater minefield, a cauldron of high-powered explosives. Not even a fission-powered ship the size of a small city would attempt to enter its waters.

James thought back to the early years of the war. Their training, Midway, the trip to the Southern Federation, his brief imprisonment with the BZ, and eventually fleeing north with dozens of refugees from Rio Negro. They had spent weeks driving through fog shrouded mountains, untamed jungles, ghost cities, and arid deserts in a mad race north. James recalled their confusion while they watched the BZ stagnate in the Southern Federation after the Federation's drone attack. He remembered panicked thoughts of a BZ mothership floating out of the gulf and lighting up the southern border where his team and the people from Rio Negro had settled, but it never happened. The BZ never attempted to chase them. They waited. The dreaded attack never materialized.

Instead, the BZ propagated across the southern continent in the same fashion as they had Africa, building a military behemoth and global powerhouse over the diverse terrain. The BZ had taken the smart, slow approach again. They rebuilt and terraformed their newly acquired land to meet their needs. Their takeover was no longer a bombastic power drive, but rather a calculated, cold, and steady undertaking.

The BZ probed their way into the Federation. Cautious compared to their original attacks. Cities were struck with precision by groups of death squads exterminating entire populations without hesitation. This was not a war of POWs, but one of cleansing. The BZ used its mass-produced army to wage the second phase of the war. Eradicate what was left of the Federation.

The Federation military was a decentralized mess. After relocating to Chicago as their home base, they were doing all they could to keep themselves together. Cities fell in mere days, extinguished by hordes of BZ soldiers with ease. It was the thing of nightmares.

For years the outlook appeared hopeless. Sentinels grew in number and were used by the BZ with alarming frequency. James, the team, and anyone who joined them fought a losing battle.

Finally, an answer came. Jon and Stacie had picked up a signal over an open HOLO network from Dolly, a former member of Brandt's command. She wanted them to join her group, called NOLA, based in New Orleans where she had consolidated troops. Without blinking an eye, the team made their decision and were there within days.

Ex-Federation, former elite training members, new sign-ups, and anyone who needed a home could find it with Dolly in New Orleans. James had been surprised to learn NOLA stood for nothing. Dolly had liked the idea of using the city's name as the symbol of their rebellion.

Another positive break came after three years of hacking the data packet. Stacie, Jon, and the rest of NOLA's brightest deciphered a chunk of the intel they found in the Southern Federation. Defensive strategies, new tech, and an implied history of the BZ revealed itself layer by layer. Thousands of terabytes remained locked and hidden away on the storied drive, and each step proved more elusive than the last. But what they had was enough. Tides started to turn.

That was over five years ago. With NOLA's support, James and the team carried out the missions he had envisioned when they left Rio Negro. Cities and towns in need of assistance requested help from NOLA. James, his team, and all the NOLA operatives crisscrossed the land on missions to stop BZ raider groups who threatened population centers. Their methods were clinically lethal and services crucial to keeping a semblance of the Federation alive. However, over the last several months fewer and fewer cities called for assistance. The occasional BZ group might be spotted doing recon or James and his team would be alerted to Sentinel forces in the area, but for the most part, it was silent.

That worried James. One tactic the BZ had perfected was the ability to remain quiet while meticulously organizing behind the scenes. The largest army ever assembled would not stop and give up after decades of planning and purposeful decision-making when they were on the edge of victory. No, they were silent for a reason. It was only a matter of time until the BZ made their move. James hoped they could discover what it was long before they did.

James shook his head when a snore from the backseat disrupted his memories.

Lowering the window, he let fresh air into their stale quarters. Open fields with rich green grass became more abundant as James descended the mountains. He breathed in the thickening air, enjoying the dry, rich scent as he drove under golden-hued trees dropping early leaves to the ground. Fall in the South. Green was still the dominant color, but the changing of the seasons was clear. Normally his trips were marred with images of displeasure, death, and gore, but at least he was headed home.

Already took care of the first part, he thought nudging the flames climbing against the dark backdrop to the back of his mind.

He always imagined the terrified screams of the men and women in their tents realizing too late what was happening. Explosions outside their doors shook the ground, and other people in their barracks mouthed mutely in the darkness. Confusion reigned supreme. Then, sudden awareness as the earth shattered and their bodies tore apart, flinging into the sky. That delay. That moment between the target's explosion and the barracks was James's idea. He wanted them to understand what was happening. He wanted their final thought to be a realization.

A *beep* came from the dash. James launched the HOLO screen with the slip of a finger and tapped a pulsing red icon glowing on the map. He was directed to a new screen and the image of a flashing drone appeared. Air activity this far east was usually the Federation or a NOLA recon group, but he did not want to take any chances. The possibility of it being a BZ drone was not a risk he could afford. James punched a request into the map.

The system took a moment to respond before it directed him to a nearby overpass where he could take cover and wait. Five minutes later he pulled under a concrete overhang watching the skies.

The blue backdrop seemed so serene and peaceful, but possibly up there somewhere sat a machine capable of disintegrating James, their truck, and the whole structure in seconds. James watched the HOLO map patiently, counting his heartbeats as the drone neared.

Finally, it arrived. James slipped out the driver's side door taking Deck's tactical binoculars. He doubted NOLA had sent the drone. *Dolly would have contacted us*, James thought putting the binoculars to his eyes. Also, their sensor would have picked it up as a known craft.

He scanned the horizon, looking in the direction the map indicated, searching for the mysterious aircraft to come over the tops of the mountains. James kept waiting. The binoculars grew sweaty against his eye sockets in the early afternoon heat and a bead of salty liquid stung his eyes. He was about to chalk the alert up to a system malfunction when he saw three drones trailed by a massive structure that blocked his view. James zoomed out until he could see the entire object overhead. It wasn't a drone. It was a transport ship. James scanned its sides and bottom, looking for an indication of its allegiance.

Who the hell owns this thing? James wondered. The BZ shot anything that did not belong to them. So would NOLA if they could, but this was too far away from the HQ for NOLA to do much about. The Federation was quite a distance away, too—at least a hundred miles north—and this did not resemble their equipment. Not to James, at any rate. The design, size, and brazenness reeked of the BZ.

Why are they sending transports north? And to where? James kept his eyes on the massive plane casting a shadow across the ground as it sailed through the sky.

Three drones flanked it on each side. *Heavy defenses*, he thought, musing over the ship's cargo. He was trying to wrap his mind around the BZ's plans when he felt a tap on his shoulder.

"Can I see?" Kevin's laconic voice echoed in the background, and James handed him the binoculars without letting the moving behemoth leave his sight.

"Flying pretty low for something that big," Kevin mentioned.

"Trying to stay under the radar, I'm guessing."

"Makes sense. Must be the first flight over land in years."

James nodded. His mind was still running in circles.

"What'd we stop for?" Jon yelled from the passenger side.

"Transport plane," Kevin replied, pointing at the sky.

"Transport plane? No way." Jon's cocky self-assurance was wiped away when he took the binoculars from Kevin's outstretched hand.

"What the fuck? What the hell is going on?"

"I've got the same questions," James replied. He returned to the truck, piecing the scene together in his mind. A BZ transport ship flying under the radar heading northeast up the coastline. It was avoiding any known Federation and NOLA outposts spread throughout the tenuously free countryside. *But where was it headed?*

James entered the driver's seat and closed the door with a *bang*. He pulled up the HOLO map. Deck woke and stretched his arms, taking a deep breath in the cramped quarters.

"Where are we?" he grumbled, peeking at the dank underpass. "This is not New Orleans, James."

"Just got out of the mountains," James replied, pecking at the screen while he worked to plot the aircraft's route.

"Oh, great, so it's only been a few hours. Now I'll never sleep," Deck mumbled in the back seat while James expanded his view. He needed to know where the plane was headed. That transport must be carrying at least a thousand troops. While the four of them had been focused on hunting Sentinel camps they had not had their radar operational. No telling how many of those had flown overhead during the last few days. The familiar sensation of battle readiness flowed through James's veins.

"Where the hell are my binoculars? Did I leave them back in camp? I could've sw—"

"Jon has them."

"And why, pray tell, does Jon have my goddamn binoculars?" Deck asked, affronted. "People taking my crap while I'm napping. Not right. I don't take his stupid HOLOs."

"Morning, Deck." Kevin's voice entered the tight space, followed seconds later by Jon, and both doors closing.

"Jon! Why'd you take my binoculars?"

"I didn't take 'em. James did."

"What?! Why do all of you have my binoculars? What is going on here?"

"We were looking at the transport ship. Chill, man."

"Transport ship? What transport ship?"

"The one that just flew overhead."

"I…what…I…" Deck stammered, confused and exasperated. James ignored him and pulled the HOLO map into the center of the truck for everyone to see.

"Here." James indicated a point at the top of the map off the coast of New Brunswick and ran his finger down the screen tracing a line to their current position. "That's where the ship is headed, and that's the route it's taking."

Jon and Kevin nodded silently while Deck looked lost and eyed the three serious faces.

"I'll work on finding landing zones in the area. See what NOLA resources we have there," Kevin said, taking out his HOLO emitter.

"I'll catalog the ship. Maybe we've shot down one of these and can get info on what they could be carrying." Jon put the binoculars into a helpless-looking Deck's hands. The techy took control of the car's HOLO and hooked them into the network.

"Good, I'll get us back home. Hopefully, Stacie and the team learned something about this on their trip."

James started the vehicle while Jon and Kevin diligently plugged into their HOLOs.

They pulled from the overhang to a sky clear of aircraft confirming the "all clear" message on the alert system.

"I guess I'll sit here with my thumb up my ass and wait for everyone to do their jobs."

"Sounds good. Wash your hands when you open the door," Kevin retorted.

James stifled a laugh while he listened to Deck grumble in the backseat. It was time to get back to NOLA. James hoped Stacie had some answers to the questions mounting in his head.

Chapter 3

Humid air entered through the truck's open windows as James and his team drove across the bridge into the city. The lake's mist washed over them, and James tasted the salt-tinged air. Egrets, seagulls, and terns floated in the estuary or sailed through the sky unaware of the military fortress hidden in the world around them.

The city rose modestly from across the water. To the naked eye, the roads leading into New Orleans appeared as would be expected by someone traveling through a military base during wartime. Those who worked in NOLA knew surface observations were not to be trusted. It was the most secure wall-less facility ever created.

There was only one way in and one way out—the causeway. Ion shields ran continually and mazes of unmapped landmines, traversed only with the assistance of NOLA's military tech, blocked all other access points. Already treacherous wetlands leading to the gulf were fortified with a web of trip wires, razor wire, and additional mines planted in the muck. To top it off, heavier artillery sunk into the grasses of the lowlands. Only the ion shields spread through the waterlogged grasslands were turned off to avoid interrupting the natural flow of the ecosystem, but their sensors could flip on at a moment's notice.

Enough C-4 in waterproof containers to pulverize the entire structure in seconds girded the causeway. Each section of the bridge was rigged with individual charges to facilitate capture if someone tried to infiltrate the city. A wealth of floating mines at various depths filled the lakes leading to the city creating impassable waterways.

Obelisk structures towered at various points along the skyline functioning as defensive pillars intended to protect against any major Sentinel attack. They pulled their power from every electric source running in the city. The idea of these fortifications originated from their BZ data packet but had never been verified. It was one test James was fine waiting to try until the real deal occurred. If those were needed, everything else had failed.

Radar sensors covered three-hundred-sixty degrees ensuring constant surveillance. At all times, pressure sensors and light-triggered alarms monitored any object coming close to the city. James knew Dolly and the rest of NOLA HQ were well aware of their arrival as they pulled up to the first set of guards.

"Wrist," a stout guard spoke curtly as he approached the driver's side window holding a scanning device. James held his fist, palm up, through the window.

The guard placed the emitter device on James's wrist and the HOLO wrapped around James's hand with a thin sheen of light encompassing his appendage like a glove. *A little much*, James thought knowing a simple iris scan or fingerprint check would suffice. NOLA used a slew of biomarkers enabled with the new HOLO sheen tech Jon and Bob had helped create. From the little James understood, it was a new way to harness HOLO tech, allowing it to be interoperable with human biology at a deeper level—another data packet inspiration. The HOLO glove pulsed three times and retreated into the emitter.

Removing the device, the guard nodded at James, "You're good to go, sir."

"Thanks," James replied as he pulled his arm back into the truck. The scan was harmless, but reminded him too much of the tech Kyle and he had been tortured with during their imprisonment with the BZ. He liked it way more when the experience was over.

"Welcome back."

James bobbed his head in response and put the car in drive.

"This always takes so goddamn long," Kevin grumbled when they arrived at the second checkpoint.

"Cheer up, bud. Oven's at the end of the rainbow," Deck quipped cheerfully, offering his wrist to the guard outside the window.

James hated the over-indulgent security measures too but understood the rationale. The BZ could easily fool a couple of sensors when entering the base and the Federation had built the rest of the tech NOLA used with some heavy influence from their BZ data packet. The extra precautions were necessary to stop uninvited Federation people from coming down and sabotaging NOLA's operation. It was over the top, in James's opinion, but he was fine going along with the process.

James nodded at the guard who finished the fifth and final scan.

They pulled through the gates to the city. James barely noticed the artillery, pulsing ion shields, towering obelisks, and 24/7 manned military presence. The two sniper scopes trained on him at all times sent a chill up his spine every time he passed the fortress's official limits. Dolly assigned everyone a personal entourage. "Just-in-case details," as Dolly liked to say. Long before entering the city, each person was watched by a pair of snipers set a hundred to five hundred yards from the causeway. *Another overkill move,* James thought, *but she definitely cares.* He passed the point where his assigned watchers were released from duty and let out a breath he hadn't known he was holding.

Any notion of war hardly existed as they drove down the boulevard. Soldiers and military presence were everywhere, but the confidence and calm they exuded was deceiving.

Bakeries, restaurants, bars, bodegas, grocers, delis, drugstores, and liquor stores were unchanged since the fall of the Federation. The tourist-driven economy of the old New Orleans with its mishmash of cultural influences was far different from the current setup with NOLA in charge, but its old charm still rang true. The team waved at friends as they made their way to the converted hotel they called home in the reinvented French Quarter.

James parked in the truck's regular spot and flipped off the ignition. The team disembarked and he stepped onto the blacktop stretching his arms over his head, feeling an urge to pee.

He left his bags and hurried into the building.

Cristina and Rich gave him a half wave as James sprinted through the bar doors towards the bathroom. He lay his forearm against the cool tile wall above the urinal while he relieved himself. *That was close*, he thought imagining the taunting from Deck for the slightest indication of a dribble.

While he washed his hands he enjoyed the little things in life for a moment, the steamy environment outside and the crisp cool air when he walked indoors, the marble-cut sink, and the lavender hand soap. Rust-colored grime and dirt dripped into the pristine white bowl as he splashed water on his face.

He admired the bathroom through its reflection in the mirror. The hotel had been a lucky find when they arrived to join NOLA. After the Federation laid its minefield in the gulf, they had used the city as a primary outpost. Ironically, to save this part of the Federation, they had precipitated its fall. Residents pushed back on the draconian measures put in place to protect the area, and the city fell into a power struggle between organized crime groups and the Federation.

When James and the team arrived, Dolly had finished wrestling the city into some semblance of societal order, but from a visual perspective it was a mess. Entire neighborhoods were unlivable due to the city's internal struggles. They were told to shack up wherever they could find space. Luckily, Deck had a nose for good bars and in his quest stumbled upon a beautiful empty hotel tucked around a maze of courtyards and gardens. It had been abandoned when the residents fled during the turf wars and the former proprietor's lush flora had taken over, but James and the rest of the team recognized the value of the property. None more so than Rich and Cristina who, while the team was away on missions, spent months of back-breaking work transforming the overgrown gardens and tragically destroyed buildings into a livable home.

They designed everything with comfortable privacy in mind. This included eight apartments, one for each team member, leaving the remaining rooms for guests. Cristina and Rich created unique areas for each person. Kevin had a massive kitchen, Stacie and Kyle's space contained a workshop and a room full of HOLOs. Meanwhile, Clint's was attached to an oversized garage for work on modifications to any sort of vehicle. Bob's held an operating room where he practiced medical procedures on HOLOs. His lack of traditional medical training made him very self-conscious, and this feature allowed him to regularly drill, ensuring confidence in any situation. It was fine, but you never knew what to expect if you walked in while he was working. Once, to his dismay, James uneasily witnessed a HOLO simulated childbirth. During the reveals James had been unsure of what he would receive, but was pleasantly surprised by the thought put into his space. On the roof was a widow's walk from where he could watch the city. Whenever he got a chance to relax he would sit carving wooden figurines or survey the activity of the bay at night. It was perfect.

The best part of their renovations though was the bar. Marble had been scrounged from burned-out buildings, looted casinos, and other hotels in the area. The bar itself came from one of the oldest bars in New Orleans's Garden District. Christina and Rich had carried most of it by hand across the city until Dolly noticed them. Next thing they knew a command of NOLA trainees was bringing the remaining pieces through the front door.

Not only did the bar ensure a place for the team to relax and hang out, but it fulfilled the mandatory requirement of having gainful employment to live in the fortress. If you weren't in the NOLA military that was a difficult task, but the bar kept Cristina and Rich plenty busy and therefore employed. The city began to feel like home for everybody, and NOLA grew from there.

James studied the intricate details of the room and settled back into his life. He knew he needed to go see Dolly sooner than later, but for the time being, it was nice being home.

When he walked into the barroom, Cristina and Rich were welcoming their partners while Kevin sat on a barstool helping himself to a bowl of nuts. James slid onto a barstool near Kevin's.

"You guys are back early," Cristina commented when Deck finally released her. The thin black-haired woman gave

James a peck on the cheek, poking him with the stud in her nose as she went behind the bar.

"We're right on time. What do you mean?" Deck asked, taking a stool between James and Kevin.

"Dolly stopped by yesterday. Said you logged the last camp and were still in the mountains. We figured you'd take a couple days to get here," Rich said. He took his place behind the bar and pulled one of the polished wood taps.

"We ran into some things. Needed to get back fast," James replied casually. He kept it short and the resulting silence from the rest of the team meant his message was clear. No one outside of them needed to know anything. Cristina and Rich had been around long enough to know when to stop asking questions. *They'll find out eventually*, James thought, feeling bad for not divulging anything, but knowing he shouldn't.

"Any word from the other travelers?" James asked. He accepted an icy draft from Rich and took a sip of the cold liquid brimming over the top. The beer left a refreshing aftertaste in James's mouth as he placed the glass on the counter.

"Nothing yet. We thought you might run into them when you were out there," Christina said.

"We would have been too far east. They haven't sent anything?" James was concerned. Lack of communication in the field was not uncommon, but it was standard practice to send messages when heading home. Stacie would not just forget. There was always a reason.

"Not that we've heard of. But we're not privy to inside info," Rich said, sliding a beer down the bar to Deck.

"You two know more than half the goddamn city. Now what's happening around here? That thruple still a thing up the block?" Deck asked, "They seem interesting…"

"They broke up, but the single in the group started a new couple group that meets by the casino," Rich answered.

"Marvelous. I don't have the stomach for it, but man that's an interesting life. James, you're a single guy. Could you be into that?"

"I'll let them handle that themselves," James replied. He was uneager to jump into a rotating set of potentially jealous partners.

"What about you, Kev? Or wait, are you single still?"

"Who knows at this point, man?" Kevin took a sip of beer making eye contact with himself in the glass wall providing the bar's backdrop.

"Caitlin and you split up?" Cristina asked, moving down the bar.

"We'll find out soon."

The door swung open and a tall woman with cropped hair and a light, gray jacket walked into the room.

"Dolly! Come on in. Have a beer. Half price!" Deck said, moving over a stool to make room between him and James.

"So kind of you Deck," Dolly said sitting on the stool and giving Deck the finger.

"Good to see you, Dolly," James said.

"You too. Thought you might come see me before you hit the bar strip though."

"Think of it as an opportunity to meet here instead."

"Then a thank-you is in order."

Rich placed a frosted glass in front of Dolly who picked it up and clinked glasses with James.

"Came back in a hurry, I see."

"It was an interesting trip."

Rich and Cristina took their cue to leave. Locks clicked as they exited. Kevin pulled the wooden shutters closed casting the room in a shadow.

Jon took over pouring drinks. He pulled out his HOLO emitter and seconds later a screen popped up showing images of the giant plane with pictures of the drones superimposed around it.

"What's this?" Dolly asked, her face scrunched in thought.

"We ran into this yesterday afternoon. I got an alert that a drone was nearby so took cover under an overpass. Next thing I know a transport ship is flying overhead. Not enough markings to outright confirm, but its size and our lack of intel leads me to think it's BZ. You hear anything on your channels about this?" James asked.

"Not a word. You saw this yesterday? Were there others?"

"Nothing else. We got lucky to find this group. Couldn't keep our radar running the whole time while we were hunting for Sentinel camps," James replied. Jon flipped through close-up images on a separate screen while video footage ran on the original screen. "Nothing from Stacie? That's not like her," James added. Worry edged his voice.

"I know as much as you do, James. Don't worry until you have to okay? They'll be fine."

James nodded. She was right, he couldn't worry about things he had no control over, but he would have felt better with some kind of answer.

"Where do you all think that ship's going?"

"We tracked them along a line off the coast of Nova Scotia, near Stacie's hometown actually," Kevin replied. "We don't have many resources in the area. It's so remote and too close to the waterfront for us to establish a permanent operation."

"What's the closest we have?"

"Almost a hundred miles away. We'd need a brand-new station to do any sort of recon."

"Who runs the one we have?"

"Teresa Perez and Liam Connelly," Jon answered pulling their images up on the parallel screens.

James's ears piqued. *Teresa?* He looked at the picture, the same intense eyes and cocky grin the woman had in person were reflected in her Federation headshot. *Of course she's there*, James thought with a smile. He remembered the tough, headstrong girl he trained alongside in their first camp. She had made it to the last round of eliminations before one of the stunners knocked her out of contention. James had always wondered how he made it when she fell short. She could have been the one in his position. *Maybe she should be*, he thought, realizing she was the one running her own outpost.

Jon and Dolly's voices broke through James's memories of his early training days. "Can we talk with them?" Dolly asked.

"I can get something working," Jon replied, tapping the light-based keyboard.

"Where have they been? What are we working with here? You know how some of these bases are," Deck said, unconvinced.

"They've got some impressive resumes," Dolly said as their listed exploits appeared on the screen beneath their pictures.

"Shit," Deck said scanning the lines of text. "She's done a lot, huh, James?"

James agreed. Both were involved in almost every front-line offensive west of the Rocky Mountains with operations penetrating deep into the edges of the open war zone on the BZ's border. From munitions destruction to assaults on BZ HQs. They had done it all.

"You two know them?" Dolly asked. Her questioning face was matched by the confused expressions of Kevin and Jon.

"She was in our first camp. Poor thing had her heart set on me," Deck replied, waving off the past with his hand.

"She wanted nothing to do with you Deck," James clarified for everyone in the room.

"Well, if I had had more time," Deck said, nudging Kevin, "You know. You get it."

"Sure, buddy," Kevin said, clapping Deck's shoulder consolingly. "Whatever you want to think." He finished massaging his friend's ego and turned to the group. "What's the idea? Make contact with Liam and Teresa, then what? Are we headed there?"

"I think we need to hear more from Stacie and the rest of the team before we make any decisions," James replied. Nods greeted him in response and James looked back to the split screens. The images of the plane, drones, Teresa, Liam, and the various pathways to the potential new outpost rotated through his vision. What kind of intervention was needed here? The road to Liam and Teresa that far north and east was a dangerous mission by itself. The unchartered BZ locations dotting the East Coast made for a tricky pathway with an increased risk of the odd Sentinel camp roaming the countryside searching for Federation targets. Then there was no-man's land, which was an entirely different game. James had no clue what was happening that far north, but recent evidence pointed to a massive movement by the BZ.

"Goddamn, it'd be really helpful if everyone would show up right about now. Clint drives like a lunatic. They should be here, right?" Deck exclaimed. He threw his hands in the air exasperated, staring at the screens with his shoulders slumped.

"Ask and ye shall receive."

A pair of hands closed on Deck's shoulders. James's eyes followed the arms to Clint's grinning face. He looked at the door to see the remainder of the team walking through it.

"Welcome home!" Deck yelled, turning around to hug their muscular engineer.

"What's this about my driving now?"

"Doesn't matter, Clint, all in the past," Deck said, releasing Clint and moving towards the rest of the team.

"Good to see you, man," James said, greeting Clint.

Kevin and Jon joined the team convening in the center of the room reacquainting themselves.

In moments like these James was always reminded of how much they had been through together.. Moments when their distance and time apart washed away with an embrace. That was what made this team work. James found himself surrounded by his friends as if the world didn't exist beyond the polished oak bar holding their drinks.

"Hot damn, first one always tastes the best," Kyle said, downing his beer. Cristina, re-entering to help Rich at the bar, filled another frosted glass and slid it across to Kyle's open hand.

"Next one'll be even better."

Kyle raised his glass in a cheer, and Cristina whipped around to slap Deck's hand from grabbing a bottle of Jameson from the liquor rack.

"Just trying to be helpful!" he said disarmingly.

"I pour the drinks, Deck, you know that. Remember last Christmas?" Cristina asked, laying out a round of shot glasses for everyone in the suddenly loud barroom.

"No, but I guess that's also the point you're making."

"Exactly. Now back off, and let Rich and me handle things."

Kevin walked behind Cristina, pulled a bottle off the shelf, and placed it on the bar as he walked back around to resume his place in the middle of the pack.

"How the hell does Kevin get to do that?" Deck said, annoyed.

"Kevin didn't cause enough mayhem and almost burn the hotel down the last time he was back here."

"One little firecracker was all," Deck mumbled.

"I think the problem was that you did it in the bar…under a Christmas tree pal," James said, hopping off his stool to join the conversation between Dolly and Stacie.

He left a sullen Deck sipping his beer while his wife watched him out of the corner of her eye.

James entered the conversation between Stacie and Dolly midway.

"How many did they bring back?"

"At least two bushels I think," Dolly said, drinking her beer.

"Nice. I mean, disgusting, but nice for someone probably," Stacie replied, tilting her glass back.

"Some people love 'em."

"Some people are idiots."

"Not all of us," James said, breaking in and hoping the conversation was about oysters and not something else he would regret owning later.

"Speaking of bottom feeders…" Stacie gave James a side hug, and he wrapped an arm around her shoulder.

"Good to see you."

"Same, bud. Kev said you all just got back, too."

"That we did. Long time in the field chasing the BZ around. We can tell you more about it later though."

"Yeah, we'll need to catch up," Stacie said, setting down her beer, avoiding eye contact.

"A lot to report?" Dolly asked, working hard to keep from asking more direct questions.

"Enough I think. Like James said, let's talk later. Looks like we have more partiers joining," Stacie said, nodding towards the door. A short woman with straight black hair in a flour-caked apron walked into the bar. She set her eyes on Kevin who turned to face the woman with a sheepish bow.

"You come back in the city and don't bother to say hi to your mother?!" the woman punctuated each of her words with sharp jabs as she stepped towards Kevin who wrapped his arms around her.

"We got home like an hour ago."

"Yeah, an hour? How many beers does that equal?"

"Not enough," Kevin said under his breath, but loud enough for everyone to hear.

The woman hit the oversized chef in the stomach.

"Good thing I have Rich here to keep me up to date on what's happening."

"What the hell, Rich?" Kevin said, whipping his head to Rich accusingly who ignored the large man's intense stare responding to Kevin's mother instead.

"Don't you worry, Violet, I've got you."

"Good man. Now pour a lady a drink."

"On it."

James turned from the scene grinning as a mound of light brown hair entered through the swinging doors.

"Long time, no see, bro," James's sister Caitlin said as she wrapped her arms around him.

"Hey! Who told you we were home?" James asked, returning his sister's embrace.

"Violet shot me a note. I knew you'd all come here first." His sister gave Violet a salute who returned the gesture.

The war had torn James's family apart. During the Northern Assault, a major Sentinel battle left wounds that still lingered, his father had died, and James was sent reeling down a path of grief. The death compounded with past heartbreaks, fueled a darkness inside of him James did not know existed. He went on constant missions, pushing the team and himself to limits testing his moral, ethical, and mental boundaries. They left NOLA, traveling to every corner of the Federation, taking orders from none, and leaving destruction in their wake. To protect James's sanity and that of the team, Bob suggested a different approach. Together, they tried to convince the surviving members of James's family to join him in NOLA's HQ. His mother and brother, Michael, refused, deciding to stay local. They lived in a resettled city, Deerfield where other Northern Assault survivors banded together in a solitary, isolation-driven existence. Mar had been working with the Federation somewhere and never responded, but Caitlin arrived as quickly as she could. Before the fall of the central government, she had gone through basic training with the Federation and fit well in Dolly's office. She was responsible for running strategic operations for missions in the field and was usually the last person James spoke with prior to leaving and one of the first when he returned. He was happy at least one member of his family was nearby, "We have to use our own canaries to find out when people come back into the city."

"You could have known because you work in the HQ office, too," Dolly said with a grin sidling up to Caitlin.

"Yes, I'll admit that helped." Caitlin observed the bar's habitants and James saw her make eye contact with Kevin from across the room.

That's still going on I guess, James thought, remembering Caitlin's casual mention of Violet messaging her.

"James, Stace?" Dolly said, interrupting James's hello, "I'm getting out of here, but can you swing by Thursday? It's going to take some time to go over all your data, but I'll have a good grasp of what's going on by then. Does that work?"

"Works for me," James replied.

"Same. The data we collected was already uploaded. Here's a hard copy." Stacie handed an emitter to Dolly who pocketed it.

Dolly nodded at the two of them and started to leave.

"You need help?" Caitlin asked.

"I've got things covered for now, but don't stay up too late. We've got a lot of work tomorrow. Besides, you have people to see." She nodded in the direction of Kevin. Caitlin lifted a middle finger as her boss walked out the door chuckling to herself.

"You should at least talk to him you know," James said, getting a swift elbow in the gut.

"Fuck. Off."

James grinned and watched his sister break into the crowd.

A rush of warm air came in and two smiling women entered trailed by a few preteens. Mariel, Rosa, and their young entourage carried overflowing bouquets of gardenia and magnolia, their cut stems wrapped in wet newspaper. Cristina and Jon rushed to help them with their fragrant armfuls. James grinned at his grandmother's inability to show up empty-handed.

He headed over to greet them when a hand gripped his shoulder. Deck stood at his side holding an overflowing shot glass. He handed it to James, and they stood, watching Caitlin walk to the bar and brush by Kevin on her way to talk with Rich who was pouring her a cocktail.

"Christ, Kevin knows how to get himself into trouble."

"Sure fucking does," James said, grimacing and rubbing his arm.

"Got an ouchy now, do you?" Deck said mockingly, "This oughta help." Without another word he clinked his glass into James's and downed the shot.

"Miss that burn, but I'll be sorry tomorrow."

James threw back his drink. A familiar warm sensation flooded his chest, and he nodded along with Deck as they made their way through the crowd to the bar.

"God, don't make me regret this already."

Chapter 4

Bulbous clouds sagged in the air. Wind was nowhere to be found, and the last hints of summer lingered. Water dripped from James's beer bottle down the back of his hands and the hazy evening sky glittered in the distance from his perch. Kyle had helped him erect an all-season gazebo on the roof, complete with glass windows to allow air-conditioned comfort when the temperature became unbearable in the swampy town.

For now, the screens were fine. James turned on the solar generator that powered electricity in the small space through his HOLO. The overhead fan's wings beat the air creating a refreshing breeze while the sun sat for its last moments above the horizon. Shadows turned into absent spaces, and in moments, the entire city was a roving maze of blackened alleyways. The noises that normally accompanied the busy streets became muted, and a different crowd replaced the daytime population. He knew he'd have to leave soon, but enjoyed sitting for a moment, as evening morphed into night.

James glanced at the sky, his mind wandering to the gargantuan aircraft they spotted a few days prior. He half expected a plane to fly overhead and imagined for a moment the distinct peal of an air raid siren piercing the night, sending the base into an organized but adrenaline-fueled battle mode.

"Knock, knock."

James, startled, whipped his head around. His hand instinctively reached for the knife on his hip.

Stacie stood outside the gazebo with her hands up.

"Easy! I wanted to walk over together to see Dolly and the gang."

James relaxed and he waved his friend inside.

"Sorry."

"Don't mention it. Comes with the job description."

James snorted.

"How you feeling?" Stacie asked, leaning against one of the gazebo's wooden columns.

James finished the last of his lukewarm beer and shrugged.

"Better now, that's for sure. You?"

"Same. A maniac woke me up yesterday at six to go for a run. 'Sweat out the booze,'" Stacie said miming air quotes. "I mean, I love the guy, but he's a masochist."

James grinned. He had seen them leaving for their run when he was finishing his. Ever since his first stint in training, James had been unable to sleep in no matter the circumstance. Even with a blisteringly painful hangover, he woke up, ran three miles, and showered before falling back to sleep. The pain was worth it when he saw Bob and Deck later that day. James recalled his friends sprawled on the common area couch for hours sipping glasses of water dosed heavily with electrolytes, lamenting their life decisions.

"He's a smart guy, that Kyle."

"You've got a problem, too."

"I guess so. Enough about hangover remedies though. Ready to head over?"

Stacie nodded and led them downstairs. The rest of the team lounged in the bar and waved as they walked outside.

The pair spent the walk to HQ in silence. James kept wondering what the BZ was doing. Sentinel attacks were down, the Federation was quieter than normal, and NOLA received fewer distress calls, yet nothing felt right. James could not pin it down, but sensed the other shoe was about to drop. The BZ's moves had always been deliberate—their attacks on Midway, Lima, and Rio, the building of the base in South America, the siege of the West Coast, the precision attacks on cities, the Northern Assault, Sentinel camps coursing through the country. The BZ did nothing by accident. This unusual calm led to something, but James had no idea what.

Before he knew it, they'd arrived at NOLA's HQ. The sign for the Commander's Palace hung over the door. Dolly's choice of such an aptly named building as her NOLA HQ impressed James. The bright blue paint was peeling, but the lit gas lamps and wraparound awnings gave the impression he was headed out for an enjoyable evening. When he stepped into the foyer, that perception abruptly changed.

HOLO screens hung suspended in every corner of the building and generators buzzed in the background. James had difficulty navigating the strange grid pattern of walkways between tables and desks where NOLA's intel analysts, strategy wonks, and tech gurus moved in a practiced hive of hyperactivity.

Everything ran through the Palace. Since its inception, this had been the scene of every major event in NOLA. From the discovery of the Sentinels' ionic weakness to the absolute latest intel maps, this floor held everything.

The original windows were blocked preventing natural light from entering the hectic room. HOLOs displayed maps, supply chain lines, battle plans, troop deployments, resource allocations, and everything in between. James's mind spun thinking about the terabytes of data flying through the air at light speed to people near and far.

This is my nightmare, he thought, intimidated by the people running the operations.

3D images of weapons, machines, medical apparatuses, and all sorts of devices sprouted from one corner of the room. James caught sight of an ionic bullet model Kevin and Jon were developing for long range Sentinel battles. When he checked his path he realized he had cornered himself amid a jumble of stacked HOLO emitters. He made his way back to Stacie avoiding distractions, following her through the organized clutter was smarter than risk being left. They received little attention as they waded amongst the sea of scrambling workers. Climbing the winding staircase James examined them, their faces buried in maps, staring at HOLO screens, or pacing with earpieces and speaking in calm measured tones, solving one crisis after another.

This job would suck, James told himself as he left the room, again thankful for the times he could work while sitting on his rooftop sipping a beer.

Organized chaos ruled the first floor, but the quiet calm of the second floor was almost more daunting. A quiet force of intellect touched every corner. Glass-walled offices surrounded an open interior of bright wood finishes. Natural light flooded the neat sections of ordered desks. For a fleeting instant the stark contrast blinded James when they reached the top of the stairs. Silent, thoughtful people walked with purpose around the room in a relaxed, but urgent fashion. It reminded James of the old police office or newsroom scenes from movies he had watched with his family growing up. Men in wireframe glasses and women wearing professional attire dominated the setting. The family nostalgia gave him a momentary sense of sadness, but he brushed it off.

No time, man, James thought, chiding himself.

"You're a little late," Caitlin said, grinning as she walked across the open space.

"Did she say that?" James asked, looking at his watch as the time changed from 1714 to 1715.

"No, but if you're not early, you're late. You know how Dolly rolls."

"She's right, you know," Dolly said from the corner of the room. The tall woman with the pixie cut walked over, her face sterner than James would have liked.

"Well, we made it."

"Late…"

"Can we get skip this whole late thing?" James asked, annoyed.

Dolly's face broke into a grin, "I'm messin' with you. Come over and pull up a chair. C's got a lot for us to look at."

James and Stacie moved next to her while Caitlin took center stage. James's sister pulled up the same images Stacie and he had looked at earlier that day as she started to speak.

"I'm guessing you two already saw and discussed this, but in the interest of covering the whole story, let's pretend you didn't. Stacie, James picked up a signal from one of the plane groups heading north that you were tracking. James, Stacie was tracking dozens of those planes in addition to helicopters and transport ships traveling off the coast.

James nodded. He was more interested in seeing what the NOLA team had put together.

"We took your data and compiled it, then we backtracked the paths you created to find their origins."

That would have been smart, James thought, wishing he thought of the idea earlier.

The lights in the room dimmed, transfiguring the wall at the far end into a mass of interconnected HOLO monitors. At once, a bird's eye view of the northern and southern Federation was on display with red, blue, and yellow rectangles covering the landscape. Most of the shapes were located farther north and east, but one blue rectangle straggled farther south.

That's ours, James thought, noticing it intersected their route home.

Long arcs beginning from different parts of the southern Federation passed through each one of the rectangles and ended at a single point north off the coast of New Brunswick. There was a map legend suspended next to the display that Caitlin referred to as she began to talk.

"Each rectangle represents BZ equipment that we're tracking. Blues are airplanes and drone groups, the reds are helicopter teams, and the yellow guys are ships. BZ resources originate from their bases all over the south. The ships are from the Atlantic coast in the Caribbean, planes come from the entire continent, and the choppers are flying from a little farther north. We know fuel and other factors play somewhat of a role, but the point is that everything initiates from the south. We tried to break past their cloaking to get satellite images, but it's an impenetrable dome over the top."

James was glad Jon wasn't there. He'd lose his techie for weeks until he figured out a way to get through.

"What about the landing spot?" Stacie asked.

"Those we have." Caitlin waved her hand, and the view changed.

James stared at a wide bay of gray blue water ringed by a rocky coastline. Behind that, he saw open land sprawling with grass everywhere he looked. It was beautiful, but it didn't make sense. Where was the BZ?

Anticipating his question Dolly held up her hand, "We don't have a live view. The Federation satellites are all down. It's been years since we've been able to do any maintenance, and they're not meant to last forever. Pieces break. We're working on redirecting another sat, but it'll take time."

James ground his teeth in frustration. He dreaded the answer to his next question. He wasn't ready to leave again after three months in the field, aware that this next trip would be God knows how long.

As if sensing his thoughts again, Dolly looked at James.

"We've made contact with Teresa's outpost. They're located too far inland for any seafaring transports, but they've sighted some of the same planes and helicopter groups that your teams saw. We need more information though, James…" Dolly's voice trailed at the end of the sentence.

"Right… When do you want us back out there?" James wanted her to confirm what he had been thinking.

"Three days. With steady progress that gets you outside Deerfield in two weeks."

James's ears perked at the mention of Deerfield and saw his sister glance at him out of the corner of her eye.

"Not much time to rest since our last fieldwork. Latest guidance is at least two weeks, Dolly."

"I know, and I wish I felt it could wait," Dolly said, holding her hands up apologetically. "But let's be real here. A massive amount of BZ vehicles are headed North. The rest of that army has gone quiet everywhere else, with a sister army doing nothing at all.

"We have a problem on our hands, James. We both know it."

The slender woman sat down, lighting a cigarette.

"I can't force you to do anything. You know that's the way it works here." She took a deep pull of air before continuing. "But someone has to take care of this and no one else has your team's experience. Up to you."

Stacie and James made eye contact across the plume of smoke rising between them.

Her look mimicked James's thoughts. They were going.

"What's our supply load?"

Dolly took another drag and nodded to Caitlin who spoke behind them.

"Three vehicles—two Humvees, and a Wrangler. Outfit the Wrangler with a .50 cal for potential support and one of the Humvees with a monitoring apparatus on top. We've requested sightings from our outposts along the road. Our goal is to map out a track for you that avoids any active Sentinels." His sister showed them a series of maps with routes branching from NOLA in a spiderweb. There were too many to count at this point, but he knew Caitlin and Stacie were on it. James was never good at listening to the details, but Stacie was in her element.

"You want us to run radar the whole way up?" Stacie asked, walking over to stand next to Caitlin.

"You got it. This way you can keep an eye on the skies while you roll."

"And what ab—" Stacie and Caitlin continued to plan.

James thought about the trip, the stress already ate away at his stomach. He looked at the screen showing the last six months of Sentinel camp sightings. He was dreading a trip with live radar.

His blood ran cold, and adrenaline pricked his fingertips knowing there were still that many Sentinel raiders out there. It was an odd mixture of exhilaration and terror culminating in pure focus. He knew the sensation well.

"Hey." Dolly nudged his leg and pointed to a chair. "They're gonna be at this for a while. Take a seat."

James accepted her offer and relaxed into a surprisingly comfortable chair.

"They really can go, huh?" Dolly said, admiring the strategists.

"Sure can…" James said and plucked the cigarette from her fingers and took a drag.

Dolly nodded and pulled a second cigarette from her pack.

"Thanks, by the way," she said, watching the strategists.

"Don't mention it."

Dolly and James sat quietly smoking while the women at the front of the room plotted the next moments of the war on glowing HOLOs in a darkening room.

Chapter 5

"Thanks, Violet," James said. He leaned back in his seat, with his stomach bulging.

"Too good, once again," Deck added, taking a long sip of wine and admiring his empty plate. "I mean, you should do this professionally."

"She does, you dumbass," Jon said, shaking his head at him.

"Not like this! This is her home, Jon. Where do you think we are?"

"But she does cook professionally."

"Yes, but you're missing—"

James stopped listening and stood, silently leaving the table. He left the garden and took his plate down the short hallway to the kitchen. After placing the ceramic plate in the sink and washing his hands he poured himself a large glass of water.

Maybe I can pee out the fullness, he thought, hoping the liquid would push the spice and gumbo from his system before they hit the road the next day.

Violet's kitchen resembled a showcase. *No wonder Kevin grew up loving to cook.*

Copper-coated pots and pans hung on hooks suspended from the ceiling. Cabinets of well-organized glassware, ceramic dishes, and culinary odds and ends covered the walls. Plants, used for both cooking and decoration, sprouted about the room and the oven's hood sported an ornamental rooster fashioned from an iron hook.

James loved Violet's kitchen. He always felt at home there.

Bob walked into the room carrying plates from the table, interrupting James's moment of admiration.

"I drew the short straw, but at least I can grab some dessert when I'm in here," he said, putting the dishes in the sink.

"Violet said something about homemade ice cream," James said, nodding at the deep freeze in the corner of the room.

"Good looking out, brother," Bob said as he grabbed a spoon from the drawer. "I'll help myself to some of that then I'll clean up."

"I got the dishes; you eat. I couldn't sit now if I tried."

"You're a saint, James," Bob said. He pried the top off a plastic container and dug his spoon into the frozen treat as he walked back to the garden murmuring as he went.

James flipped on the hot water and plugged the sink while he searched for a sponge.

"You doing dishes?" Caitlin asked, carrying in another stack of plates.

"That's the plan. Need a sponge though."

"On the left over there," she said, pointing at a stainless-steel rack on the windowsill with a sponge and hanging dishtowels.

"Thanks for that," James said, pouring some soap on the sponge.

"No worries. I'll dry."

The two chatted while they washed the dishes. James scrubbed the pots and pans while Caitlin dried and put them away. James was impressed at how well she knew the room, realizing how much time she must spend with Violet.

A steady stream of people came in and out of the room, getting beers, replacement wine, dropping off more plates, or in Bob's case, searching for a box of pastries Violet had brought home from the bakery.

When they finished, the siblings surveyed their work.

The countertop had transformed from a crush of soiled kitchen implements into a pristine, cream- colored granite surface. James ran his hand across its top rubbing his fingers together when he was done. His fingertips squeaked with cleanliness. *Perfect.*

"Ready to hit the road again?" Caitlin asked.

"No. Not our call though."

Caitlin nodded. "Deerfield though, huh?"

James froze. He knew this was coming.

"I know."

"You think they're still there?"

"I hope so."

"Are you going—"

"She wouldn't leave the last time, Caitlin," James interrupted, frustrated. "I can't pressure Mom and Michael to do anything they don't want to do."

"She may say yes this time." Caitlin dug in, ready to make her argument.

"And if she says no? They like it there. It's their home." James was not about to force his mother and younger brother to leave.

"It's the most dangerous part of the Federation. We've got to get them out of there. Dad wou—" Caitlin caught herself.

The two made eye contact and whatever tension had been building melted.

"I don't want to get a message about them is all," Caitlin said, her eyes cast towards the doorway.

"I know." James remembered the day after the attack.

He had been on the road when NOLA HQ pinged him. Caitlin's shaky voice had broken the news of the Northeast falling. City settlements from Philly to Boston had been hit by Sentinel raiders in a mass attack. James, Stacie, and Deck had family in those areas, and were ready to fight, but cooler heads and a stern message from Dolly had prevailed. It would be a legitimate suicide mission for them to attack at that moment.

James and the team spent two days waiting and a third sprinting north with a fresh squadron of Sentinel hunters called in by NOLA. The destruction was horrific. The cities were mass graves, the earth stained by death. Finally, at the tip of Maine, a hundred or so miles south of their current target, they were able to eradicate the Sentinel horde. When the fighting ended, James had learned of his father's death, and for the first time, a cruel anger boiled inside of him.

That was the moment James designed their no-limits approach. It was his expression of pure pain. Grief had run its course, its mantle assumed by vengeance.

Since then, James kept the note his father had given him years ago closer than ever. He knew he would open it one day, but it wasn't time yet. At this point, he wanted his mom and brother in NOLA with him and Caitlin. Mar was a different story that James tended to ignore for the time being. *Damn Federation*, James thought when Caitlin's voice intruded into his thoughts.

"At least mention them coming here." Caitlin wiped a finger under her eye and grabbed a bottle of water from the fridge.

"I will."

Caitlin nodded and headed back to the party her dark hair blending with the night.

James leaned against the counter, tired.

2300. Goddammit, James cursed when he glanced at the oven's digital clock. Tomorrow at noon they would head into a desolate land once brimming with life. Echoes of a lost world were everywhere in the dark and noiseless areas outside the city. It was a strange paradoxical sensation to feel isolated when surrounded by his closest friends. More than seven hours of sleep would have been nice, but he knew his internal clock would have him up at 0600 at the latest.

So much for a long night's sleep.

"You good in here, man?"

Clint and Bob were coming through the doorway. Bob held an empty container with, James assumed, the tragic remnants of Violet's homemade ice cream.

"Yeah, tired is all. I may head out."

"I'll join you," Clint said. "I'm stuffed and beat."

They bid their goodbyes to the rest of the team, ending with long hugs from Violet and Caitlin.

The night was quiet. Yellow lampposts cast their glow across cobbled streets, and the three friends watched rats scurrying between the shadows.

"That one looks pregnant," Clint said, pointing at a particularly bulbous rodent squeezing its way into a gutter.

"Rat king," James said imagining a colony of rodents bowing in front of a large rat on a throne.

"That's actually what it's called when a bunch of rats get their tails stuck together. They twist into such a knot that none of them can escape, and they eat each other and then die."

Clint and James made dubious eye contact and glanced at Bob who was still searching for the city pests.

"That's revolting, Bob," Clint said, his face a mask of disgust.

"Seriously, where did you learn that?"

"Just a fun fact. Now I gift it to you two," Bob said with a grin.

"Keep 'em to yourself from now on. Two more…three!" Clint shouted as another group ran across the smooth cobblestones.

"There must be thousands," James said, wondering at the world they must inhabit below ground.

"Probably closer to millions," Bob said casually.

"All right, stop giving us facts, Bob," Clint said, shaking his head.

"Trying to spread knowledge."

"Some knowledge is better left unknown."

James bobbed his head in agreement as they turned the corner to the hotel.

The tip of a cigarette glowed in the darkness ahead.

"You've got a visitor I think." Clint nodded at the figure standing outside the bar.

Dolly's silhouette came into view under a cloud of smoke.

"Gentlemen," Dolly said, gesturing at them with her cigarette.

"How's it going, Dolly?" Clint asked.

"Pretty good. Best of luck tomorrow. You two mind if I have a word with James?"

"No problem. See you tomorrow, buddy." Clint turned inside, giving James a clap on the shoulder. Bob did the same, the door swinging behind him as he followed Clint to the bar for a nightcap.

"What's up?" James asked. He put his hands in his pockets and watched the shrewd commander's face in the darkness. *What does she want?*

"Can we talk somewhere?"

James motioned for Dolly to follow him around the corner to where they parked outside Clint's garage. Their vehicles were packed with every piece of equipment imaginable. Clint liked to travel with his entire toolset, and Bob had loaded enough medical paraphernalia to set up a full operating theatre wherever they went. It was funny to James how the team worried so much about being unprepared when they were better than anyone at improvising.

"Should be okay here." James waved his hand over a sensor and dimmed light illuminated the area.

"I want to show you this." Dolly slipped an emitter from her pocket and pulled up a HOLO map showing a series of shifting icons popping on the screen.

"What's this?" James asked.

"The Sentinel raiders. They're everywhere, James. They're covering every square inch of space between here and the north. Just…waiting."

James's heart rate quickened and his eyes tightened. *Why was she doing this now? What is this?*

"Nothing we haven't seen," James said, nonchalantly reaching for her cigarette.

She handed him the glowing stick. "Yes it is. They're not attacking or even readying themselves for a siege. They're rotating, changing positions. It's constantly re-forming arrangements, breaking apart, and reforming again. No discernible pattern. This is the highest concentration of Sentinels we've seen since the Northern Assault. This gets more dangerous by the second."

James kept quiet. He knew this exercise. Her mind spiraled, and James waited.

"We can wait a few weeks for those satellite images to come in, right?" she said, breaking the quiet.

"What happens if they set up jammers?" James asked, handing back the cigarette.

"We send you up."

"Only going to get worse."

"James, the BZ hasn't been this active while also remaining silent since Midway. I'm worried."

"It's too late to back out now."

"Not yet. There are things we still don't understand about the BZ. The Sentinels—they're the tip of the iceberg. The general…" Dolly cut herself short and glanced at James, "All I'm saying is that data packet has a lot we don't understand. I'd know—I shaved ten years off my damn life working it."

James grinned, remembering the days on end Stacie and Dolly spent digging into code hacked apart by Jon. Those sleepless days turned into weeks, that turned into the first floor of the Palace. Time had a way of making the extraordinary mundane.

"I know, Dolly, but I ca—" James started, but Dolly cut him off.

"I know. I won't stop you, but keep that in the back of your mind. There's more we don't know than we do."

James nodded and looked at the ground. It wasn't like Dolly to get cold feet at this stage. He'd watched the woman go headfirst into a front-line tank assault with a smile on her face. He took her cautions as seriously as his own.

"We'll get it."

"I know. Just be careful."

"Always are."

"That's a lie."

James grinned. "Well, you try keeping Deck careful."

"Fair enough," Dolly said. The woman smiled, took a final pull from her cigarette and dropped it in the bucket next to the door.

She nodded and James brought her around to the hotel entrance. The rest of the team had joined Bob and Clint inside. Rich and Cristina resumed their spots pouring drinks for the team and the rest of the patrons, lucky to be in the bar at a time when everything was free.

Dolly turned to James.

"See you in a few months, James. Call if you need help."

CHAPTER 6

Clouds of smoke billowed. A wind funneled gaseous fumes into his face and James choked on the chemicals. Oily, inky, poisonous. Elements of death.

He lost his vision in the foggy residue from the fire, and the warm brush of highly concentrated air and debris whipped his face. He shut his eyes. Ash brushed against his skin, singeing his eyelids. Sound was irrelevant, and James wondered for a second if he would ever see again when he reopened his eyes.

The scene changed. A landscape of charred plastic, metal, and earth stood where the smoke had been seconds earlier. Embers were scattered amongst bits of earth smoking from the sheer heat of the recent flames. His legs carried him into the wasteland. His eyes teared from the heat, smoke, and ash.

His foot struck something hard, and he looked down. Part of a boot poked out from under a pile of burnt rubble, the rest of its ensemble lost beneath debris.

James moved on, confused by a myriad of thoughts, suddenly wondering where he was, how he had arrived here.

Why am I walking so slowly? His head was heavy, and he had the strange sensation of carrying an immense load throughout his body.

Without warning a glimmering caught his attention. He lifted numb eyelids to locate its source when out of the corner of his eye he spotted another flicker.

His next steps were interrupted by a rush of wind, and a metal disc with a distinct gray shine hovered in his path. Fear flooded his senses as another joined. Then another, and another, and more until he was surrounded by a legion of hovering discs circling him. Watching him. Waiting patiently for their moment.

Panic gripped his chest. The impulse to run stagnated somewhere in his spine and a cold immovable force seized his body in its grasp.

There were too many of them. Too many. There was nothing he could do.

He blinked. His heart hammered in his sternum and a cacophony of horror filled his ears with pounding, paralyzing his body. A roar of flames grew as the discs floated, unchanged, unmoved, deadly. Blocking any hope.

James woke up. His chest heaved with anxiety, and he loosened his clenched fists. Blood rushed into his knuckles as he released his hold and subtle realization flowed into his consciousness.

You're here.

Getting up, he sucked in a deep breath and left his tent. The half moon lit the ground. James walked to the edge of the stream near where they had made camp.

He sat on the stream bank admiring the sky.

Dreams, or nightmares more like it, had plagued him for over a year. He often spent his nights in the field staring at the stars after waking from a horror show over which he had no control.

Scenes varied from a fire-torched earth, dead bodies of people he knew, flashbacks to his imprisonment and torture at the hands of the BZ, or Sentinels hovering, like tonight. He exhaled and his breath misted as he attempted to calm himself. He hated the dreams, but it was pointless lying in a sleeping bag. Leaving his tent, sitting, and focusing on something other than sleep or blocking the gruesome images from his mind was the way he handled the situation.

He dug in his pockets for his self-prescribed therapy. A semi-shaved wooden block and his buck knife. He held the partially carved figure to the moon and inspected his handiwork. The bottom half was nearly finished with the scales of the mermaid's tail filling the forked end of a carefully detailed fin. He dug the tip of his knife into the soft wood and etched another mark in the curved tail. His mind wandered as he painstakingly continued to shape the mermaid.

They had left NOLA two weeks ago. A trip to Deerfield should not take this long, but Dolly's final words played a major role in James's decision-making. He routinely changed routes to skirt the edges of cities or trek through untamed forests. All that to avoid run-ins with Sentinel camps roaming the countryside. Every night James and Stacie waited while Jon downloaded a fresh dataset for them to comb over for the next day's journey.

The BZ camps were organized in semi-circles looping in and out of one another, overlapping like crescent moons, locking and interlocking at random. Their advances left so much guesswork it was difficult to push through, and beyond Jon's cloaked data pulls the team navigated blind. Deck traveled on top of the Jeep for a bit every hour with his enhanced binoculars, keeping an eye out for Sentinels while Jon recreated trails using older maps to get them through the riskier pathways.

Twice they had almost walked into converging Sentinel camps. Both times James's heart had practically stopped beating. The team had not gotten close enough to see anything, but James knew enough about those camps. Large tents hosting the human operators of the deadly weapons, the silver discs that glinted in the sunlight. Their simplicity was made more sinister by the lethal humanoid figures they became.

James envisioned the rest of their journey after his briefing with Jon and Stacie earlier that night. They would follow a straightaway along an old train track hugging the waterfront. Sentinel camp movements were unreliable, but the water gave them a natural defense. Only when they were close enough to run would they swoop to the interior and risk contacting the Deerfield team.

His eyelids drooped and his head fell forward. *That's it.* He collapsed his knife and shoved both items in his pockets.

His sleeping bag had gone cold, but he didn't care. He hoped he could get a couple more hours until his body forced him awake.

The morning came faster than James preferred, but he had slept until daylight. There was nothing worse than lying in bed waiting for it to come.

He helped himself to an MRE pack and started the portable coffee machine. When the trio of beeps alerted him, James poured a cup of steaming liquid and sat against a tree in the grove. He enjoyed the silence and waited for everyone to wake. The team was usually quiet when they emerged from their canvas shelters mumbling good morning as they walked off to relieve themselves or pour their own coffee. Morning routines had evolved to become solitary affairs, an aspect of the team James deeply appreciated as he took a swig of bitter liquid.

"This is miserable," Deck grumbled as he ducked through his tent opening with a blanket wrapped around his shoulders, his teeth chattering. "What is it, negative twenty?"

"It's forty-five, Deck," Jon replied as he sipped his coffee.

"What's the feels like?" Deck asked, suspicious and seeking validation.

"Fifty actually," Kevin spoke up, winking at Jon.

Deck's eyes slanted in Kevin's direction. "Liar."

"Come on, bud," James said. He pointed at the coffee. "Half a day to go and we can't get there soon enough."

"Can't feel my feet," Deck mumbled while he tossed the blanket in the back of the nearest jeep.

"You don't have a lot of natural survival skills, do you?" Clint asked, throwing his packed tent into the trunk over Deck's shoulder. "Hate fast driving, can't deal with the cold... What else don't you like?"

"I don't mind heights," Deck said, offering a defense.

"I guess that's something," Clint said, shrugging.

James glanced at the rest of the camp. Kyle and Stacie were already loading their tent into the back of the pickup and Bob was filling water bottles from the stream.

Almost there. The same thought had been teasing James for days.

Twenty minutes later they were ready to move. The HOLO screens depicting their route hung in the air. James looked at the path for the hundredth time in less than twelve hours.

"Could you mark the contact point?" James asked Jon, pointing at an invisible junction on the road.

"Done."

A blue triangle popped up on the trail four miles from their destination. James had no idea what to expect when it came to the city's defenses, and he would need to talk to someone on the inside before they started their approach.

"Stick to the waterfront. If you get separated get to that contact point as fast as you can. If you're pursued, break radio silence with our future hosts. I don't know what Deerfield has for active defenses, but they know we're coming," James said. The team nodded their agreement. They had heard the same speech a hundred times. *Gentle reminders could save their lives*, he reasoned.

"You got it, dude," Clint said, giving him two thumbs and a dopey grin.

"Yeah, yeah," James said, waving off the obvious sarcasm. "What've we got Deck?

"Signal ahead." Deck's voice had dropped the pathetic whine from earlier.

"What?" James wasn't sure if he was serious. Yet, they were so close… *Not now.* "Sentinels?"

"Not sure. Could be some campers. Maybe Nomads or Exils."

James gritted his teeth. Nomads were not a problem. These were people who focused on taking care of themselves outside of any city-state protection. The Exils were another story. They consisted of criminal groups kicked out of the city states or people from former NOLA affiliated outposts who had stopped responding to calls after losing too many people fighting the BZ. Overall, Exils were decentralized, independent, and selfish. They upset the meager supply chains, attacked independent city states, and were known to set traps for roaming NOLA troops on missions. They had nothing and took what they could, be it gear, food, or any other supplies available.

Supplies were not the Exils' sole target though. James remembered the early days of the Federation's fall when the criminal empires of the Exils gained power. Human trafficking was a trade they plied across the country, taking over small towns and selling their women and men to the highest bidders. NOLA's rise was what brought them back in check. Some managed to exist on the fringes of society, but their threat was far from its original peak. Whenever they took one of the trafficking camps, James had made sure the deaths were slow.

"Keep an eye on it. What do you think?" James turned to Stacie who was staring in the direction of Deck's binoculars.

"I'd guess it's Nomads."

"BZ troops aren't so stupid they'd keep a signal alive in a field," Kevin said, checking the chamber on his light machine gun.

"He's right. Probably friendlies. And if not friendlies, at least not BZ." Kyle added, pulling an arm over his head in a stretch.

"Go around?" James asked.

"Safest bet," Stacie said shrugging. "You're the boss though.

"Jon?" James said, turning to find their techie.

"On it." Jon appeared at James's shoulder with his HOLO screen ready. An overhead image of the area sprang to life and Jon spread the light-based map in the middle of the group giving them a 3D field display.

The stream ran into a larger lake a few hundred yards to their right. There was too much of a drop on the land next to the lake for them to drive along the edge. James trained his vision from the top of the hill to the lakefront and back to the homes nestled in the countryside.

"I can't get a live view. Too dangerous without knowing who's there," Jon said while he flicked his fingertips around the screen. "Buuuut I can do this."

Green, red, and yellow swaths of land sprang up along the ground.

"Green is for safe pathways. Even ground and plenty of space to book it if needed. Yellow's risky, and red, well…I think you get it."

Not much green there, James thought as he surveyed their options.

The town stretched too far to the left to drive all the way around without having to recalibrate their entire route for the day. Driving through abandoned homes and neighborhoods was not a big deal, but not knowing the inhabitants was enough to deter him from doing that. And although he wasn't comfortable with its proximity to the houses, the only option that avoided delaying progress was a path up the hill and along the steep drop to the water.

James nodded, "Good work, Jon. Let's take this path." James pointed at the stretch of yellow between the houses and the water, "Far enough from anything to avoid stirring up a problem we don't want. Stace, you, Kyle, and Kevin, take the pickup. Jon, Clint, and I will grab one Jeep. Bob, you drive with Deck in the other. Jon, check if you can get a local signal. A live image would be awesome right now. Stay well clear of those houses. Got it?"

Silent nods answered James and the team moved with practiced ease to their spots. Within a minute, James was in the front seat of a Jeep. Clint jumped into the driver's seat and Jon hopped in back.

James tapped the wrist control for his headset and heard a bell tone as the team's communications synced.

"Ready?" he asked.

"Ready," Stacie and Deck responded in unison from their respective vehicles and the team started their drive.

James jostled over the bumpy terrain. They headed uphill away from the outcrop of houses. *Different kind of childhoods now*, James thought looking at the playset in one of the yards. A yellow slide and a pink castle adorned a strip of overgrown grass in back of a broken wood fence. Their once bright paint was covered in grime and dirt from ages of neglect with weeds wrapping around the edges of the doorway to the castle.

"Signal still ahead," Deck's voice came over the group intercom.

"BZ? Federation? Gotta give us more, Deck," James replied. His hands clenched and unclenched on the hilt of the rifle propped between his legs.

"It's weird. It's stable and almost a beacon. Not an SOS, but someone's looking for attention."

James listened, digesting the information. *Who's sending signals?*

He saw Kevin lean out his window with a riflescope to his eye.

"I can't see anything," Kevin said,' pulling his head back in.

"Jon? Eyes aren't working."

"I've got nothing."

"Keep trying."

The neighborhood became clearer as they drew closer. The houses in the cul-de-sac were intact. This wasn't unusual as BZ armies did not care about razing the cities and towns they demolished. When the Sentinels attacked they sliced cleanly through their target and moved on to their next hit.

"People," Deck spoke over the intercom.

"How many?" James looked above Clint's head to get a peek out the window as his mind picked through scenarios.

"Well, person. One girl…or woman, I guess. I don't know, but it's a lady and she's waving to us."

James's jaw hurt. They'd barely been up for half an hour and already it felt like he had chewed through a pack of Juicy Fruit.

"Weapons?"

"Nothing visible. Maybe under her jacket."

James was quiet. It could be a lone Nomad who needed help. Someone stranded in the middle of a neighborhood. This wasn't a BZ move. It didn't seem as if they were risking a run-in with Sentinels. He made up his mind.

"Clint, Jon, and I will head down to check it out. Deck, you and Bob trail us. Stacie, Kevin, Kyle, you find a good place to keep an eye on things."

"You got it," Stacie said, as the pickup veered uphill.

"Stay alert," James said to no one in particular.

"I'll do what I want," Deck replied.

James shook his head and grinned at Deck's ability to remove any pretense of seriousness from a situation. "Just do it."

"Whatever…"

"He's a fuckin' pain," Clint said. His eyes never flinched and he watched the houses spring up on the streets as they hopped over the curb onto the asphalt.

"At least he's our pain," James said, peering warily at the windows of empty homes.

"Masochist."

James turned his attention to the road where the woman stood watching their approach.

The familiar feeling of hot metal cooling in his gut resurfaced, and an increased level of focus sharpened his senses. He hoped he hadn't made a mistake.

CHAPTER 7

She's calm.

James's eyes were glued to the figure in the middle of the cul-de-sac. Her hands were tucked in her pockets, and she leaned against the passenger side door of the truck.

The woman's dark brown hair was pulled into a high bun with stray strands tucked behind her ears. Her face was pinched into a discerning stare, inspecting the team's approach. She wore an olive jacket and black pants with worn boots.

She let off an air of suspicion which comforted James. As if her hesitation around strangers made her less threatening.

"Pull in slowly and park so I'm facing her," James said to Clint. His eyes did not waver from the one-person welcoming party.

James released the grip on his rifle while he checked the pistol holster strapped inside his jacket. *All there*, he thought as his hand met metal and plastic.

Clint pulled to a stop following James's instructions.

Stacie's voice came through his earpiece. "In position."

With his eyes still trained on the woman James addressed the team. "You stay here." Then, deciding it didn't look great carrying a long gun to meet an unarmed stranger, he pushed his rifle to the side.

"Yessir," Bob replied.

"Anything in the area yet, Jon?"

Jon's face glowed with the light of his HOLOs. "Nothing that I see. She looks to be alone on here."

James nodded. "All right, I'm going."

Avoiding the impulse to change his mind, James swung open the door.

The woman did not flinch. She remained steady as she pushed off the truck while her visitor approached. James shut the door, purposely flashing the handgun protruding from under his jacket.

As he walked towards her he took in his surroundings, focusing on the truck. It was beat to hell. The cab looked as if it had been stripped of any creature comforts and the exterior was rusty in spots where the paint had been eaten away. The grill, however, looked to be intact.

"You James?"

James was taken aback. *Who is this?*

"What?"

"Are you James?"

James glanced back to gauge his team's reaction. They shrugged, and James wondered again why he was the one who always ended up in these situations.

He looked back at the woman. Her hazel eyes were analytical and probing, the hue shifting in the light from gray to brown to green. He lost concentration, deciphering the different colors while trying to summon a response.

"Are you James?" she asked again, enunciating each syllable.

"Yes," James replied, regaining composure.

The woman stepped forward and held out a hand with fingerless gloves. "Teresa and Liam sent me to guide you north."

James reached his hand out tentatively.

"Why didn't she tell us that?" he asked, unconvinced.

"How do you know she hasn't tried? You've been traveling dark the whole way here. Plus, we didn't know when we last talked how strict Deerfield's gotten."

"Pretty risky putting up a signal here."

"I've got sensors up from the connection to Deerfield," she said, brushing him off.

James wondered if he heard her correctly. *She's still connected to Deerfield? We're fifty miles out.*

She moved to the other side of the truck's cab and opened the door to the back seats. "There's nothing within seventy-five miles of us, and that's likely a group of exiles waiting for the next supply drop to pass through the area." She reached inside the cab and walked back around, handing James three emitters.

James accepted them, inspecting the devices casually. "What are these for?"

"Plug them into your nav systems. They're routes through the defenses. Deerfield won't send specs over a connection."

James nodded. He understood and appreciated their caution.

Aren't we following her? he thought, remembering why they were even here.

"Wh—" James started, but the woman cut him off.

"The city has a shifting minefield and the nav system keeps you on route. Even following me, you need one of these to get you through," she said, pointing at the emitters stacked against his stomach. "Traffic's slow, but Deerfield doesn't have the firepower of NOLA or the other settlements farther south, so they're extra careful even if it's a pain in the ass for everyone else." She added the last part with a bite of sarcasm.

James bobbed his head in understanding. *What the hell is a shifting minefield?* he thought as the woman walked away again to the other side of the cab.

Another emitter flew at him from the other side of the truck, and James caught it with his spare hand. He flipped the rectangular device upward and Teresa's face looked at him from the HOLO screen.

It had been more than eleven years since he had last seen her. Wavy hair framed her face and smile lines added to her age, but her cocky grin remained in place.

"Hey, buddy, good to see you," she said, reclining in her seat. "Glad you made it."

"So are we. Sorry to keep you waiting."

Teresa shrugged. "No worries. BZ camps have been acting strange. Heather'll get you here in no time. We can talk more in person."

"See you soon."

Teresa nodded as the screen disappeared.

James tossed the emitter back to the woman on the other side of the truck.

"I guess that makes you Heather."

"That it does," she replied. She closed the door and came back to the other side. "Who wants to follow first?"

"We'll follow," James replied, adding for the team, "Deck?"

"What's up, lambchop?" Deck's voice came over his earpiece.

"Can you come grab these emitters?"

"It'd be my honor. I'll be right there to retrieve, oh, great one."

James shook his head and heard the door to the Jeep shut.

Deck appeared a second later next to James.

"Plug this into the nav system. The other one's for Stacie." James pushed the emitters into his hands. He wanted to move things along, wondering if Deck's casual approach might bother their upcoming hosts.

"Right, right. And you are?" Deck asked Heather, holding out his hand.

"Heather," she replied. "Guessing your Deck?"

"My reputation precedes me," Deck said, winking at James.

"Oh yeah, Teresa told me what a smooth talker you are." Heather's wry undertone and subtle eye roll were lost on Deck.

"I'm sure she did," he said. Speaking to the group over the intercom, "Did you all hear? Or should I repeat for you?"

"She's fucking with you." Kevin's response came too fast for James to stifle a laugh and Deck's face broke into a scowl.

"Jealous ass," he muttered as he walked back to his vehicle.

James ignored the comment and spoke to Heather, "We'll follow you."

"You want to ride with me?" she asked. "Plenty of room."

James glanced at his truck as Jon got out and moved to the front seat. James threw the remaining emitter to the techie's outstretched hand.

"See you there," he said to his team as he hopped in the passenger seat of Heather's pickup.

There was something strange about the whole situation. Not bad, just different. James couldn't put his finger on the trust he had in this stranger. Someone he had met in a barren, war torn countryside neighborhood.

The cab was as empty as it appeared from the exterior. Everything but the seats and gear shift had been ripped out. A glance in back revealed metal flooring and two jump seats strapped in a waiting position.

"Down to the studs, huh?" James said as Heather locked her emitter in place. The screen sprang to life filling the empty center console with opaque light.

"Speed is everything. Besides, I still have heat," she added. Her fingers moved on the screen until a map appeared. Their route was illuminated with topographic readings and CGI renderings of potential barriers. Outcrops of houses and towns formed the beginning of their journey until they hit the highway, the corridor to Deerfield.

"Why not use live satellite images?" James asked.

"Too unreliable. Central NOLA's lucky with all the power you guys pull. The farther north you get, the satellite coverage is sparser. Everything's been pulled to cover gaps in coverage farther south, destroyed, or hacked by BZ. Deerfield uses an old composite view from satellites before the BZ invasion. They rely on people like us for manual reporting and a small fleet of drones to keep their coverage zone up to date."

As she spoke, Heather checked the route, pulling the screen to read through her path. The road was straightforward until a dense line appeared in the middle of the highway. Diagonal lines and a soft red hue highlighted the area with a single clearing of roadway left blank.

Must be the minefield, James thought. What threw him off were the hundreds of objects floating in the red-tinted area. They moved aimlessly bumping off the boundary to the pathway, arcing away naturally, coming back to the path and bumping off again.

James had never seen something like that, but Heather was unfazed.

Done with her reconnaissance she looked at him. "Ready?"

"Ready."

Her hand yanked the car into gear, and they rolled off.

James peeked in the sideview mirror to see Jon waving while the rest of the team moved from the top of the hill.

After ten minutes of driving by yards, neighborhoods, and overgrown athletic fields, the truck pulled to a stop. The landscape had changed to a twelve-lane highway.

Heather put her hand out her window motioning the rest of the team forward.

Clint pulled alongside James and put his window down.

"Travel right behind us, no farther than ten yards no closer than two." Heather's voice commanded a level of gravity that set James's nerves on edge.

"You got it." Clint nodded, and he looked at James quizzically as he rolled up his window.

Without another word, Heather moved the truck forward.

James glanced at the HOLO's depiction of the area and compared it to the reality. According to the collected graphics, the roadway was well maintained. After a single look, though, James knew that was not the case. Evidence of major attacks spread across the road. Although damaged, the asphalt was still drivable.

Their path consisted of miles of blacktop lined with walls of concrete and steel girders. An airport with planes heaped in twisted piles of melted steel stood off to one side. Telltale signs of abandonment were everywhere. Ivy crawled over buildings and thick fields of browning grass brushed in the breeze. Bombed portions of the road were filled with rocks and cracked cement walls crumbled where they stood. James remembered the scorched-earth defensive tactics of the Federation during the BZ's Northern Assault. City-state commanders blew up every piece of infrastructure possible to stop the waves of Sentinel attacks. Memories of shattered buildings and all out carnage came back to James as they drove the same highway.

A flock of birds flew overhead, and the breeze kicked in from the east, sending a rush of salt-tinged air through the vents in the car. *Low tide.* James grimaced at the scent.

"Where are these mines?" James asked. "We've driven fifteen miles now and there's nothing."

Heather pointed at the HOLO and in the air without taking her eyes off the road.

Confused, James followed her finger and gazed at the sky through his windshield.

"See for yourself."

What the hell is she talking about?

James looked between the screen and the air above them. Clouds were moving in a slow dense mass. Nothing beyond fluttering leaves were apparent in the empty space.

Finally, the HOLO screen came to life. An oval figure buzzed near their position on the map swinging away in an arc. Three more appeared at the edges of the screen doing the same, and James looked out his window to spot them.

As he strained his eyes to get a better view, he spotted something. A disc, gunmetal gray and unimpressive, floated thirty feet above their heads. It brushed against the edge of their car's route and bounced away, repelled by an invisible bumper. It was replaced moments later by another.

Were those Sentinels? James watched, puzzled, as the objects bumped into the invisible field along the edge of their roadway and looped back around for another pass.

The number of discs on the screen multiplied as they continued to drive, the pathway becoming more erratic. James gripped his handle, and Jon murmured over the team's intercom.

"Motherfucker…"

"What are those things?" Clint asked. "They look like Sentinels, but…"

"There's no way." Stacie's voice sounded less certain than it had ever been.

James watched the sky with fascination. *What had Deerfield done? Were they sending their own Sentinels?*

"They're the mines." Heather's voice broke James's concentration, and he looked over at his companion. She nodded her head skyward. "The old Sentinel shells. They're the mines. Tell your team to stay inside the lines."

James nodded and relayed the message to his team.

"They're using old Sentinel shells as goddamn floating mines? Kinda genius…" Deck trailed off.

James agreed. *Talk about owning your trauma*, he thought, watching the unassuming metal objects playing bumper cars above his head while destruction from prior attacks was on display below.

The edges of the pathway widened, and the truck slowed to a stop. Heather waited while Clint pulled beside her.

Jon put his window down. "You could have warned us about those things," he said bluntly.

Heather shrugged and shook her head apologetically. "I know, I know. The techs at Deerfield reprogrammed Sentinel shells to act as floating mines. I assumed driving through it with me would be okay. Also, how else am I supposed to describe a field of mines that use constantly shifting electromagnetic fields to re-form a path controlled at random by Deerfield's security algorithms?"

"I'd say exactly like that," Jon replied with a bite.

"Either way, welcome to Deerfield."

Jon rolled his window up while they waited for the pickup and Jeep to pull up behind them. Kyle's thumbs-up signal from the driver's side gave them the go-ahead.

Heather tossed the car into gear and rolled up her window. "Let's head into town."

Before pulling away James saw Deck in his mirror rolling his eyes at their host.

The old highway winnowed to a thin strip of road forcing the vehicles to travel in single file. Gray cattails, reeds, and muddy soil surrounded them on both sides. The vegetation swayed in the breeze and James's gaze followed the rolling furrow to the edge of the salt marsh where the world seemed to stop.

"Holy crap," James muttered under his breath.

A wall of multi-colored steel storage containers loomed in the distance. They were stacked off-center at least seventy high with cranes designed to build skyscrapers braced against them, welded permanently in place. Cords as thick as a man's chest hung from their walls at intervals.

Ion charges, James realized tracing the wires to intermittent underground wells towards their power sources. A seventy-story wall hooked up to an ionic charge was something James had never heard of.

"That'll fry a Sentinel or two, huh?" Stacie's voice crackled over the speakers.

"Only takes one Northern Assault to keep your guard up," James replied.

"Huh?" Heather said, glancing over at him.

"Oh, sorry, intercom," James said, tapping his ear.

"Ahhh, talking about the walls. Pretty impressive," Heather said, looking ahead at the approaching defensive behemoth.

"Certainly is. Are those ion charges?"

"Yep. It takes too much power to keep them running all the time with the geothermal heat they use here. Fortunately, the warning system is pretty advanced, and they take only about ten minutes to heat up. When they're on though"—Heather shook her head in wonder—"it's something to see."

"You've been here for an attack?"

"I've run here when we've come close," Heather spoke, carefully choosing her words. "Deerfield doesn't like us visiting their doorstep."

"Makes sense."

"It does until you need a place to go."

James nodded and glanced at his host, wondering how much experience she had in the field. If she was anything like the Teresa he had known, Heather would be more than capable. Maybe even as good as James's team when it came to battle readiness. *Good to have someone like her on board*, James thought, staring at the structure in front of them as they parked.

The lot was empty, interrupted at random by rusting streetlights held in place by crumbling cement blocks. James was surprised the structures still stood. Humps of stained metal, presumably melted cars, littered the area and aging concrete filled the cracks in the pavement. James started to wonder, *Where the hell was this incredible Deerfield?*

He admitted he was impressed—taking BZ tech and using it for their own defenses. *Clever*. James knew from experience that discovering how to neutralize the humanoid figures in the Sentinels was progress but turning the devices back into weapons—that was a different level.

"Here we go," Heather spoke as they approached a wall of shipping containers. Spaced fifty-or-so-odd yards apart were the standard ion pillars. Thick bundles of cord connected the massive structures to one another. A gate opened between the containers and a series of iron chains let down a draw bridge. A group of suited guards waited with rifles poised on their shoulders. James felt the eyes of the men through the sights of their weapons, and he glanced at Heather. Her face remained calm and impassive as she rolled down her window.

She put her head out and yelled, "Get out of the fucking way."

She put the window back up, muttering, "Assholes knew I was leaving and have to make a goddamn show every time someone comes in here."

A soldier at the front of the line lowered his rifle and walked towards them. He went to Heather's window.

"Miss, you know we have to do this every time." His voice was exasperated, and he held a sensor in his hand. "Can I get your wrist please?"

Heather rolled her eyes and held her arm through the window.

"I get it, but every time? I've been gone three hours." The guard ignored the comment and, when a green light flashed across his screen, gave a thumbs-up to the rest of the guards who lowered their weapons.

Motioning to his team and standing aside, he said, "Can never be too careful. Have some people waiting for you inside." Then, addressing James he said, "Welcome to Deerfield."

James nodded as a series of metal walls pulled back to reveal an opening that reached more than three stories leaving a bridge of containers suspended overhead. A wide passageway greeted him, and he stared in awe at the entrance to Deerfield.

Chapter 8

Heather's truck pulled between Deerfield's military outfit. She nodded at the guards as they waved the other vehicles through the entrance.

The bridge rose with a groan, darkening the space inside the metal box. James glanced at Heather. Their guide appeared unperturbed at being stuck in a car surrounded by fully armed strangers in an inescapable cell. *I guess not strangers to her*, he reasoned and fought the uneasy sensation of imprisonment. The gate finished its ascent with a shudder. Lights flickered on and James found himself staring at another wall of metal shaking with movement.

The second drawbridge splayed out revealing the world hiding on the other side of the crates.

Thousands of people milled about an open space full of storage containers stacked in clusters. A stadium towered over the area casting a shadow across the ground in the late morning sun. Tangled noise reached James's ears first. Machinery clamored, electric generators hummed, and dozens of muted conversations combined into a blanket of sound. It was as if the city had not fallen, but erected walls around itself to hide from the rest of the world.

"Cars on the line, Heather," a voice called. James's driving companion signaled recognition as she pulled off to the left.

Four rows of vehicles ranging in condition from decrepit to well used lined the walls. Heather drove along the row closest to the city.

James's eyes were glued to the scene. *Where did all these people live? This must be the largest settlement in the Federation,* he thought, realizing he hadn't seen this many people together in one place since the attack on Midway.

He scanned the various sections of the city, trying to take in as much as he could until Heather pulled into a spot, interrupting his fascination.

She turned the car off and looked at him with a grin on her face, "Pretty crazy, right?"

"What the hell? Last time I was here… I mean…" James was at a loss for words and Heather nodded, looking back over her seat.

"It's the only safe haven. Everyone, unless they were part of an outpost, came here after the Northern Assault. It's a real city," she said. Her eyes locked on the contained metropolis, a hidden longing trapped in her voice. "Come on, I'll show you around."

"That'd be great. I've got some people to find, too," James added, wondering how he'd ever find his mother and brother in such a place.

"Easy. Let's check in with the guards and return our nav systems. Then we can do whatever you want."

The rest of the team pulled into a trio of empty spots farther down the line, and James signaled them to wait. Getting a series of thumbs-up and one middle finger, James followed Heather towards the gate. The guard who had greeted them waited with his rifle clipped to his chest.

"Heather," he said. He cautiously scanned the group waiting by their vehicles. Standing straight James kept a steady gaze.

"Martin, how goes everything in Deerfield?" Heather asked sweetly.

"Who are they?" he asked pointedly, ignoring the friendly approach.

"Team from NOLA," Heather replied, dropping her honeyed tone.

"Why?"

"Why what?"

"Why are they here? What are they doing in Deerfield?"

"We're headed north," James cut in. He hoped speaking would somehow improve the situation. Judging by Martin's brow furrowing into a frown, it hadn't worked.

"North? What the fuck is up north other than outposts with her kind?" Martin replied, bobbing his head in Heather's direction.

James caught Heather's eye. She nodded slightly to James, giving him the floor. Remembering his sister's notes from their briefing earlier in the week about remaining cautious James quickly considered how to respond. *Just don't freak them out*, he thought.

"Routine check, BZ's moving all around farther South so it was slow going getting here. Asked Heather and her crew if we could rest here before heading the rest of the way to their HQ."

Martin's face remained a stone, but his body language softened as the tense moment from seconds earlier dissipated.

"We've seen the formations they're using over our drone imaging. How long has the trip been?"

"Little over two weeks now. Needed to get off the road," James replied. He had not anticipated this level of scrutiny over NOLA visitors.

"Long trip."

"Certainly was. Glad to be here, that's for sure," James elevated the gratitude in his voice, hoping to sound more like a grateful, weary traveler than a soldier headed on a mission.

"You'll need to talk with our leadership," Martin said.

"Sure thing. Should I get the rest of my team?"

"No need," Martin replied and turned on his heel.

James glanced at Heather who returned his look with an eye roll before following the large man to an open-topped Jeep.

James turned to his team and pointed to the vehicle. Stacie waved him off, and Deck stood straight and saluted as James stepped into the doorless truck.

Without waiting, the driver took off in the direction of the city.

James expected some conversation or even a brief tour of the settlement but got nothing from his new hosts. Heather sat silently as well, so James turned and took in the sights.

As they neared the stacked shipping containers, James began to get a sense of how the settlement was organized. Sections of steel containers, their sides replaced by plexiglass, depicted scenes of a lively grocery store, a few delis, a restaurant, a bakery, and a couple of general stores. Clothes merchants dotted the road intermittently, and James was again taken aback by the feel of a true city. A tickle of hope ran down his spine as he gazed at the people milling about ignoring the stranger being escorted to the center of their city.

James wondered how they managed to feed, clothe, and safeguard all these people. NOLA benefited from its proximity to the wetlands, which provided a steady source of farmable shellfish. The warmer climate allowed for growing vegetables year-round, and the local farming communities they defended helped maintain their food supply. But Deerfield was far bigger than NOLA. At most, NOLA served and protected 30,000 people if everyone was home from missions. Deerfield was something else entirely. Triple the population with a third of their security force on loan to other settlements in an enclosure surrounded by an unfriendly environment with few natural resources.

James shook his head, trying to wrap his mind around their operation. His questions were answered when they entered the arena. Formerly a host to thousands of sports fans, the field and stands had been replaced with stationary platforms stacked on top of one another, mounted every ten feet or so on long poles. Each platform contained large wooden boxes teeming with vegetables, their vines flowing freely between the poles. A web of metal catwalks connected the platforms and workers walked between them carrying equipment to and from storage lockers. Small drones, akin to the roaches Jon had designed for reconnaissance, flitted between the platforms. Meanwhile, sheep and goats munched casually on patches of overgrown grass and fallen crops under the suspended farm.

"What the…?" James was breathless. Using the existing infrastructure from the old stadium they had built a perfectly sustainable, vertical farm system.

"Pretty cool, isn't it," Heather said.

"I've never seen anything like this."

"The bioengineering is the craziest part. Plants ordinarily unable to grow here are thriving. What a world, huh?"

"What a world…" James repeated as his mind flipped back to snow-covered tropical vines hanging over the courses at Croyton's training compound.

The driver pulled into a tight corridor and drove onto a set of spiraling ramps circling upwards until they reached the top of the stadium. As they drove along the corridor, James looked over the expanse, marveling at the ingenuity, design prowess, and skill needed to put it all together. From this height, the residential housing surrounding the other third of the stadium was in view. Tall columns of stacked storage containers had been constructed into metal apartment buildings. People sat on their porches or rooftops talking and relaxing. The day was unnaturally warm, and everyone was outdoors enjoying the weather. James's body relaxed as he witnessed its effect on the people.

The Jeep stopped abruptly, and Martin exited, opening James's door.

James nodded at the impassive face of his host and followed him to an unimpressive wood door.

Martin knocked twice and held his ear against the waxed surface. They waited patiently until the door handle turned, the door opened, and Martin pointed inside. Heather led James in and the tension that had been melting away seconds earlier resurfaced in a torrent.

Three of the walls were covered in wood paneling. Images of data tables, graphs, and other statistical references rotated on the screens of the HOLO monitors suspended at three-foot intervals throughout the room. On the far wall was a set of glass French doors that looked out on the farm system. The tops of the crop laden platforms exposed themselves as he followed Martin and Heather deeper into the room. They strode through the doors and admired the expansive operation.

James was stunned by the sheer magnitude of the enterprise. In the dense space, an interlocking set of growing surfaces had been created out of circular platforms held up by poles and jutting out at intervals alternating in height, some at least ten stories high. Dozens of crop variations gave off a kaleidoscope of color in the immediate vicinity. Drones flew from platform to platform carefully inspecting each of the crops.

Completely enthralled by the entire operation, James was startled by the hand waving in front of his face.

"Helllooo! Ah, there you are," Heather said grinning.

"Sorry," James replied, embarrassed by his lapse in attention, "I've just… This is incredible."

"Hopefully you'll see more of this soon." James turned towards the new voice. A figure stood with its back to the new visitors tucked behind five rows of folding chairs.

A slightly built man with a graying five o'clock shadow and receding hairline turned around. He had on a gray hoodie and worn jeans with white sneakers. The look was unassuming and unprepared.

Motioning for James to join him, he said, "Come on down. Martin tells me you've been on the road for a while now." James glanced at Heather and led the way down the short staircase to meet the man on the balcony.

James held out his hand and introduced himself. "James. My team and I are making a run north to do some recon, but would like to stay here a night or two if that's okay?"

The man took his hand and held it lightly. His skin was paper dry, and the muscles underneath differed from those of a soldier.

"Welcome. My name's Arthur. We're happy to have you here." His smile was warm and continued through their shake.

Arthur's eyes were deep and probing. The intelligence they held was palpable.

"Thanks, Arthur. This is an incredible setup you have here."

"Yes, we've come a long way in a few short years." Arthur looked over the fields. His eyes roamed the stalks of vegetation as if he was looking for one specific item but never planned to find it.

"Certainly is. I haven't been here since—" James caught himself. *Why bring up the most painful memory for these people?* he thought, chastising his lack of forethought and hoping Arthur didn't notice.

Arthur spoke as he sat in one of the stadium chairs, gesturing for James to do the same "Rebuilding what's broken is a good step towards healing, James. No need to hide your words here. We all remember what happened to our community. It's why we behave the way we do. Insulated and self-contained."

James sat while Arthur continued, "After the Northern Assault, we could do nothing but mourn. Our lives had been crushed by the attack, but we realized we couldn't stop living. There was too much at stake. A few of us banded together to repair the stadium with the intent of turning it into a farm. More and more people joined, and before we knew it, a city formed. Odd to think, a city of farmers, but that's really what we are.

"You know we harvest over five hundred varieties of fruits and vegetables each cycle? There is a constant rotation of plants grown, harvested, and reseeded on the platforms. It's a perfect self-sustaining ecosystem. The townspeople either run businesses or work the farm. Everyone eats the food we harvest and helps to keep each other safe inside the walls."

He paused looking at James with another peaceful smile.

"Sounds…lovely," James responded, instantly regretting how stupid he sounded. *Lovely, really?*

"It is." Arthur paused and looked back over the field. One of the roach-like bots plunged through the air, then hung stationary off a long vine overflowing with peas. It fluttered there for a second before swooping away in the blink of an eye.

"You know James, we normally don't welcome visitors here." Arthur's voice grew quiet.

"I understand that, and we appreciate you letting us come here. We only need a night or two. After that, we're out of your hair," James replied. He could have told him more, but he was cautious to keep details light. *No need for him to know why we're heading north.*

"We allowed you in because of our relationship with our northern outpost friends," he nodded his head in Heather's direction who kept her gaze averted eyeing the fields intently but listening to their conversation, "Teresa's group has done a lot to help us, and we owe them the courtesy of our occasional hospitality."

James nodded. "We won't cause any trouble," he answered, wondering where the conversation was headed.

"Right, I know that. I assume we wouldn't be able to do too much about it if you did, although I'm sure Martin would say otherwise. No, James, the reason I bring this up at all is that we don't want to be considered a refuge to anyone. We can't be involved in the war." He continued, "Again, out of courtesy we'll shelter your team for a night or two, but in the future, if you're ever running from problems or need assistance, we're the wrong place to turn. The people in this settlement have suffered enough."

They're not kidding about this whole isolationist thing, James thought, remembering old analyses from the NOLA analysts on Deerfield and the city's uncommunicative nature.

Arthur looked at him with his eyebrows raised, waiting for a verbal response.

"Yes, completely get it." James nodded and Arthur dipped his head in a nod.

"Excellent. Well, please enjoy your stay here."

"Thank you. We're happy to be here." James stood to leave and was halfway up the staircase followed by Martin and Heather when he turned around.

"Do you have a directory? I'd like to find some people. I've got family here."

"Of course! Martin would be glad to guide you to your mother and brother whenever you wish," Arthur smiled his warm, peaceful smile.

I guess he did his homework, James thought, knowing he hadn't mention exactly who in his family he wanted to find. Arthur was proving to be a step ahead of him.

They drove past a line of workers changing shifts outside the stadium. Their faces shined with sweat, and they waved tired hands at the car as it passed.

James returned the gesture and strained to see if he could make out either of his family members. *Needle in a haystack,* he realized as they drove past dozens of workers switching shifts.

A few minutes later, they pulled up next to the team who looked like lions bathing in the sun, draped over the seats, bumpers, and hoods of their vehicles. *Kind of a lazy look,* James thought as Clint's head rose sleepily from its resting place on the windshield.

The mechanic tapped Kevin on the arm who opened his eyes and rolled off the edge of the pickup's hood. He walked around back to rouse the rest of the troops while Clint hopped off the hood to greet them.

"What's the word?" Clint asked, ignoring Martin and his driver.

"We can stay for a couple of days."

"Whereabouts?" Clint asked.

"Not sure yet. Captain?" James asked turning back to the roofless truck.

Martin pointed at a cluster of containers set aside from the main neighborhoods.

"Overflow quarters. Heather can show you the way. Plenty of space for all of you." He reached into the back seat and laid a binder on his lap. He fished a set of cards from the packet and handed them to James.

"Vouchers," he explained. "Food, water, the basics—this will get you what you need."

"Any way we can refill with biodiesel?"

"Anything you can trade for it?" Martin asked, tossing the binder into the back seat.

"How about a few mobile solar arrays?" James asked, quickly running through their inventory in his head and recalling their surplus items.

"That'll work. Drop them at the gate. I'll let our team know and they can fill you up."

"Thanks for that."

Martin nodded and nudged his driver who circled around and stopped in front of James.

"By the way, your mom lives with your brother in the east field section. Eastern groups are between shifts right now, so you might be able to catch them before they head back to the fields."

"Appreciate it," James said, adding, "How do I get there?"

Martin pointed towards a pathway leading into the city, "Walk that way. No vehicles allowed other than Deerfield transportation."

Martin tapped his driver's shoulder, and they left without another word.

James felt the rest of the team's presence as they closed around him.

"Guy's kind of a dick." Deck said, yawning.

"He's got a tough job," James replied, trying to give Martin the benefit of the doubt.

"Everyone's got a tough job. He's still a dick."

"Could be an off day," Clint reasoned.

"Nope. He's right. Martin's a dick," Heather said, walking to her truck.

"I knew I liked her." Deck smiled. "So, big man, what's the deal? What's the plan?"

James explained his discussion with Arthur and watched their reactions carefully. When he finished he waited while they pondered his words until Kevin spoke up. "I say we see your family and get the fuck out of here ASAP. It's obvious they don't want us here."

"They don't," Heather said. She leaned against the Jeep inspecting her nails, listening to James's recap

"Why? We didn't do anything," Stacie asked, her face scrunched in a frown and James could tell she was trying to make sense of the situation.

"The people of Deerfield have been through a lot, and they don't want to give the BZ a reason to target them. They've figured out what works for them. They trust nobody and want no one to consider them a stopping point. I'm barely welcome, and I grew up a few hours away and know everyone involved in the Northern Assault who moved here. Arthur's protective."

"Those fields though. The amount of relief they could provide everyone," Jon said, staring longingly at the stadium farm in the distance.

"They don't care. Deerfield's in it for self-preservation. That's it. They've been destroyed once and they're taking no risks."

James nodded. He understood. Hide and wait for the world to figure itself out. No need to go on the offensive.

"Regardless of their 'friendliness,'" James said, interrupting the group speculation, "let's get moving here. Clint, Bob, and Jon, get the cars filled up. Try to negotiate a few extra canisters if you can. Good to have backup. Stacie and Kyle, head into town and find replacement gear to replenish what we used getting here. Check if they have iodine tabs. We'll need more purifier supplies as we get farther north. Deck and Kevin, come with me. We'll see what we can get with these things." James passed out the rations cards and they inspected the light metal cards with interest.

"Any questions?"

"Can I join?" Heather asked.

"Of course. We'll need a guide." James was happy she offered. He could use her insight and felt oddly calmed by her presence.

"Anything else?"

Silence greeted James.

"Meet back here in three hours."

The team headed off to their various tasks and James grabbed an empty pack from the pickup's bed. He was pulling the canvas bag from its storage place when he felt a hand on his back.

Startled, he jumped around and slapped it down, realizing only a second later that the massive bearlike hand belonged to Kevin.

Taking a breath James spoke, "Jesus Christ, Kev, you scared the shit outta me."

"Sorry, man, didn't mean to. I just..."

James looked at him, not sure what Kevin needed.

"When you see your mom and brother, mind if I join?" he asked, his voice hesitant.

"Of course," James replied. "It's why I wanted you with me."

"Thanks, man," Kevin said, a wide grin on his face. He clapped James on the back harder than he realized. James winced, rubbing the spot between his shoulders as he followed the friendly giant to meet Heather and Deck.

CHAPTER 9

Shadows filled the gaps between the metal boxes lining the sides of the streets. James's group wound their way through the well-marked paths of the city's infrastructure. Clouds gathered overhead limiting the sunshine that had been so brilliant in the preceding hours.

Their shopping trip doubled as a tour of the city, courtesy of Heather. Every turn brought the heavy weight of watchful eyes as much as the people who pretended not to notice them. Cautious and hesitant acceptance was the population's model for dealing with outsiders. James tried to understand their mindset whenever he went into a shop. *We may be the first strangers here in months*, he thought as a trio of children stopped in the street to stare at them. Heather didn't seem bothered by the extra attention, and James worked to ignore it.

If she doesn't mind it must be normal.

After the first few shops, James got used to the constant monitoring and started to relax. He wanted to enjoy exploring his first city since Midway.

Deerfield was a circuit of right angles and straight lines. With detailed descriptions from Heather, James felt he understood the layout. Each district was broken up by residential areas which were identified by an alpha-numeric code. Residential areas were occupied by the farm workers and infrastructure maintenance teams. Merchants lived above their shopfronts and the defense force resided in a set of barracks.

The segmentation and planned execution of the city were astounding. Every street had an entrance to a series of underground tunnels which Deerfield retrofitted from old transportation lines in and out of the arena. Within an hour, the entire population could disappear underground. James loved the simplicity of their arrangement and envied the self-sufficiency of the city. The underground schemata and its implications only reinforced the cautious nature of the inhabitants so prevalent in the city.

Dolly needs to see this, James thought as they ducked underground to examine a pristine shelter stocked with provisions that would last the settlement months, or years if needed.

They stopped at a corner and James looked from his screen to get a sense of their surroundings. He oriented himself on the map Heather had downloaded for them before she returned to the overflow barracks. James looked diagonally across the intersection from where they stood. *AC-056*. His mind hummed as he stared at the house.

"Over there," James said, pointing to the residence across the street.

"What are we waiting for?" Kevin asked, checking the roadway for the bicycle trains that served as the settlement's transportation system.

"Yeah, what's the holdup?" Deck said, glancing at the other homes along the block.

"Nothing," James answered, but his legs were rooted to the spot. Why was he nervous about seeing his family? He saw Caitlin all the time. Family had always been a constant in his life. Why did this feel so different, so momentous? He forced his foot forward, aware of Kevin's eyes on him while they walked to the front door cut into the thick metal plating.

Although the houses appeared the same, they each revealed the unique personalities of their owners. Clean and simple designs adorned the metal walls, an aesthetic that gave his mother away instantly to anyone who knew her. A basket of neatly cut ivy hung from each window and cream-colored shades were drawn across the plexiglass panes. Frosted lace covered the small opening at the top of the entrance and the knocker was fashioned in the shape of a lion's paw. *That's Dad,* James thought recognizing his father's influence on the design.

He lifted the iron knocker and let go, causing an unappealing *clang* as it hit the metal door. James grimaced at the noise, wishing he had used his fist instead. In seconds a lock slid, and the door opened revealing a long-haired, younger, replica of himself. Taller for sure, but undoubtedly Michael. The resemblance was uncanny.

"Mind if I come in?" James asked and Michael's face broke into a grin. He grabbed James by the shoulders and enveloped him in a hug. James returned the embrace, shocked by Michael's size. At their last goodbye, Michael had only reached his chest. Now James was smothered in his younger brother's arms.

"Michael?" a voice called from the back room and Michael released James. Both were speechless as they stood in quiet observance of each other caught in the moment as five years of separation dissipated. James's mother called again.

"Michael? Who's here? You have an early shift with me, so don't think you can be out all night again. Last time you barely managed to wake up." James's mother walked in and stopped in her tracks.

Seconds later, James's face was buried in the crook of his mother's neck while she shook.

"Geez, Ma, don't need to cry," Michael said, putting an arm on his mother's back.

"I'm not crying," she said. Pushing herself off James, she wiped an eye.

James saw the smile spread across her face and the happy tears of laughter collecting in her eyes.

"Well, stop laughing so hard," Michael said, and James's mother swiped a hand at her youngest child.

"Shut it, Michael. Oh, James! You brought friends, Kevin! Deck!" James's mother draped her arms around his companions, greeting them as if they were her children.

Kevin bent his large frame over the doorway to receive the hug, and Deck embraced her like he would his own mother.

James's mother had a soft spot for Deck. After his family had died during the Northern Assault, she had taken him in like a son. They linked arms and walked into the house.

"Place looks great, Mrs. Coffey," Deck said, picking up a decorative squirrel statue from a table, inspecting it, and putting it back on a different table, "Love what you've done with it all."

The woman waved him off, fluffed some of the pillows on the living room couch, and pointed for them to sit.

"Pshh, all the houses are the same here—metal boxes with two bedrooms, one bathroom, a kitchen, and a living room. Larger families get more, but everything's evened out here. Deerfield runs a tight ship. Surprised they let you in," she said, raising an eyebrow subtly at James.

"Just up here on a check of a few outposts."

"Sure you are, honey," James's mom said, patting him on the cheek while pushing him into a chair.

"What's that supposed to mean?" James asked, affronted.

"It means you're a bad liar. At least to me," she responded. Her attention switched to the others as she ushered Kevin and Deck onto the couch, "Now coffee, tea, beer, water, wine, the hard stuff? What can I get you all?"

"The hard stuff will do fine," Deck said, relaxing in his chair.

"Water for all of us," James said, eyeing Deck across the coffee table.

"Hmmphhh," Deck snorted audibly but didn't put up a fight.

"Back in a second."

The room grew awkwardly quiet as James inspected his family's living space. Drywall covered the metal plating, and James noticed his mother's favorite shade of eggshell blue adorning the space.

"Michael, what've you been up to bud?" Deck asked, relaxing in one of the wingback armchairs.

"Working on the farm, but I've got my eyes set on joining the Defense force," Michael added. He nodded at the corner of the room where a rucksack and worn black boots sat ready.

James's stomach dropped, but he held his tongue. *His decision*, James reasoned. It wasn't his place to comment.

"Good for you, man. Tough line of work," Kevin said.

"You guys would know. I'm not sure if I want to stay here though. Might be better off where I can do more."

"Run around and get shot at like the rest of your siblings?" James's mom interrupted rejoining them in the living room.

James stomach tightened as he accepted the water she handed him.

"That's not the point, Mom." Michael sounded exasperated, and he looked at James with pleading eyes. James shook his head curtly in response. Michael gave him a burning glare before turning back to their mother.

"James thinks it's a good idea."

Whipping her head around, she stared at James whose mouth hung open in surprise at his brother's momentary burst of insanity.

What the hell, Michael?! His eyes shifted between his mother's surprised hurt face to his brother's hopeful stare. *Lotta good coming home,* he thought, taking a long sip of water.

"Umm, James, you eventually need to swallow, bud," Deck said from across the room, grinning into his glass. Even Kevin couldn't suppress a smile. James scowled at them planning revenge as he turned back to his warring family.

"Well, Michael, I think, as long as you're here you should keep working on the farm," James started, his mother's face morphed into a righteous nod and smile, "But…if you want to learn our trade, Martin seems like a good guy."

Michael's face brightened as his mother's ire towards James returned, and he looked quickly out the window.

"Great weather…" James said. He wanted to push past the conversation. Within ten minutes of reuniting with family for the first time in more than half a decade, he was refereeing disagreements. Not his ideal return.

"It is beautiful, James," Deck said, leaning back and looking out the window. "So what's with the farm, Mrs. Coffey? Why doesn't anyone else know about it?"

James was happy for the reprieve from the family turmoil even if he did have revenge percolating in his mind for the smart-ass scout.

"That's a good point. Mom?"

James's mother sighed. "Arthur's a good man, but he was completely broken during the Assault. I don't know the whole story but heard he lost everything. Wife, children, home, life. Everything. He didn't just need a fresh start; he needed to feel protected. Secured so no one would ever take it again. That's who he is. A broken man with a plan for total secrecy. It's a strange way to live I suppose, but he cares about everyone and everything here and does all he can to make sure everyone's safe."

James listened, nodding along.

"Everyone works there?" Kevin asked as he refilled his water from the pitcher on the table.

"Almost everyone," James's mother replied sitting on a chair next to James. She placed her hand on his arm. "Defense is a different working group, but that's the extent of it. The goal of the settlement is survival. That means food and shelter. It's a collective movement." She waved a hand at the room, "All this was put together by everyone living here. The walls of the city, the structure of the town, the crops, the animals. All of it." Her voice trailed at the end and James caught Michael's eyes shift to the carpet.

"Nice little place," Deck said, nodding and taking a sip of water.

"Depends," Michael said, speaking to the carpet.

"Depends?" James asked. The tone and the mood in the room shifted.

Michael's head perked up and he looked at his mother whose eyes drifted.

"Depends on if that's all you want. No real option other than…this," Michael finished his sentence glancing in their mother's direction. The temperature in the room turned icy.

"Michael, I——" James's mom started to speak as a loud knock interrupted the conversation.

Michael and his mother looked at each other confused. Another knock sounded and Michael opened the door cautiously.

Three men burst into the room.

In seconds James was on his feet, his hand on the hilt of the knife that he kept in the back of his waistband. Kevin and Deck stood ready as well. Three more men entered, and James stared down the barrel of two rifles as Martin entered through the doorway followed by Arthur.

The older man's eyes swept the room falling on each inhabitant in turn. He settled his gaze on James and nodded exiting the house.

Two of the soldiers grabbed James's arms and led him outside. Martin stood behind Arthur at attention.

Arthur's silver hair grew dark gray as rain drops pelted his scalp.

"You led the BZ to us, James."

"What? We haven't seen any BZ our whole trip. Avoided them the whole way." James was confused. *What is Arthur talking about?*

"That's not what we're seeing."

On cue, a soldier stepped between Arthur and James holding an open HOLO screen. It showed a group of Sentinels swarming the town where they had met Heather.

"That's miles away, Arthur. How do you know it's because of us?" James was confused. How were they blaming James and his team for the Sentinels?

Arthur's eyes never wavered. "They must have picked up your scent somehow. We know better than most what an attack would mean. They're too close for comfort. You need to leave. Immediately."

James's stomach dropped. *Leave? Now?*

"Arthur, please. They're miles from here. We need some rest and then we can—"

Arthur held up his hand stopping James. It was useless.

"Your team has already been informed and are waiting at the gates."

"What's going on there, James?" Deck called out casually unable to hide the stress in his tone from James.

Not the time for a debate, James thought, fighting the impulse to argue further.

"Turns out it's time to get going." James glowered at their hosts as he headed back into the house. With a reassuring smile, he hugged his brother and mother and walked out, followed by Deck and Kevin.

Arthur's uncompromising stare trailed James as he entered the front seat of the waiting car.

The driver threw the vehicle into drive, but before they pulled away, James held the man's arm and turned to the city's leader.

"Arthur, we've been in the field since this whole goddamn war started. We fought at Midway, we did recon in the South, and we responded to the Northern Assault. If the Sentinels are getting this close, you've got a problem on your hands because I sure as shit know we aren't the reason they're here. We know how they operate and can hide from them better than anyone else."

"Could be true, but I'll feel better when you're gone." Arthur's smile delivered no happiness, just the smug self-assurance of a man who saw no need to question his own tactics.

"Good luck," James muttered and he released the driver's arm. They pulled down the narrow street waving goodbye to his family standing in the doorway of their steel home.

The team was outside the packed trucks, waiting for them when they arrived at the gates.

"Welcome back! How's your mom?" Clint asked grasping James's hand and pulling him from the passenger seat.

"She and Michael are good. Would have been nice to visit a little longer though," James said staring at Martin who ignored their presence, "Let's get the fuck out of this place."

"Heard that," Stacie mumbled as she walked by him.

"Anyone wanna ride with me?" Heather asked the group.

James grabbed his pack and tossed it into her backseat.

"Everyone keep comms in your ears and move as fast as possible. Heather and I have lead."

Affirmative responses greeted him as James hopped into the passenger seat. They drove to the gates and entered the darkened cavern again this time to exit.

James was furious. Deerfield was supposed to have been their break. A quick oasis in a desert of unknowns and danger. Now they had to go back into the world with no rest, no extra gear, and no food in their stomachs. He had seen his mother for all of ten minutes. Five years for a ten-minute reunion.

Fucking Arthur, James grumbled in his head, *blaming us for something without considering other possibilities.* James knew they couldn't have led the Sentinels to Deerfield's doorstep. It didn't make any sense. *How would Sentinels track us? But what was it they were picking up on?*

Jon's cleanup had been perfect. No one could find their tech prints. They wouldn't have led the Sentinels anywhere other than their camp. *So how the hell did they pick up on the town?* James was stumped and he didn't know enough to doubt Heather yet, but he needed someone to figure out what was going on.

Sounds like a job for Stacie, he thought, making a mental note to have her to look into it.

Gray skies and rain hid the setting sun trying to greet them outside the walls.

Martin approached their truck, and Heather accepted an emitter from him through her open window.

"This will get you all out. The drive will self-destruct when you're beyond the minefield."

"And if Sentinels are on the other side?" Heather said, handing the thin metallic device over to James.

Martin grinned and made eye contact with James. "Good luck."

With that, the defense commander left them.

James watched his back, muttering curses at their former host under his breath and hoping his brother would steer clear of the Deerfield defense force.

If anything just to avoid that loser, James thought as he secured the emitter on the console.

The screen displayed the pathway leading from the settlement and Heather threw the car into drive.

They took off at a slow pace on the thin trail between the invisible bumpers of the minefield. The mines were undetectable in the rain, their gunmetal coloring camouflaged by low hanging clouds.

When they reached the end James looked into the side view mirror at the winding pathway back to Deerfield, the walls were barely visible behind the fog that hung in a dense blanket above the ground.

"What's the move now?" Deck's voice rang over the headphones and James glanced at the HOLO screen in his lap. He had maintained his connection to the settlement but expected to lose it any second. The map showed a maze of old highways and roads with heavily annotated pathways carved into the area by NOLA and outpost holders alike.

He poured over the map searching for the best option.

"Give me a minute here, Deck."

"Yes siree, bob."

"We can retrace my route," Heather suggested. Leaning across the center console she tapped on one of the pathways snaking farther east and straightening into a line directly north.

"It's a little roundabout at the beginning, but eh, infrastructure here is screwy."

James nodded, inspecting the notes and diagrams from other travelers. Nothing significant stuck out to him. James decided to trust their new guide.

"I'm sending you all the route we're taking," James said, dropping the highlighted path into a shared drive for the rest of the team. "We'll keep leading at a fast pace. If anyone has trouble speak up, but try to limit comms. Sentinel camps might be close." *Didn't even get a chance to properly scan*, James thought, worried about the possibility of a sneak attack, but it was their only choice. They had to keep moving.

"Got it, boss," Deck spoke for the whole group, and Heather sped up as she descended the cracked rampway north.

Chapter 10

Anger beat in James's ears, and they drove in silence witnessing the post-apocalyptic destruction from the Northern Assault.

Mangled guardrails and large craters were constant reminders of the violence that had bled this area of life. Moss covered slabs of concrete blown randomly from other locations were common. The strangest looking trees, bent from the explosions years ago, had wrapped and warped around various structures as they continued to grow.

"Sorry about that." Heather broke the silence with a side glance at James.

"About what?" James asked, realizing how quiet it had been.

"Deerfield, Arthur, Martin. They can be…picky."

"That's the truth. No clue what they're talking about with the Sentinels though. You?"

"Nope. You don't seem prone to leaving trails in the open."

"Quickest way to a fast death," James said. He looked out the window at an outcrop of skyscrapers.

"Right," Heather said, allowing silence to retake its hold over the truck cab.

James's attention was captured by the abandoned city they approached. Years of neglect had dulled the shining glass windows. The tops of three buildings were gone entirely, exposing their interiors to the elements and giving them the appearance of jagged bones in the fading light. As always, James was taken by the suddenness of the end. People had simply picked up and left, fleeing an unknown threat.

Evidence of the Northern Assault mounted as they drove. Heat licked the edges of his imagination as they passed a melted gas station.

"So how did you and Teresa meet?" Heather asked, pulling James's attention back inside the truck.

"Basic training. She was the last in our group to be eliminated. Deck and I were the only ones who made it out."

"Ahh, you *are* the ones I thought you were. I was in one of the camps."

James's eyebrows raised. He had assumed she had been trained somewhere in the Federation, but going through Elite basic was different.

"Really? Where?" James asked.

"Southwest. Desert land. Very different from what I'm used to."

"Which was?"

"This," Heather said, waving her hand at the landscape. "Well, the Northeast at least. My family was from Boston."

"Nice. They still there?"

Heather shook her head. "Northern Assault. They were the last group to be attacked before the cavalry arrived."

An ache formed in James's throat, and he looked at his lap.

"I'm sorry," he said, pushing thoughts of his father from his mind. He remembered the towns, the bodies, the burnt landscape overcome by fear and death. Mass execution by an unstoppable volume of BZ HOLOs. It had been too late for most when the ionic blasts were set off destroying the remnants of the enemy.

"Thank you, but it's not your fault." Heather's voice dropped. "I was on the other side of the country fighting along the border, trying to keep the western settlements running. Thought we were doing a good job. Low attack rates, fewer Sentinel sightings. Hell, there was even news coming out of NOLA about the ion updates. It was a miracle." She shook her head and bit her lip. "All a mirage."

James nodded. The BZ had staged the perfect assault. Lulling the enemy into a false sense of security, pulling back their forces, and flipping a switch. The Northeast had been theirs for the taking. *In some ways it still was*, James thought.

"We were too late."

"There was no way to be on time for that one. Can't think about it. Have to move on." Heather's stiff back and white knuckles sent a different message, but James nodded silently and kept his eyes on the road.

They drove beneath an underpass and through a neglected traffic light, the dull metal relic swung in the wind. James peered down a city boulevard as Heather blew through the intersection. Blackened windows of brick and cement buildings hugged one another in reflected pools of darkness in the stormy gloom. Most were intact, with the occasional sign of fire or water damage in the older buildings. They drove past a standalone brick building with a white sign hanging askew with the letters *PIZ* still visible in faded red paint.

Stiff gusts of wind struck the side of the pickup pushing them around the broken asphalt as heavier raindrops pelted their windshield. Heather remained steady at the wheel. James was thankful he was driving with someone who knew how to handle the rough weather.

Darkening clouds moved in their direction from the west, changing colors as evening approached. They entered a residential neighborhood where trees swayed dangerously overhead. Heather tried her best to maintain their speed.

"I'm not sure it's a good idea to drive much longer," Heather said, swerving to avoid a branch, "No light, and these streets haven't been kept up for years. There's no telling what's out there. Add that to the massive storm brewing and we could have a big problem."

"Agreed. What's the move?" James asked, deferring to the area native.

"There're some houses farther along this road I've stayed in on other trips. We can camp for the night. Keep going in the morning.

James would have liked an hour or so to plan their stop, scan the area, and make sure there wouldn't be any problems, but they'd have to make do.

"Let's do it," James said. He tapped his wrist control for the team comms. "Listen up, everyone, weather and road conditions aren't good enough to continue safely, so we're gonna pull over. There's a place to rest in a few miles. Jon, can you run a quick scan? Stacie, find out if there's been any activity around here. Check logs from other NOLA outposts or old Federation files. See who else has been through the area."

"Got it," came their synchronized responses.

"Deck?"

"Yes, dear?"

"Pull up a map. Find a decent place to stay for the night."

"On it."

"Kevin?

"Yep?"

"Do we have anything you can throw together for a quick meal when we get there? No heat."

"Yep, I'm on it."

"Great, the rest of you, get ready to lock the vehicles and make a run for it." James pressed the side of his face against the cold window to get a better look at the intimidating clouds growing steadily overhead. "I don't think this thing is going to hold off."

"And I just had my hair done…" Deck muttered over the headset before the channel went silent.

"Lead the way," James said to Heather.

Deck picked a house in an unassuming neighborhood where families would have been happily living a few years earlier.

Many homes lining the block were well groomed although their previously manicured lawns were overgrown. Still, the shades of gray, blue, and white depicted a pleasant suburb. Even amongst the neat and tiny houses the remnants the war had left stood out at random intervals along the street. Holes in the road and ruined houses marred the once peaceful area.

When they parked, the team hurried inside, taking only a few personal items. Rain pummeled James as he sprinted to the front door and entered with ease. James stepped into the foyer that led to a recessed living room. A stagnant odor hung in the air and the eerie sight of an intact living room covered in layers of dust greeted the team.

It's like a museum, James thought walking into the room and running his hand along the back of a chair. Dust floated to the floor and crumbled on his skin when he rubbed his fingers together. He climbed the stairs on the opposite side of the room. Conditions on the second floor were the same, abruptly abandoned and uninhabited for years.

"Owners must have left during the attacks," Heather said, ducking her head into a room with an unmade bed.

"Hope they got out," James replied, noticing a playhouse erected in the corner.

"That's all we can do," Heather replied, leaving without further inspection.

Bunk beds and a bin full of children's toys were in another room. A lone stuffed elephant lay in the middle of the carpet. James picked it up and carefully laid it on top of the others, forcing away the image of a terrorized family throwing their toys into a bin and fleeing their home. He tore his eyes from the room and followed Heather back downstairs.

"Clear upstairs," he said to no one in particular.

Bob flipped a light switch and to James's surprise it turned on. *That's strange,* he thought, touching his pistol.

"Relax," Bob said, noticing James's reaction "Clint plugged a battery pack into the house's power grid."

James breathed a sigh of relief as the engineer returned from the basement.

"There is a sweet ping pong table down there. I'm happy to kick anyone's ass who wants me to," Clint said, throwing his tool bag next to his pack.

"We can see about that after I eat something," Bob said, impatiently eyeing the spread Kevin was putting together.

"Where the hell did this thing come from?" Kyle asked, standing by the front window stretching one of his legs. "Late in the season for a thunderstorm."

"Never too late around here," Heather said, joining him by the window.

"Guess not," he replied, shrugging. Finished with his stretching, Kyle walked over to Stacie whose nose was buried in a HOLO.

"Watcha looking at, Serial?" he asked, leaning against the wall and peeking over her shoulder.

"The signal around here, it's…weird." Stacie's face scrunched into a frown and James's danger alert piqued.

That's not a good sign, James thought, self-consciously scanning the room where the rest of the team lounged. Heather caught his eye and nodded towards the adjoining room.

"Check if the fridge is running?" she asked, creating an exit for them.

"Not yet," James answered as he followed her.

They entered a galley kitchen decorated with black-and-white checkered tile reflecting the dim light from the other room. James opened the cabinets one by one, getting different scents from each depending on their contents, soap, plastic, moldy bread. More reminders of the previous inhabitants.

James opened the fridge. Empty, except for a stick of rotting butter and what appeared to be dehydrated apples. Heather poked her head into the remaining cabinets and opened the sliding French doors to the yard, closing them quickly to prevent rain from getting in.

"Why'd we come in here?" James asked. He squinted out the window, trying to discern anything other than flying plant debris. Gail-force winds dipped trees to the ground simultaneously ripping any remaining foliage off their branches.

"Signal misfires aren't normal. Every time there's been one before…" Heather's voice trailed off as she stepped towards a door at the far end of the kitchen.

A sliver of light emanated from a thin crack at the bottom.

James held his breath as Heather turned around and made eye contact with him.

Then, taking in the room, she inspected the ceilings and windows deliberately stepping closer and closer to the thread of light.

James's heart pounded in his chest, uncertain about what to do. Stay and take on whatever's behind the door or alert the team?

The wind reached a new level outside, moaning against the trees. A fresh gust whipped through the air and the windows rattled in place.

Shadows from the doorway lengthened as Heather passed her target and crept along the wall. In the window, he caught her reflection and waited as she counted down on her fingers while wrapping her other hand firmly around the doorknob.

James stood ready with his hand clasped around the hilt of his sidearm. As Heather opened the door James raised his gun and pointed the muzzle at the opening. Inside, a lone HOLO glowed with the word HELLO written across it in bright blue letters, a yellow smiley face twirled in a circle underneath.

What the—

"GET DOWN!" Heather's shout pierced the air seconds before the scream of shattering glass broke the room in half.

Chapter 11

A shove sent James flying backwards slamming into the tiled floor.

Air was sucked from his lungs on impact. Two pairs of hands gripped his shoulders and flung him from the kitchen.

Shards of glass and bits of drywall covered the ground. A gash above the kitchen door exposed its frame. James struggled to get his bearings as slivers of wood floated in the air around him. He regained his breath and tried to steady his racing heart as thunderous noise filled the chaotic space.

Shouts of confusion and a deafening barrage of semi-automatic gunfire filled the room. He put his hand to his forehead, and it came away with rust colored liquid smeared on his skin. Hot breath filled his ear, and he realized someone was shouting.

Turning he saw Stacie trying to get his attention while Heather covered them with selective handgun fire.

"JAMES!" Stacie yelled, her eyes an odd mixture of panic and perfect calm.

James held a hand up acknowledging her. "I'm back," he said. Taking a deep breath he assessed the condition of his body. His head pounded from striking the ground and his shoulder burned as if shards of glass were stuck in his tendons.

"What's the deal? Where's the team?"

An explosion came from the kitchen, and Heather threw her body over the two of them as chunks of drywall showered their heads.

"Out front. We need to move," Heather said. Replacing her spent magazine and maintaining focus on the kitchen. "I'll cover. You two go. Now."

Without waiting for a response, Heather let off a round of fire into the kitchen.

Stacie grabbed James's bicep and pulled him to his feet.

He stumbled over mangled pieces of house material as they sprinted towards the door stopping in their tracks as gunfire cut through their intended route. Stacie whipped him against the hallway wall for cover while she poked her head around the side to peer into the living room. She let off a round of fire as Heather sprinted around the opposite corner diving behind the wall as bullets tore the path to pieces.

Breathe in, breathe out, breathe in, breathe out. James worked on regaining control. Every time he moved the heat of his stomach contents warmed the back of his throat and his vision swam from the effects of a definite concussion. He concentrated his breathing further.

He shook his head violently and gritted his teeth. *Get it together.*

Willing away the impacts of the attack he reached for his sidearm, racked a bullet in the chamber, and assessed the situation.

They were pinned in a hallway by an unknown number of hostiles. The rest of the team waited outside. James considered their options while Heather and Stacie kept their enemy combatants busy.

There was only one solution.

"Stairs!" he shouted over Stacie's shoulder.

Stacie nodded her assent. "You go first. Cover us and we'll join you."

James signed to Heather, hoping she shared their language: *Stairs. Cover me.*

Luckily, she nodded in response. Gesturing silently, Stacie counted down, and on one they let off a cover round as James took a deep breath and sprinted to the stairs.

Chunks of banister pelted his body and the thud of bullets burying themselves in the wood emphasized the missiles' near hits.

When he reached the top of the stairs, James looked into the living room. A mist of paint dust and minuscule splinters of wood hung in the air and coated his tongue. Lying on the ground were two black clad bodies in wet combat gear, their faces covered in masks. James breathed a sigh of relief. *No one we know.*

Stacie emptied a magazine and pulled back around the wall. James signed to her:

Move.

Without hesitation, Stacie sprung towards the stairs as James's gunfire erupted, aimed at the same spot where Heather pumped bullets.

James continued his assault as Heather followed, sprinting from her position. She practically flew, puffs of dust trailing her after each terrifying impact of shrapnel marked her every step. When she reached the top James turned and looked down the hall. Stacie was outside the kid's bedroom he had inspected earlier.

Slowing, James caught his breath and checked his magazine.

Gunfire sounded through the thin windowpanes, its intensity ebbing and flowing with the wind's direction.

A bolt of lightning illuminated the room casting a pale glow across their faces. They stood breathing heavily awaiting more assailants. James glanced at Stacie who caught his eye. They knew they were trapped.

Cracking glass broke James's thoughts and he felt something strike his calf. Catlike, Heather's hand shot to his foot as Stacie dove into the bedroom. Splinters of wood erupted in the air and shards of white paint sprinkled the ground. Heather tossed something into the hallway and lowered her head. James followed her lead, ducking as a scream from an unsuspecting victim came from the hallway.

"Nice toss," James said, looking at the spot by his boot where the grenade had been seconds earlier.

"They're coming up the stairs," Stacie said. Using a piece of broken mirror from the floor, she peeked around the corner.

Working one step ahead, Heather brought an overstuffed tiger to the door.

"James, when I throw this out, wait for them to bite, then take them all out."

Stacie held the glass so Heather could see, and James got into position. The creak of the carpeted wood floor caused a rush of adrenaline to enter James's veins. He fought to keep his heartbeat in rhythm and took a deep breath of the paint layered air as Heather lobbed the orange cat into the hallway.

A meat grinder of flying metal barbs tore it to shreds, and seconds later James popped around the corner releasing a slew of bullets at the three soldiers, stunned in confusion at the white balls of fluff floating innocently to the ground.

Their bodies dropped and James, hearing movement on the stairs, reacted. Running to the nearest body, he yanked a grenade off the figure's belt. Swiftly pulling the pin he flung it down the stairs and simultaneously dove through the nearest doorway.

Three seconds later an explosion rang followed by the telltale sound of a grunt confirming a hit.

James lay on the floor for five heartbeats before he moved to the door and poked his head around the corner.

Empty stairwell.

He turned to Stacie and Heather who had taken positions on either side of the hall.

Stacie gave him a thumbs-up, and James lifted his sidearm as he turned to the stairway. Crumpled bodies lay on the first floor in unnatural positions, with pools of blood gathering around their torsos.

"All clear," he yelled to the women.

Stacie brushed by him, followed by Heather.

"I'm going outside to back them up," Stacie said, as she checked her magazine and ran out, not waiting for James or Heather to respond.

"Grab our gear. We need to leave," Heather said, already in the living room. She pushed a body over with her toe and bent to check the face of their assaulter.

"Recognizable?"

"Never are," Heather said with a sigh, pulling the mask back down, "But Exils, I know that much. Federation trained I'd bet. Maybe by proxy, maybe directly. Either way, we need to get the fuck out of here. They've got backup nearby for sure."

"Great," James said. He grabbed four of the packs and tossed them over his left shoulder. Clenching his teeth through the burning pain, he hoisted another two over the right.

"Grab the other two for me?"

Heather picked them up and slung them behind her. At the front door, they heard the peppering of gunfire. Sounds of active shooting were unmistakable but it seemed to be dying down.

Let's hope, James thought.

"On me," Heather said, looking him in the eye.

"On you," James replied with a nod, returning eye contact.

Heather held the doorknob loosely in one hand waiting for a longer break in the melee. She yanked the door open in a rush and stepped out.

"Get to cover!" she shouted, sprinting towards the parked trucks while letting off a few rounds into the grove of trees across the street.

James followed. His heart pounded as bullets whipped by slicing the air around him and hitting the concrete. The twenty-yard run felt like the length of a football field. He slammed into Heather's truck, fighting the pain that shot through his arm.

This thing is going to be annoying, he thought pushing his mind past the agony and grinding his teeth.

"Nice of you to join," Kevin said. He sat against one of the truck's tires clutching his leg. Sweat ran in rivulets down his temples and the normally stoic chef clenched his jaw.

"Kev! What happened?" James asked, throwing down his packs quickly forgetting his own injury.

"Shot twice in the leg. Bob was near me, so he took care of it, but hurts like a motherfucker."

"Goddamn it."

"'Goddamn it is right. We're pinned down, man."

James analyzed the scenario and tried to come up with a way out of the situation. They had to leave. Two of them were injured, and the other six were God only knew where.

What the fuck is happening?

Truck lights flipped on and the pit in James's stomach lessened.

"Get in!" Clint yelled from the front of the pickup.

Great timing, James thought, squinting from the harsh light.

Two people appeared next to James.

"We've got, Kev. You two, get in the bed," Kyle shouted over the scream of bullets hammering the driver's side door. Bob knelt next to Kevin inspecting the damaged leg with a coolness James dreamed of commanding.

Can't just watch him work, James thought, mentally chastising himself.

James grabbed Heather's shoulder and yelled, "Let's go!" They picked up the gear and sprinted to the pickup as bullets flew overhead.

James threw his packs into the back of the truck, and someone pulled him up.

"Glad you made it out," Deck shouted over the deafening combination of explosions and the storm.

"Same," James replied. He reached into the armory behind the truck's cab and pulled out a rifle. He clicked off the safety and racked a bullet in the chamber, focusing his scope over the top of Heather's truck above where Kyle and Bob were getting ready to lift Kevin. A group of black-clad figures walked through the yard across the street, letting loose a steady stream of rifle fire.

Hurry up, guys. Clenching his teeth he started picking off the encroaching group of shadows.

An elbow bumped James's, and he looked over to find Heather with her eye on a scope.

"They've got a rocket!" Deck cried out.

James's eye twitched until he spotted the offending party.

He was too late. His finger flicked the trigger as smoke appeared from the back of the missile as it tore through the air straight for the engine block of Heather's truck.

Horror unfolded in slow motion as the explosive propelled towards the truck with the helpless group pinned against its side. James's stomach dropped into his groin, and a sickening lurch filled his throat.

No sound escaped his mouth as he tried to yell a warning to his three friends stuck behind the car destined for death.

Flames shot into the air, and James looked in confusion as Kyle and Bob ran for the pickup with Kevin hopping between them.

The Jeep parked in front of the demolished pickup became a pile of molten steel with dark smoke funneling into the wind over the devastation below. Air filled with burning rubber and gasoline seared James's eyes as he hauled Kevin over the side of the truck bed.

Squealing tires screeched as Clint poured on the speed. They flew from the scene, racing through suburban back roads and whipping around corners. *Glad he's the one driving*, James thought, looking at the neighborhood they were leaving behind.

The weight dispersion of the truck did not seem to bother Clint as he pulled through drifts with expert precision. Following in the remaining Jeep, Jon gunned the gas to keep up. Stacie, half hanging out the passenger window, continued taking shots at the ghostlike people emerging from the darkness.

Flames from the demolished Jeep could not be seen in the inky black night and the rain continued to pour. James gripped a leather cord holding the armory in place to keep from being thrown from the truck and leaned in relief against the side of the cab. He exchanged a thumbs-up with Kevin as Bob disinfected the man's wounds with quick bond bio-tape.

"Close one," James said to Heather. The woman's face was anything but relaxed. Her eyes searched the darkness with a fervor replacing James's momentary relief with anxiety.

"They're coming. They always do." She put the rifle scope to her eye and scanned the area. As if on cue, a roar resounded from the right, and turning, James was shoved to the floor of the truck as Heather let off a series of shots at the oncoming lights.

How am I always in the wrong place? James thought, rubbing his injured shoulder.

Pushing to his knees and bracing himself James picked up his rifle and stared down the scope.

Three pickups carrying heavily armed combatants trailed by a group of dirt bikes followed them.

"We need a way to take them all out," Heather said. She shot at the driver's window of the first truck only to have her bullets repelled by its protective glass.

"No shit. Any ideas?" Deck asked, stabilizing his rifle on the bed's rear door, and aiming for the bikes. He took out the tire of the first one and the bike skidded to a bone crunching stop against the side of a tree. The other bikers took the hint and slowed to follow the armored vehicles.

"Here they come," Clint's voice crackled over their earpieces, and James watched the trucks pick up speed.

Windswept rain blinded James, mingling with his sweat, and the salty liquid stung his eyes as it dripped down his forehead. The lead car closed the gap, and James saw the glint of two mounted muzzles. His stomach twisted in a knot as he searched for what to do.

Without warning the Jeep barreled into view. The off-road vehicle slammed the pursuing truck, knocking it off the road and sending it careening into a house. Steel and glass exploded as Jon whipped the Jeep back onto the path, gunning the engine to catch up to the team.

James saw their opening and yelled to the others in his truck, "Take out the bikes!"

Flashes lit the darkening night as James concentrated on the weaving daredevils treading dangerously close to each other.

Three of the riders had been exposed by the loss of the truck and were caught in no man's land with nowhere to hide.

James fixed his sights on the lead rider and waited for the bike to tilt, the perfect moment to nail the front tire. Seconds after the bullet hit, the driver flew through the air, helpless against gravity. The bike flipped and, as James had hoped, fell into a second rider knocking it from its perch and under the tire of the final biker who landed in a faceplant on the slick asphalt.

Three down.

James focused on the remaining two trucks that had converged in the middle of the road protecting the bikers from the sniper fire peppering their advance.

Wind and rain kicked up another notch as Clint skidded into another turn onto a wide-open highway. Gusts pushed them around the unruly roads jostling the team in the back from side to side. The Jeep sped ahead of them, and James braced his torso as he crawled to the front of the truck bed.

He opened the window to the cab. "Clint, what's the plan?"

"Jon's leading us to a bridge ahead. Maybe we can lose 'em on the other side, but these jackasses are persistent. We're going to need to take them on soon," he said, pointing to the fuel gauge that showed a quarter tank. James nodded his head grimly. There was no telling how much longer that would hold with the fuel they were burning.

"Keep it going," James said, patting the bulky mechanic's shoulder.

"Keep them off me," Clint replied, checking his sideview mirror and switching lanes as potshots glanced off the bulletproof glass.

"We're working on it." James slid the window shut, and he looked behind the truck.

Both pickups chasing them closed in, and their companion dirt bikes had driven off.

"Where'd the escorts go?" James yelled over the wind in Deck's ear.

Deck pointed at the ridge trailing the side of the road, and James watched their chasers pop out at random from the tree line.

Smart strategy, James thought, wishing he had a bike at that moment.

A hand tapped his shoulder, and he turned to Heather whose eyes were glued over the front of the cab.

"Bridge is around the corner. If we can make it over that we can get into the woods and away from them."

James nodded and gritted his teeth. *Come on, Clint.*

They swung around a curve, and James was weightless. On two tires now, the truck slanted diagonally on the rain-soaked roads. James was certain they were going to flip when the bed bounced, the rubber tires hugged the road again, and James's stomach returned to its natural position.

James took shots at the trucks' windshields. *If I can't break them, I might as well be as annoying as possible*, he thought and the rest of the team followed suit, forcing one of the trucks to reduce its speed.

While reloading, James peeked over the top of the cab and saw the bridge in front of them. *Almost there.* Beaten and aged, the open-air bridge took up eight lanes and spanned a wide river. They would be completely in the open when they crossed, but they had no other choice. The other side was safety.

James racked a bullet in his chamber and aimed back at the pickups still chasing them.

His numb fingers squeezed the trigger.

Just a little longer, James breathed, anxiously waiting to be over the bridge.

"HOLD ON!"

The shout came from nowhere, but suddenly James was airborne. The truck flew underneath him, and he floated into pellets of cold liquid. Time sped and he landed in a heap as his body rolled to a stop.

Everything hurt. Driving sheets of rain and cold air whipped his body into weak submission. His hand lay in a pile of mush emitting liquid when he pushed it down. James desperately hoped it wasn't a part of him. A pair of hands examined his back, and he fought with every ounce of strength to turn over.

"What the hell…?" he said as he saw Bob's face.

"Hold on a second, you got thrown from the back of the truck. Clint had to swerve away from a missile shot."

Slowly processing he concentrated on the words. *Thrown from the back of the truck? How was he still alive?*

"Lucky you landed on the grass," Bob said, nodding at the wet spongy material James had felt seconds earlier.

"We've gotta get back," James said urgently.

Satisfied with his exam, Bob held out his forearm and James gripped it. The medic pulled him to his feet with a surprising amount of strength and led James back to the group. When they got there, Deck handed him a rifle. "Can't keep flying off like that, pal."

"I'll remember that for next time," James grimaced. "Can we move yet?"

"Clint's fixing the pickup now," Deck said as he headed back to the line, firing at the Exils advancing across the bridge shielded behind their armored trucks.

James crawled over and joined the firing, positioning himself between Heather and Deck as they did all they could to halt the well-defended enemy whose bulletproof vehicles provided all the cover they needed.

"Rocket!" A shout came down the line and James saw the shooter's head fly back as one of their bullets took him through the skull seconds before he fired.

Heather ignored a clap on her shoulder from Deck as she kept her eye pressed to the rifle scope.

"We've got two more up!"

James acted first this time and tapped his trigger three times taking it out.

Stacie shouted, "Enemy armor's up!" An ion shield popped up, rain soaking its exterior.

They were screwed.

"Get over the bridge!" James shouted.

He grabbed Heather's arm and tried pulling her away, but she shook him off.

"Not yet."

"We're going to lose this one. Let's go!"

"Not yet," she growled, tapping her trigger three more times. James gritted his teeth, and began firing at anything that moved.

The Exil team assembled their weaponry, protected by their transparent shield. Each time a streak of lightning illuminated the scene, the image of a distorted cannon gun glinted through the shield.

"Motherfucker," James mumbled as a shadow figure ran to the machine, pulled back on its ammo loader, positioned himself behind the sight, and aimed at the team's pickup.

Driving wind blinded James's vision. He held down the rifle's trigger, willing one of the bullets to break through the enemy fortifications. Hoping he'd be able to fight his way out and wondering if this was the last time.

Sweat, blood, and rainwater stung his eyelids. As he waited for his inevitable death, he heard the boom of a heavy gun.

Seconds later, he tasted the salt from his skin in his mouth. Cold metal brushed against his palms and his numb fingertips felt the trigger pumping bullets at their attackers.

Opening his eyes, he witnessed a scene he hadn't expected. The gunner and his machine lay in a mangled twist of metal. The trucks were on fire and the black-clad attackers were sprawled across the ground, dead or dying.

James stared in confusion as the dirt bikers scrambled away from a rain of bullets tearing their bodies apart before falling from the ridge into the river's raging waters.

Muffled sounds and a host of light flooded the area as three canvas-covered trucks skidded onto the bridge.

Two people emerged from the lead vehicle and approached him.

It took a second for James to recognize one of the faces and he couldn't help but smile.

"Hey, James," Teresa said, nodding. "Looks like you've had an eventful trip."

PART II

CHAPTER 12

Morning arrived with a wave of confusion.

What happened?

Recognition and memories filled his consciousness as his brain awakened. Exils, stuck on the bridge, heavy guns, then Teresa. *Great timing*, James thought, wondering how many more of those moments he had left.

The raging downpour from the previous night was over, and James shook his head, adjusting to the brilliant morning. Rain-soaked earth squished under James's hands as he sat, and his breath froze when he exhaled. Remnants from the storm littered the scene with bits of leaves and small branches covering the ground. A damp moldy scent hung in the cold air, making it hard for James to pull himself from the warmth of his sleeping bag. Orange sunlight lit the sky, revealing a cloud-dappled horizon. A swollen river roared hundreds of feet beneath the bridge blending with the constant buzz of the forest.

The telltale *clang* of mechanics at work alerted James to the presence of others. He glanced at the sleeping bodies sprawled out nearby. Clint was the only one of his team missing. Their saviors from the previous night were already up, no doubt adding to the background noise.

James stretched his arms and watched a family of squirrels chase each other on a leafless tree, puzzled by the human activity absent from the area for so long.

"Watch it!" someone shouted from the Exils' overturned pickup.

"Ahh, you're fine," Clint's voice cut through the air. James exited his sleeping bag and headed over to inspect.

"Could have taken my freakin' head off, man," an unfamiliar voice came from the same spot.

"But I didn't. Now help me hook this thing up."

"Lotta goddamn thanks I get," grumbled the unidentified voice. Heavy chains dragged across the asphalt rattling the morning stillness.

"Hook it to the pick—" Clint started to speak when he was cut off.

"Clint, I know how to winch an engine block."

"Fair, I don't have a lot of other gearheads on the team. None actually."

"I'm handy," James yelled out, sarcasm edging his voice.

Two grease-stained faces popped up over the edge of the truck. Clint grinned, "No. You aren't."

"Well, I could be."

"Sure you could, bud." Clint wiped his hands on a rag as he nodded at the man wiping his face. "This is Liam, Teresa's husband."

"How's it goin', man?" Liam asked. He had a five o'clock shadow and a mullet of dark brown hair hanging off his head. His wore a goofy smile and showed his blackened hands to James. "I'd shake your hand, but you wouldn't want that. Call it a raincheck?"

"Works for me. What's going on here? Where's everyone?"

"Teresa and the rest of the crew are farther back cleaning up the mess. You all did quite a number on that group of Exils," Liam replied.

"They didn't pull any punches either," James said, glancing at the bodies strewn across the bridge.

"They're here for themselves, that's it. Glad you were able to get through."

James nodded, the stiffness in his shoulder returned as he rotated the swollen appendage in its socket.

"When'd you wake up?" James asked Clint.

"Heard this guy messin' around with the truck. Didn't want some amateur screwing it up," Clint said, getting a shove from Liam. "Turns out he's a pro."

"Need any help?"

"Yeah, grab this chain for me. We're taking the engine with us. Never know when you could use the extra parts," Liam said. The mechanic tossed him the end of the heavy iron cord. James clenched his teeth when he caught it, a shock of pain echoing to his elbow. *Need some help from Bob,* James thought, making a note to ask the medic to look at his shoulder.

James followed Liam and hooked the chain to the winch at the front of the canvas truck sitting on the other side.

"Keep pulling the extra cordage out of the way. Can't let it get stuck in the gears. It'd make for a horrible day." Liam nodded at the empty spool in the back of the truck.

"I'm on it," James said in a more confident tone than he felt.

Liam patted his shoulder, and James observed as the two engineers turned on the winch that then lifted the engine into the air. They guided the steel apparatus over the walls of the truck bed and into the back where it settled with a groan.

"All right, let's get some coffee and clear these bodies up," Liam said, wiping his hands on a rag hanging from his belt.

"Sounds good," James replied.

"Looks like someone beat us to it." Clint pointed to Kevin dragging his banged-up leg around the fire while he steeped a pot of coffee over an open flame.

Bob sat at the edge of the circle, rifling through his bag as James and the two mechanics approached the camp.

"How're you feelin', big man?" Clint asked grabbing three tin coffee mugs from the open bag.

"Been better," Kevin answered, shrugging. He poured dark steaming liquid into the mugs Clint held up to him. "Lucky Bob was there."

"Luckier that rocket misfired," Bob added. "How's the arm, James?"

James shifted his shoulder, wincing as a stab of pain rippled to his elbow. "It's moving."

"Not well though." Bob stood. His face was a mask of analysis, and he motioned for James to sit on the ground.

James obliged, taking a cup of coffee from Clint as he did.

Bob's hands probed the back of James's shoulder and the joint around it. "Cracked your collar bone when Heather shoved you down. It'll take a while to heal. I'd normally suggest resting for a while, but we don't have that luxury. I'll have to help you manage the pain."

"That'll do. Thanks, Bob."

"Right, I'll grab a couple of pain blockers. Kevin, we're getting those bullets out in ten."

Bob walked away as Kevin lowered his body gingerly into the seat next to James.

"Good we've got him," James said, nodding in Bob's direction.

"Speak for yourself. He's not going to dig around in your leg," Kevin said sullenly eyeing his bandaged thigh.

"Good point. How'd it happen, anyway?"

Kevin shrugged. "No clue. One second I'm near the car; next second I've got two hot coals under my skin and blood pouring like a faucet." He took a sip of his coffee. "I was worried they'd hit an artery. So much blood."

James glanced at the stiff, rust-colored pants Kevin wore.

"Looks like you've been trying to paint a barn. Bob's in the right place a lot of the time."

"Harbinger of injury, I think," Kevin said half joking, "He certainly has a different level of calm."

James nodded, recalling the unflinching face of their medic from last night, "That's the truth."

"Where's coffee?" Deck interrupted their conversation, and James turned to see his red-eyed scout looking lost standing next to the circle.

"Over here, bud," James said, holding the pot in the air.

"Gracias, boys," Deck poured himself a cup while he surveyed the damaged surroundings, "Quite the evening, huh?"

"Yes, it was," Kevin said, leaning back on his elbows as he waited for Bob to return.

"Happy Teresa and her people got here when they did. Poor lass is probably still heart stung over me," Deck said, gazing forlornly over the scene of destroyed trucks and littered bodies. "I'll have to let her down easy."

"I'll help explain," Liam said, with a slight grin.

"Ahh yes, one of her team. I hear she's got a husband. I'm sure he's a great guy. Has to be to mend her broken heart."

Liam waved off the comment, choosing to continue his anonymity. James kept his mouth shut enjoying the show.

"She doesn't know what she's missing I bet. You Deck?"

"My reputation precedes me," Deck said, winking at James. "Must be talked about a lot around here."

"Clint mentioned you. Teresa's probably still too heartbroken to mention your name."

"Of course." Deck sat on the ground, oblivious to Clint, Kevin, and James struggling to keep from laughing as he continued his self-aggrandizing.

"You know, I always thought we'd meet again. She missed her chance." Deck looked away wistfully immersed in deep thought, and Liam remained sympathetic listening in earnest to Deck's recollection of Teresa's hidden affections.

"If only she knew."

"I'll drink to that." Deck raised his glass to Liam who returned the gesture over the low flames. Deck, sipped his coffee, glancing at the area. "Where's everyone else? Bob's gotta be up?"

"He's getting some pain blockers for James and grabbing his equipment for Kev's leg," Clint replied.

"Eesh, that's gonna suck," Deck said, wincing at the injured chef's wrapped thigh.

"Thanks, Deck," Kevin said, shaking his head.

"And our heroes? They off to find the rest of the enemy?"

"Yep, should be back any minute," Clint said.

"Well, guess we can relax for a bit. What's Teresa's husband's name again? Lyle? Lorne?"

"It's Liam," Kevin said, a cocky grin plastered on his face.

Deck, missing the smirk, nodded. "Gotcha. He around?"

"Somewhere," James said, deciding to let the joke continue.

"Hey, Deck." Bob entered the circle and sat in front of Kevin.

"Bobby boy, how you doing? I see you're tending to our injured comrades. Can I help?" Deck asked.

"Might need your help during the removal, but we'll see. Hey, Liam, do you have any extra med supplies we can use? I need extra gauze," Bob said, unaware of the earlier conversation.

"I gotcha, man." Liam hopped to his feet and walked towards one of the pickups.

James turned to Deck whose face had morphed into a pale shell of itself. His ears burned bright red and his lips pursed together in a strange mix of emotions James could not decipher. Calmly, the scout placed his coffee cup on the ground and looked at each person in turn finishing by making eye contact with James who stared back at him innocently.

Deck picked his coffee cup back up and blew a wisp of steam from the rim as the rest of the team bit their lips to keep from laughing.

"You know, guys, it's nice to know when you step in shit before you walk into someone's house," Deck said with a flourish.

"Yeah, but it's way funnier this way," Clint replied as Liam walked over with gauze tossing it to Bob.

"Here ya go. I think Teresa's almost back. Might wanna get yourself cleaned up, lover boy," Liam said, winking at Deck who looked at the ground.

Liam walked away as the rest of the team broke out laughing while Bob glanced at them, confused.

"It's official. I hate everyone," Deck grumbled, sipping his coffee, ignoring the rest of the group.

Ten minutes later, James met Teresa on the bridge. Her team had returned and were moving the mangled scraps of metal from the night before to the side of the road. James lifted the body of a dead soldier under the armpits and moved it over to the pile started earlier by Teresa's team.

James watched it roll limply into a fellow corpse burying its face into the neck of the other body. He stared at the heap of flesh, realizing all too well he'd see the scene again in his nightmares. Clammy flesh more like slabs of fat hung over each other, overflowing onto the asphalt. Faces, arms, and legs burned beyond recognition, with skin bubbled and charred to a crisp, lay perfectly still in a heap on a broken road and became image scorched into James's retinas. He knew how close he had come to their fate.

"James, how's that arm?" Teresa's voice pulled James from his thoughts, and he turned to greet the stout leader.

"Not too bad. Broken collar bone."

"Yikes, that sucks." Teresa stood with her hands on her hips, breathing heavily. He was surprised how similar she was to the person he had known during training. A decade of war can do a lot to a person, but Teresa had kept her core. Confident verging on cocky with a determination James admired. He remembered the tough woman waiting for her turn outside a medic tent bleeding to the point of unconsciousness.

"It's just time and pain. What'd you find back there?" James asked, nodding in the direction of the town.

"Same as always for these groups. Supplies, vehicles— anything worth a damn all gone. Only thing left behind is the damage they deal. Broken gear, burned-out buildings, spent ammo…bodies." The last word hung in the air as Teresa continued. "Operations influenced by pure self-interest." Teresa guided her team with hand signals while she spoke.

"Exils a big problem around here?" James asked. "Not many hanging about NOLA and those we have are harmless. Disorganized former criminals for the most part." James watched two of Teresa's soldiers pull a crate of .50 caliber ammo from the cab of the dead Exil's truck.

"Only gotten worse. More and more Federation AWOLs seeking a life out from under the thumb of the powers that be. They're too paranoid to join us and too disillusioned to sign on with any local city states, so they become independent. Unaffiliated groups of highly trained military personnel solely motivated by survival." Teresa turned and looked James in the eye. "They're a dangerous proposition, James. You guys were lucky you encountered the weather you did. With the way they were trenched in around here, things could have been much worse."

"Best thing was having me around though." Heather sauntered over to the two of them and leaned against the truck.

"That's a good point. Girl saved your ass," Teresa said, grinning.

"Certainly did. Fucked my shoulder in the process, but I owe you one." James tipped his head in respect at their guide.

"Anytime. My bad about your arm," Heather said, true concern on her face.

"All's fair in the middle of a war," James said, waving off the apology. "Would have been my head if you hadn't."

"Hey! Enough talking over there, what's the move?" Liam walked over with his hands on his hips.

"We all done?" Teresa asked, glancing around the burly engineer at the activity slowing on the bridge.

"Engines all removed and in our trucks. They're picking up the rest of the supplies now."

"Let's push the empty trucks into the water and burn those bodies. Then we can hit the road."

"We'll take care of that," James said, motioning for Deck and Clint to start pulling the truck off to the side of the road. "You two get some coffee."

"You're a hero," Liam said, clapping him on his good shoulder and walking over to the fire where Kyle, Stacie, and Jon stood sipping their morning brews.

"Send the rest of my team over here when they're ready. We'll be done soon. Deck's already gotten most of the supplies from the truck bed."

"Deck?! Wow, it's been so long," Teresa said, shaking her head and smiling.

James noticed Deck's back straighten at the statement.

"I completely forgot about him. Is he here?"

"HA!" Clint coughed a loud laugh, and Deck's shoulders drooped as he pushed the chuckling mechanic out of the way and grabbed hold of the mangled truck's front end, grumbling under his breath.

Still laughing, Clint said, "Yeah, I'll bring him over to say hi."

Teresa looked confused but nodded and walked away.

The cleanup went smoothly with the six of them hauling bodies and scraps of metal into various piles, but James missed the carrying power of their doctor and his patient. Bob and Kevin sat off to the side with Bob concentrating deeply on Kevin's leg while the patient gritted his teeth through pain. James was glad his own injury would not require such hands-on treatment.

As their final task, James helped Clint use a jack to push the Exil's truck off the bridge. The vehicle was surprisingly light without its engine. It splashed a hundred yards below them eliciting a loud *crack* upon hitting the water.

With the mess cleaned up, James walked over to his medic and chef, grimacing at the sight of Bob's hands covered in blood. Kevin's face had drained of color and the ball of muscle on the side of his jaw was a knot the size of a jawbreaker.

"Come on, Bob, you've gotta finish," Kevin grimaced, his voice shaky from exhaustion and pain.

"Almost done, buddy. These rounds shatter on impact so I..." Bob's voice broke off as he dug his fingers deeper into the wound and, with a final grunt, pulled a glinting fragment of sharpened metal from under Kevin's torn skin. "Got it."

Relief washed over Kevin's face. He took a deep breath as Bob wiped his hands and injected a pain blocker into the chef's leg.

"That hurt like you wouldn't believe."

"I know. I'm sorry, man. I was fishing close to that artery and needed to keep an eye on your blood pressure. Couldn't risk you on heavy meds. Changes now," Bob said, disinfecting the cut. He applied bio-tape around the wound that morphed to match the chef's skin, assimilating as if it were a piece of Kevin's body.

"All good over here?" James asked, clapping Kevin on the shoulder.

"Yeah, finally," Kevin said, his head lolling back on his shoulders as the effect of the painkiller took over.

"Hollow points. Nasty little things." Bob said holding the twisted piece of metal to the sunlight.

"Glad you got it all out. I'm gonna grab Teresa, let's get out of here."

"Got it." The two replied in unison. He waved at the rest of the team pointing in the direction of the fire and mimicking driving. He received a thumbs-up from everyone but Deck, who, suffering from a bruised ego, held up a middle finger.

Maybe I'll have Deck drive with Teresa and Liam. James grinned to himself thinking of the potential conversations they could have as he walked over to their newest hosts.

CHAPTER 13

Marble flooring ran into another blank stone wall as James and Deck turned the corner.

"Goddamn it!" Deck exclaimed, frustrated.

"We'll figure it out," James said, but he was as annoyed as his friend.

Headquarters for the outpost were housed in a Gothic estate in the middle of the countryside. The square building enclosed a courtyard containing trampled gardens and cracked slate walkways crisscrossing the space. Wrought iron gates blocked the archways preventing entry and exit. James wondered what it would have looked like in all its grandeur, polished, pristine, and cultivated. It seemed more suited for a wedding than headquarters for soldiers fighting an infiltrating army. What remained of the décor was palatial. Romantic, ornate statues topped the walls, and a belltower sat at one corner of the building. James often felt he was living in a medieval castle when he walked through the bolted wooden doors to the main hallway.

The operations command center where Teresa and her team worked was clean and fully equipped, complete with current technology. Living areas had been well maintained, and even in the abandoned sections the windows were intact and the walls free of graffiti. The layout was another story. Every day James lost his way in one corner or another. Shifting staircases, hidden doorways, hallways to nowhere, and rooms that appeared at random were commonplace. After a week, James had yet to find a way to operation headquarters from where he and his team were housed without leaving the building, walking around to the main door, and re-entering. It was too late to ask for assistance and he had been able to hide this shortcoming in his meetings with Teresa. But with the heavy rains the last couple of days though, that was getting harder to do.

Either way, although the HQ setting was more fitting for a fairy tale than modern warfare, James enjoyed the regal feeling he got while planning operations amidst gargoyles as HOLOs floated through the air.

"James, let's face it, this place sucks. Can't even get to the meeting rooms the same way twice. How the hell are we supposed to run operations here?" Deck's hands were on his hips, and he was becoming more agitated as he walked down the hallway, "I don't even know where the bathroom is outside our rooms. Seriously! The freaking bathroom, James. I'm peeing in random corners."

James stopped and looked at his friend with concern, "You're peeing in corners?"

"No. Well, yes once. It was a window and late, and… It's this damn building!" Deck said throwing his hands in the air and lashing out at a random doorway with his foot.

"That's disgusting, man. Why not ask one of us for help? What if someone was walking there?" James shook his head, making a note to wear shoes when he left their room and look up when turning corners.

"That's not the point. Listen, there have to be other buildings in the area that we can fortify. This place…" Deck's eyes scanned the walls with suspicion and anger.

"I know, but it's only been a week, man."

"That's six days too long to continue getting lost."

"Hey, what are you guys doing? Room's this way." Heather popped around the corner and pointed at a random door that, when Deck pushed it, revealed a newly exposed hallway.

"Of course it is," Deck mumbled under his breath, walking ahead of James.

"You sure he knows how to find things in the field?" Heather asked, an amused grin on her lips.

"You'd be shocked, but he's the best I've ever seen. One time he guided us through an entire Sentinel camp in broad daylight. He's something special," James said, as Deck threw his hands in the air again when he arrived at another dead end.

"If you say so," Heather said as Deck punched the false doorway only to bend over clutching his fist in pain. "Let's help him before he breaks a wrist."

Heather guided them through another door into a small auditorium. The musty scent of old paper and dust filled the air. Stadium seating took up half the space. Three V-shaped sections of chairs with plush, but old, red velvet cushions led to a platform set up with a dais and some HOLO emitters. Behind the seats were large windows letting in the late afternoon's yellow light through mottled panes casting shadows across the stage. James's team was seated on the right side of the auditorium while Teresa's command filled the remaining seats.

Liam and Jon manipulated HOLOs combing through images as James walked over to his team. The jumbled maps with handwritten notes scrawled across the bottom were moving too fast to make any sense so he decided to wait. He and Heather followed Deck to a row of empty seats in the front and filed in after the still-grumbling scout, leaving an extra chair at the end.

"Nice of you to join us," Clint drawled.

"Deck got lost," James spoke quickly, getting a scowl from Deck.

"Oh, that is low," Deck said, slitting his eyes in James's direction. "You'll see. Next time I can't find the bathroom at night…"

"Can't find the bathroom at night?" Bob asked. His glazed eyes peered at Deck around the corner of Kyle's long curly hair.

"Never mind, Bob. Just a saying."

"Never heard it."

"That's because it's not a real saying," Stacie said impatiently, cutting the conversation off before asking James, "Teresa have what she needs?"

"She's got it covered," James replied, placating the type A personality occupying Stacie's brain.

"Glad we're finally doing something. Been going crazy waiting around here." Kyle stretched an arm over his head. "Feels like we're wasting time."

"Not Teresa's MO," Heather spoke, a self-assured nod accompanying her words.

Stacie glanced at James who nodded, backing Heather. She was fiercely loyal to her commander, and James was not about to doubt the intentions or strategy of a group who had helped them so much since their arrival.

"Good." Stacie leaned back in her chair and Jon settled into the seat next to Heather as Teresa walked into the room.

James observed the stout female commander flicking through the images on her HOLO. *She looks in charge*, James thought. Her focused preparations accompanied by the quiet in the room told James a lot about the kind of command she had over the people who served at the HQ. She was the boss. When she looked up, silence took a front seat.

Teresa began, "Let's get into it. It's been a week, but in case you've been asleep, drunk, or otherwise incapacitated, we have some new guests. Treat them like you would family."

"I'll treat them better than that, ma'am," A deep voice belonging to a short muscular guy sporting a buzz cut and a voluminous black beard spoke from the other side of the room.

"Good to hear it, Oz."

"My mom was a real—"

Teresa held a hand up. "We get it, Oz."

"Just saying is all."

"Okay, so, like I was saying, treat them like family, unless of course your family sucked, then please treat them better. Does that work for you?" Teresa asked, lending a stern eye towards Oz who grinned and bowed his head sheepishly.

"Anyway, I'm sure you're familiar with their faces. They've been in this for a long time and will be here for the foreseeable future. NOLA sent them to work with us on the BZ's recent active streak up here."

A shuffle sounded through the room. The reaction was palpable. *They know us*, James thought, analyzing the furtive glances probing his direction.

"Before we dive into all that, we're going to get a post-op from the Exil attack." Teresa waved in James's direction. The pit of his stomach dropped.

Was I supposed to talk? Sweat pooled in his palms, and he tried remembering if Teresa had asked him to speak when he felt Heather's arm brush his as she got up. Jon swung his legs into the aisle and James's heart rate slowed.

"Thought she was talking to you," Deck whispered in James's ear. James gave him a jab with his shoulder as Deck stifled a laugh.

Teresa stepped aside as Heather took the podium. Pictures from the attack circulated across the screen. A beige house with missing windows popped up on the HOLO displays.

"The attack started fifteen minutes after we arrived…" Heather detailed the fight for the command, pulling up more images as she spoke. James had already heard everything. Embedded Exils living in the area, very aggressive, must be getting desperate, supply chain risk is elevated… Teresa, Liam, Heather, and his team had reviewed it all for the past week. He couldn't listen to it anymore, so he took the opportunity to size up the rest of Teresa's command.

It was the first time he had seen everyone together in a single space. There were usually about a hundred people living at the outpost at any given time. Ranging from tech savants to field experts, they all had enough battle experience to fill volumes on war with the BZ. To his surprise, most of them had come from basic camps, like Teresa and Heather. The rest were either ex-Federation, like Liam, or recruits from the West Coast after it fell. The latter normally got sent to NOLA for training given their lack of battle experience, but the ones here possessed the skills Teresa needed. Her tech guru, Rhia, had already gotten into Jon's good graces when she showed him how to create independent network connections to the outpost, even when in the field, something Jon had struggled to do for years. He had been so impressed, in fact, that he had complimented her, taking James and the collective team's breath away. Skills varied across Teresa's teams from field engineers to security forces, but an undercurrent of competence was felt at every level.

"Thanks, Heather," Teresa said as the images flickered back to a neutral gray. "Now, for our guests in town." James waved casually to the crowd, receiving a few nods and a slight curtsy from the eccentric Rhia standing on the opposite side of the room.

"As I said earlier, they're here because of those transports." A rustling echoed through the room, and discomfort swelled. "NOLA wants to find out what's going on, and we're the ones to do it. They'll be running recon missions to the BZ camp. We're their supporting cast and home base. Whatever they say, do, or need should be considered a direct order from me, understood?" An icy silence filled the room, and tension entered James's forethought. Eyes shifted and faces stared blankly at the floor.

"Ma'am, are you suggesting we engage the BZ?" the buzzcut spoke up, his face an emotionless mask, but the implication underneath his words was clear. This was an unpopular move.

"I am not Oz, but thank you for asking. This is a mission of non-engagement. Their objective is to determine what the hell the BZ is doing way up here and as such will be observing BZ camp activity. All we have now are these photos."

The screen showed a desolate tundra with runways cut into the rocky landscape. James stared at his first view of the new BZ camp.

Different from last time, James thought, examining the terrain. Gray, brown, and beige owned the landscape cast into an even more colorless void given the near constant presence of clouds overhead. Mountains hung in the background, and rivers cut their way through accentuating the scene with sweeping torrents of glacial water. The site appeared bare, but the runways and their associated warehouse structures implied the level of interest the BZ had taken in establishing themselves in the north.

"Why the hell would they want to look at that every day?" Rhia's high-pitched voice bounced around the room.

"Their orders," Teresa said, readying herself for something James didn't know was coming.

"Their orders!" Rhia shouted. "They're going to wake a beast we have no way of killing. No offense, Commander, but you weren't anywhere near here the last time the BZ took interest in the north."

"Now hol—"

"What? You thought we'd all be okay with this? Deerfield and all the other undergrounds have been planning for exactly this possibility since the last attack. These people are going to create a problem that we can't defend against, and this time everyone will die. What happens if the Sentinels come back or the BZ uses the same tactics from their first attack? What then?" Rhia's voice grew sharper, and she stood, adding emphasis to her words.

James glanced around the room. Rhia had the backing of her teammates and James sensed the support gathering. Teresa looked around the room exasperated, and anger lit her eyes.

"Listen to me, Rhia. This is why you signed up, right? To take it to the enemy. The people who killed your family, right? At least, that's what you told me."

"I did, but I think it's better to wait and watch. Plus, the Exils are a bigger threat to us here than anything else. The BZ is building. All we need is recon."

"That's what they'll be doing."

"They don't know what to do here." Rhia scoffed. "This is a whole different game, and you know it. There are thousands of those gray-suited motherfuckers over there, and we—"

"Jesus Christ, Rhia, I get it."

"No. You. Don't." Rhia's words were emphatic.

The two women glowered at each other, their faces taut with anger.

"I know what you lost." James stood. He had no idea what he was doing, but all eyes turned towards him.

He waited for Rhia to disengage from her staring match with Teresa before he continued, speaking to her from across the room.

"I do. We all do." He gestured at his team who sat avoiding eye contact with the crowd. "We were at Midway, some of the few who made it out alive. We were in the South during the deadly drone attacks. My father was killed in the Northern Assault, and I was too late to help. And I know the risks we're taking by getting close to the BZ camp. We will do everything in our power to stay under their radar to get as much info as possible, but I'll need your help. Our techs have designed a system to avoid problems while observing movements in real time." He watched as Rhia's suspicion changed to interest, "We've done the whole surveillance thing with the BZ and know with confidence how their camps operate. The risk is greater with Sentinels now more than ever. We understand our approach must be smart and cautious. We need to get as close as we can while remaining safe. That's the goal. We're not here to poke a sleeping bear, but we need to know what it's going to do when it wakes up. We can't do that sitting back on our asses."

He nodded to Teresa who pulled the next image showing Rhia's network design inlaid with Jon and Clint's roach cameras.

"Your secured tunnel networks will enable us to deploy our cameras and continually monitor the BZ full time. We're close enough that we only need small parties at the line every few days. The roaches can trigger us whenever something major happens. Meanwhile, we study the area and position more satellite coverage over the land. This limits our exposure to Sentinels, BZ surveillance, and other BZ defensive measures.

"You're one hundred percent right, Rhia. The last thing we want to do is disrupt the BZ army and start a battle we know we can't win. If we don't know exactly what they're doing though, we fall behind. If we fall behind, we lose. So, for now, our only option is to observe, anticipate, estimate, and plan. And we need your help. What do you think?"

A sense of heaviness engulfed the room, and the slender woman considered his words. He imagined her envisioning the possibilities and held his breath, hoping she would understand and accept the plan

"You've got a chance."

"All we need," James replied, nodding at Rhia and back at Teresa to continue.

"Nice work there," Heather said, patting his leg. James took a deep breath, not sure he hadn't lied to everyone, including himself.

CHAPTER 14

Hazy outlines of maps displayed about the room produced an array of mottled colors on the stone walls of the mess hall.

"So what do these lines mean again?" Deck asked, pointing at the outer edges of their BZ target.

"Tells us hypothetical boundaries," Stacie said. As she spoke, her focus remained on the map and she flexed the image into different angles.

"And this?"

"Pathways."

"And what about these circles?"

"Suspected defenses," Stacie replied. The strategist's jaw line tightened as Deck poised his finger above the map again.

"And what about—"

"How the hell are *you* our scout?" Stacie asked, the frustration in her voice unmistakable.

"Yeesh, lighten up," Deck said, raising his eyebrows and walking to a different map. "And it's because I can navigate the actual terrain, not just read it on some dumb map. Also, your keys are ridiculous." Deck added over his shoulder. He walked away glancing back to make sure Stacie wasn't pouncing on him in retreat.

Kyle squeezed Stacie's shoulder as he followed Deck to the other set of HOLOs.

Good peacekeeper, James thought as he tried to ignore the jabber. Refocusing, he traced a line down the face of the map along the forest boundary outside the BZ base. Yellow dots appeared where his finger had been.

"Here's where we need to establish a marker for our surveillance. Get a little closer every time."

"Right, set up our roaches here and here," Stacie replied, punctuating her thoughts with two red stars, "We can add more in the future, but we should keep things simple until we have a better idea of their defenses.”

“Agreed. What about comms?”

“Rhia and Jon are working on something.”

“Will it get through BZ space undetected?”

Stacie waved the question away. “You ask Jon. Every time I bring it up he gets pissed off.”

Sounds right, James thought, knowing their techie’s temperament all too well and lamenting, *We could use Rich here*.

“What’s our path into their territory?” Stacie asked, spreading out the forest view with her hands.

“I was wondering the same,” James replied, examining the dense woods. It was hard to tell since their satellite images were old but given the lack of human intervention in the area, he imagined the passage was less than ideal.

“Deck, come back over here,” Stacie said.

Deck reapproached the table, his face skeptical. “Yes…?”

“What do you think of these woods? No obvious path through, and I doubt there’s more than animal trails in the interior, so the trip won’t be easy. I want your opinion.” Stacie looked across the table at their scout earnestly, and Deck, taking the hint from the stern faces of Kyle and James on either side of her, let the moment pass.

He looked at the map zooming in and out of various points between the HQ and the BZ fortress. After some time of quiet manipulation, he froze the screen and drew a pair of parallel lines in a curving shape through the wooded area.

“Given the gradient and level of aerial coverage, this should be a good route to start with. Not a lot of up and down, no signs of water underneath, or at least nothing we can’t easily cross, and it’s a mature part of the forest. Not going to be a ton of growth underneath there, especially this time of year.”

James was impressed and glanced towards Stacie and Kyle who nodded along.

“Good, nice work. Thanks.”

"It is my honor," Deck said with a stiff bow.

"How goes it, everyone?" Kevin entered the room carrying a full burlap sack. He slammed the sack on the counter separating the kitchen from the hall with a thud, brushing the residual dust from his hands and shoulders.

"How's it going, Kev?" Kyle asked leaning against the table, stretching his calves. "Big bag you got there." Kyle nodded at the package.

"Twenty pounds of oatmeal. Breakfast for tomorrow," Kevin said, patting the sack emitting puffs of dust that floated onto the wood top in a thin coat.

Since their arrival in the North, Kevin had taken the role of HQ chef. Cooking for the garrison one second and meticulously designing explosive devices the next made for an interesting life, but he seemed to enjoy bouncing between occupations. HQ loved it too, and Oz had made a special point of finding the best possible ingredients to bring home to Kevin.

"Anything special planned?" Kyle asked.

Kevin shrugged. "Oz said he would try and find some frozen or freeze-dried fruit. Figure we can put it in the pot."

"That'd be amazing," Kyle said, his voice reflecting the tasty dream playing across his tongue. James thought the same."

"What are we missing here? What else do we need to run this op?" Stacie asked no one in particular.

"Hmm, you know who's great at this stuff? Caitlin," Deck said. His eyes danced in the direction of Kevin who showed no reaction at the mention of James's sister.

"Okay… That might be true, but…" Stacie replied, confused.

"Don't you think so, Kev?" Deck asked.

Kevin stopped what he was doing and turned to the group. "She'd be great for it." Sounding as puzzled as the rest of the team looked.

Deck nodded and looked at the three non-team members in the room.

"Ahem. Hey, you. Yes, you." The trio, at first unaware of other conversations, were now alert and cued into the situation.

"Umm, we're trying to have a private talk. Would you please leave?"

They looked at each other, baffled, and James, unable to understand what was happening himself, shrugged in a wordless apology.

Mystified, they stood from their table and walked out of the room with Deck following to close the door after their exit.

The scout turned around and faced the team with a surprised look on his face. "I've always wanted to try that, but legitimately never thought it would work."

"What the hell, Deck?" Kevin asked, glancing at the others perplexed. "What are you doing?"

"What are *you* doing is the question? What's with you and Caitlin? It's been years since this whole relationship thing started, and you better have answers."

"What for?" Kevin asked, defensiveness edged his voice.

"Mrs. Coffey wants to know."

"She does?" James asked. It was his turn to be confused, and he stared at Deck with skeptical disbelief.

"Yes. She does."

"Really? She told you that?" Stacie asked, folding her arms.

"In a way. There were a lot of implied questions."

"About me and Caitlin?" Kevin asked.

"Well, it was mostly about things in the kitchen, but I could tell what she was getting at."

"Oh, so she didn't say anything about them," Kyle said, returning to his stretching.

"She said things! Not directly, but like I said, implied," Deck spoke with a mysterious tone.

"Whatever, Deck," Kevin said, waving him off.

"Oh, come on! Gotta give your friends a morsel of information! Hell, I saw you leave the living room to talk with her in Deerfield. That has to be something," Deck said, grumbling into the table.

Kevin's ears burned red, and although James was interested, he knew it wasn't his business.

"Leave it, Deck," James said, turning back to the map. "We've got a lot of work to do here."

As Deck started to reply the doors swung open and Clint walked in followed by Oz.

"What's going on in here? We heard you asked for the room?" Clint asked, glancing at the collective group with puzzlement.

"Deck's bugging Kev," James said, squashing the conversation.

"Looking out for my adopted family is all," Deck said, holding his palms up defensively.

"Pain in the ass," Kevin mumbled under his breath, returning to his oatmeal prep.

"What's up?" James asked Clint, switching topics.

"Oz got something for you."

"Yeah? What's that?" James asked, eyeing the baritone smuggler.

"Frozen fruit?" Kevin asked hopefully from the kitchen.

"Not frozen fruit," Oz replied. "You all should come with me. Not a far drive."

"We need gear?"

"I've got it in the truck."

"All right," James said. "Deck, Kyle, Stacie. You three come along for the ride. Clint and Kevin, mind staying here?"

"No problem with me. It's freezing outside," Clint replied, meandering over to a HOLO display and manipulating the map. "Besides, I've got some engine work to do on Oz's delivery trucks."

"Appreciate it," Oz said, nodding at the mechanic.

"Kevin, you okay sticking around here?" James asked again.

Kevin bobbed his head in agreement. "You got it."

"Let's roll."

Gray skies hugged the tops of the trees as James and the team rode over root strewn pathways on the makeshift forest roads Oz and his team used for their smuggling routes. They alone knew how to navigate the winding paths intersecting and looping back on one another in the dense foliage. James was happy to have the leader of their group operating the vehicle. They drove for over forty-five minutes and James was getting impatient.

"Almost there," Oz said, detecting frustration in the cramped vehicle. "Through this holly grove is all."

The truck ran through a series of holly trees retracing the trail Oz had no doubt used earlier that day. A stillness hung over the space and, sensing danger, James's skin prickled with fear. The space emanated nothing more than your everyday forest, but the isolation gave James a foreboding impression.

They tore their way through the thick, needle ringed leaves until breaking into a clearing. Five tents stood in a wide space. Choppy ground, hurried abandonment, leftover supplies, and rutted tire tracks instilled a sense of suspended urgency. James gripped the handle of his ionic knife and toyed with the power button. Even with so few clues James had been in enough of these camps to recognize a BZ HQ.

Oz stopped the car, and James exited the vehicle soaking in the camp's layout.

A cold drizzle started, and drops of freezing liquid fell from heavy clouds. James wiped a hand across his face wicking away raindrops. The tents were empty, their flaps partially pulled aside leaving empty chasms of darkness dotting the area. Leftover, useless gear was everywhere. Broken cords, empty magazines, and sodden medical supplies littered the ground, blown about and caught by the shelters. The scene was not normal. James tightened his grip on the knife in his belt.

"Left real fast," Deck said, pointing at a set of destroyed generators stacked along the side of a tent.

"Sure did. No reports of them being here though. Couldn't have been us who attacked them," Oz said as he picked up a piece of soiled bandage off the ground. "No sign of actual struggle either. Shell casings absent, no bodies, nothing."

James nodded along, but it didn't make sense. Something was off. It wasn't the same setup as previous raider camps. The tents were too small, with insufficient generators. The scene didn't add up.

"Not raiders," Stacie said, bending next to a generator. She pointed at the markings on the side, "Wattage would barely power a live Sentinel for a half hour."

"The hell was this place?"

James turned in a circle, the droplets of cold rain added to the unsettling mood of the camp.

"Not going to learn anything standing here," he said and walked through the flapping doors of a tent. His feet crunched on the dry soil inside, and it took a second for his eyes to adjust to the darkness.

Empty metal tables with folding chairs haphazardly arranged around them. Grooves in the dirt floor showed where equipment had been dragged during their hasty move and discarded cords snaking under the tent walls indicated where HOLO emitters had been erected. The white walls were bare without a hint of adornment, physical or otherwise.

Big heap of nothing, James thought, disappointed by the lack of clues.

"My god, what is that smell?" A retching sound followed Deck's voice.

James exited to find Deck standing outside with his hands on his knees. Kyle lifted the collar of his shirt over his nose and mouth, removed the ion knife from his waistband, and clicked on the power button disappearing behind the flap. James watched the knife's glowing bright light as darkness enveloped the entrance to the tent.

"That was horrible," Deck said. He stood and wiped his hand across his mouth. "I mean, I've smelled things, but that…" The scout shook his head, unable to finish his sentence.

"Stay here and keep watch. Oz, stick with Deck. Stacie, Kyle, and I'll check it out."

"Don't have to ask me twice," Deck said, recovering from the assault on his olfactory system.

James peeled back the tent opening and pulled his collar over his nose similar to Kyle.

He stepped inside, letting his eyes adjust to the interior when the scent struck. A rotting, corporeal stench ripped into his senses. Even with his shirt as a filter, James could barely stand to stay in the space. He gulped in air to avoid breathing through his nose. It was impossible to deny, something had died in that room.

"Over here," Kyle called from across the room and James walked towards him followed by Stacie. The glow from their knives guided them through the room, and so far they had not bumped into anything. The tent was surprisingly deep, James realized as he reached the far wall and turned a corner.

Quite the building, James thought as he rounded the turn and found Kyle examining the new space.

"What the hell was this for?" Kyle asked as he stood in front of a stage with three tables. No other adornment crowded the area to help them guess it's strange design.

James approached the raised platform, pocketing his knife. Once on top, he ran a hand over one of the tables. Cold and smooth, but with veins of residue spread across. The smell was stronger now. His thoughts drifted to some of the first images they had recorded of the BZ sacrificing one another and torturing villagers in the Southern Federation. A silent alarm triggered in his brain.

"We could use some more light in here," James said, more to himself than anyone else.

Seconds later, light flooded the room. James blinked in the brightness and glanced back at the tables.

"Better?" Kyle asked, standing in a corner next to a plug and holding a cord in his hands. "They must have left some juice in the batteries they buried," Kyle surmised dropping the cord and joining James and Stacie near the tables.

In the halogen light, James ran his fingers back across the tables. The residue was visible now as a dull rust colored sheen. He smelled his fingertips. Amid the putrid odor, James could discern the familiar scent of iron. *Blood.*

"Operating tables?" Stacie asked, examining the lights and the stage.

"Torture," James said, edging his voice with finality.

"But who?" Kyle asked.

James answered with a shrug.

"And what is that smell?" Stacie asked, replacing her shirt over her nose and mouth, "It's…"

"Like death," Kyle finished her sentence examining the platform they stood on. "Hold on a second." The construction savvy athlete hopped off the raised bar and bent to the ground. He tapped the side of the dais, eliciting a barrel drum response. He looked at James and Stacie. "It's hollow."

"I'll help you try and move it," James said. He jumped off the platform and bent next to Kyle. Stacie took a position on his other side, and with a wordless nod from Kyle, the three dug their fingers under the edge of the platform and pulled upward.

A rush of trapped air crashed into James's nostrils, and he doubled over to protect his face as millions of tiny projectiles rammed into his eyes and mouth.

He dry heaved, trying to catch his breath and settle his stomach. Blinded, James fumbled to escape the sickening odor and the blanket of terror trapped under the metal platform.

"This way," Kyle shouted in the darkness and James followed the sound pawing in front of him, holding his breath.

When he made it outside he inhaled deeply and wiped his teary eyes. He turned to watch a cloud of flies stream from the tent flaps. Deck ran around the corner, startled to see the three of them sputtering and spitting, doing their best to keep food in their stomachs.

"What the fuck is in there?" he asked with wide eyes.

"There's some sort of operating table I think," Kyle replied, spitting on the ground as a fly buzzed out of his mouth. "When I was looking at the platform's surface, I noticed vents. We lifted it and the flies came out."

"They must have thought the ground would soak up the blood," James said, trying not to imagine the experiments they had been running.

"Blood can't penetrate frozen ground," Stacie said.

"It must have congealed when it warmed again, and the smell started. Flies joined and next thing you know there's a horror swamp growing under their stage."

James's stomach flipped when he thought of what it might look like under the platform. "Let's check the rest of these tents. We can come back to this later."

The group nodded their agreement and went into two of the other tents with layouts similar to the first one James had entered, empty with only tables and chairs. Neither contained the same kind of gruesome platform. *They keep their experiments contained*, James thought grimly as he walked to the last building.

The final structure sat at the back of the camp. It was squat and rectangular with one visible flap. James tried to open the entryway, but it was secured.

Suspicion swept through James's gut as he pulled out his knife and flipped on the ionic pulse. He pushed the tip of the blade through the opening and ripped down, cutting through the sealant.

He expected a similar rush of flies and rank odor to emerge from the dark area, but only silence and musty air leaked out. Inching his face closer, he caught an unpleasant whiff of something that he couldn't pinpoint. He parted the flaps and entered the room. It was an empty space with vertical poles erected throughout. The odor he had detected earlier grew stronger. Albeit not as revolting as the insect-infested blood stage, it left an unpleasant taste in the back of his throat.

"Smells like a zoo in here," Deck said, putting the crook of his arm over his mouth. Realization crashed into James.

Sweat, mixed with untreated human waste and grease. His holding cell under the ground in Raspin's Southern HQ flooded his memory. Darkness, pain, fear, and hatred filled his mind. He clenched and unclenched his hands as he stepped further into the room.

He glanced at Kyle whose faraway gaze told James that his friend was coming to the same revelation. These were the holding cells for whomever the BZ had tortured at those tables.

"What is this place?" Oz asked, examining one of the poles in the room.

"A jail," James replied, bending next to another one and picking up a cord from the ground. It was long and flat with buckle adjustments. It looked like a simple belt, but James remembered the devices well. It was identical to the one he had worn around his neck during Raspin's experiments cutting off his airway to the point of unconsciousness time and again. Memories swirled beneath the surface, and he stood abruptly.

"Take as many samples and videos as you can. If we get some of that blood for Bob to test, great. Let's get out of here in an hour." James walked towards the exit and opened it. "Kyle and I will see if we can get those generator batteries out of the ground."

James held the flap and Kyle exited the room. James noticed Stacie's knowing gaze follow her boyfriend.

"All right, well, what should we do? I mean, there's not a lot here, but maybe Dolly will want someone else to come take a look," Deck asked, scanning the room as the realization of its significance sunk in.

"She'll be good. Burn it."

"James, I get what this is, I do. But can we—"

"Burn it."

James's voice turned to iron as he spoke. Deck and Stacie nodded, looking around the room as James left, actively fighting his past as he walked away.

CHAPTER 15

Wood smoke stuck in James's nostrils, and he rubbed his nose hoping to remove the caked-in scent.

He took a test sniff, annoyed when the smell lingered in the background even after hours outside.

Where's a tissue when you need it? he thought, blowing hot air on his hands. Despite the latent smells James still wished he was in front of the black iron stoves at the outpost. *Better than the tents,* he thought grimacing at the memory of the tents from the other week.

The sun was still due to appear for the day. Invisibility was a necessity anywhere outside their base. Ghosts were their mentors.

James's cupped his hands to his mouth trying to resuscitate his frozen fingers.

I miss Rio Negro, he thought, reminiscing about the South. Roaring fires late at night, cooking ears of corn to sizzling perfection, and slathered in spices, sauce, and cheese, or a freshly killed pig roasting in a pit of hot coals for hours.

Instead, he waited for daylight, huddled in a thermal blanket as Kyle napped and Jon prepped their field connection. Even with the bone-chilling cold, it was nice to be outside for a change.

There was always something to do these days. At HQ he was busy reviewing images from the roaches, analyzing BZ troop movements, talking with NOLA, or planning future recon trips. They had made significant progress, more than James ever hoped they'd achieve. Since the discovery of the torture camp near their HQ, the base had been on high alert. No one from Teresa's various teams were familiar with the BZ's incarceration tactics. To them, the BZ only killed; they took no prisoners. James and Kyle were intimately familiar though, and it had only taken a second inside the jail's tent flaps for James to recognize the horror of his previous cell. He had focused on the field, thankful that Teresa dedicated a custom team to investigate the images of the BZ torture camp. James was happy to separate himself as much as he could from the nightmares burned into his memory.

Field activity gave plenty to keep him busy. Rhia's network joined with Jon's roach tech gave them much needed coverage. An invisible boundary had been established by Jon's mapping tech that created a dome and allowed the roaches to simply fly back within range to drop off material, automatically downloading their collected data to protected servers. This eliminated the need to recharge or manually download from the source.

It also gave the outpost the advantage of recon without the danger of maintaining a permanent field presence. However, some human intervention was still required at the border to monitor the stationary sensors and cameras set up near the BZ base. Small teams accompanied Jon and Rhia in the field to transfer data from the devices outside the boundary directly into storage drives to upload back at the HQ. The increased hazard of sending people into the field was worth the risk.

For the last month they had recorded hours of footage detailing the BZ's activities giving context to the satellite images Dolly and the NOLA team compiled. Troop buildup continued to mount, but battle preparation was not the primary reason for the BZ's northern presence. They were doing something James had only witnessed after the fact: terraforming. It was incredible watching their machinery move the land, reshaping it for purposes James had yet to understand. He was fascinated with the footage.

The BZ had broadened their Sentinel tech and built machines that shifted the earth using granular electric webbing. Long arms of electromagnetic nets carved, shifted, and shaped the land. James was floored by the results. In mere weeks barren tundra that had existed for millennia transformed into a brand-new landscape. Rivers and water systems re-engineered the geography, altering existing mountains and islands, repurposing them as fortresses, armories, or bunkers.

The interior of the structures were still a mystery, but James's and Kyle's unique experience as prisoners in a BZ headquarters gave him some clues. He imagined honeycombed bedrock twisting and turning under the earth in long passageways with unfinished cement floors, rock face walls, and dirt-packed ceilings. Nature and construction meeting at a strange crossroads.

The horizon came to life with the first rays of sun kissing the edge of the earth. James was relieved, *Hurry it up, Jon*, he thought watching his breath billow thick clouds in the dry, frigid air waiting for Jon to give them the go ahead. They were vulnerable this close to the BZ's base.

The Exils had become more aggressive. Oz, the bearded guy with family problems, headed the supply team. Liam called him the leader of the "smugglers." Oz and his team ran trips to depots farther South to keep their operation running smoothly. The smugglers were responsible for obtaining supplies. From weapons and medical equipment to food and toilet paper and anything else it took to maintain a viable post. They risked crossing no man's land with Jeeps and pickups, each time collecting and carrying four identical loads. The redundancy ensured the outpost would be stocked in case one of the smugglers went down. Until recently, that had been a precautionary step. Now, the Exils set traps and had come close to catching Oz on his last trip. Luckily, Teresa's sniper teams had intercepted his pursuers in time, but every day became more dangerous.

James poured cold coffee from a thermos. He sipped the icy liquid pretending the steam came from the cup and not his frozen breath when Kyle stirred. "We ready to go?"

"Let's give Jon a few more minutes," James replied, gesturing towards their hyper-focused tech.

Kyle nodded and rolled his sleeping bag as James poured him a coffee and pulled up a HOLO for them to study while they waited.

James had developed a soft spot for Rhia and Jon. The genius of their combined solution made it possible to finally do reconnaissance of the BZ without risking everyone's life. However, it was too complex for anyone else to maintain. James barely understood what a network tunnel did, let alone keep one running and out of sight of the BZ's scanners. Keeping the lights on was a constant balancing act for the two techs, one of whom was also needed in the field each time the teams had to check the stationary cameras

Lack of sleep and constant pressure added to their stress. Their short tempers made them difficult to live with already. Now it was impossible. James had decided a few more minutes of quiet wouldn't hurt Jon's mood. *Maybe he'll be nice today,* James thought ruefully, remembering Jon's sharp tongue and muttering annoyance at the lack of proper shelter the previous night.

"Anything from HQ today?" Kyle asked, stretching a leg on the ground.

"Nada," James replied, shaking his head. "Must be quiet back there."

"No news is good news," Kyle replied, peeking over James's arm at the HOLO images pulled from the roach network. "Brings back memories, huh?" Kyle nodded at the newest picture, a wide cement opening at the base of the mountain descending steeply and disappearing into the darkness.

"Not a place I'd like to return to," James said, shaking his head. He remembered the flaming piles of bodies, thick clouds of smoke, and concussive explosions. Their escape from the BZ's jungle HQ still haunted James more than he cared to admit.

"Can say that again. Whenever we get close to their base, I feel like I'm waking up with that collar around my neck."

James looked at the ground, overly familiar with the sensation. "Hasn't gotten better for you either?"

"Stacie tries to help, but…"

"Right."

"In a weird way though, I get excited to see what they've done. It's like I feel closer to it because I somehow know it."

James nodded. He had the same sense. His experience made him feel as if he was a part of the building. As if his time as a prisoner and the torture resulted in something more beneficial than personal anguish.

"I get you. I wonder what they've been up to. Beyond what the roaches bring back."

"That river. I swear it's going to be completely diverted the next time we get here."

"Really?" James asked. "I think it's the mountain. They have a whole new bed car—"

"WOULD YOU TWO SHUT THE FUCK UP?!" Jon's red eyes whipped towards the coffee drinkers, and James stifled a chuckle at the disheveled techie. Jon's curly hair expanded in patches all over his scalp and the tightness in his jaw emphasized the stress he dealt with on a regular basis. His appearance was that of a strung-out poodle dangerously close to chomping at anyone who put a hand next to its mouth. To his personal annoyance, James could not help but find the sight amusing.

"Sorry, Jon. We didn't want to disturb you," James said, biting the inside of his cheek.

"Yeah, our bad, man," Kyle said, swallowing his laughter.

"Fuckin' jackasses," Jon mumbled, turning back to his HOLO.

Grinning to themselves, James and Kyle rolled their eyes as the techie returned to his work.

I'll give him a couple more minutes, he reasoned, pulling up shots of their path to the BZ's base.

Two hours later they were climbing over barren earth interspersed at random with lichen-covered boulders. A light breeze brushed his face. James gritted his teeth against the cold. Instead of a pleasant touch on a sunny day, the wind carried sharpened icicles stuck to every waft of air. The frigid temperature of the tundra had a way of escalating even the simplest of weather patterns into an untenable climate.

Kyle signed back to James from further up the hill:

No sentries; active worksite.

James replied with a nod and kept moving, but his stomach bubbled with excitement. An active worksite meant he got to watch the BZ in action reshaping the world with their machines. He scrambled faster up the frosted earth.

He arrived at the summit and stood next to Kyle, who was looking through a pair of infrared binoculars. James shifted his rifle to a more comfortable position and gazed at the glinting spectacle in the angular Arctic sunlight.

The BZ's operations were a marvel. When at rest, the construction scene looked like a ritualistic burial site for ancient civilizations. Obelisk structures stood in the center of the latest project. On top of each column sat twelve fin-like spokes that turned in a continuous clockwise rotation. During their downtime they appeared to be broken or poorly designed wind turbines. However, when in operation the world changed around them even in the most extreme conditions. As the arms of their fins sprouted a wall of mesh, a net-like cloth that extended and dropped to the ground, hanging across the surface, suspended in the air by an invisible wire. As the turbine circled, the mesh brushed against the ground and ever so slightly reshaped the planet beneath it. Electromagnetic currents pushed frozen earth, stone, water, and any material in its way, molding the world one sweep at a time.

Today, three turbines spanned the plain. They were focused on the networks of water that ran in torrents of dark blue glacial liquid. These waterways had spent eons slicing the land to their specifications, dropping sediment and eroding the harsh landscape into sloping banks and wide deep pools. Charged webbing washed over the area, pushing the earth and straightening the turns creating parallel pathways of water. The new designs drove the rivers in faster streams spraying extraneous liquid onto the surrounding ground, creating ice rinks along the banks.

"What are they doing?" Kyle asked more to himself than to James, but James agreed. *What was all this?* The land that had been a jumbled mess of islands, mountains, hills, water passages, and barren desert had become organized. A neat row of mountains lined up along the northern edge of the tundra. Flat plains stretched until they reached the new rivers the BZ had etched into the stonelike ground. *It was a design, but for what?*

"Cameras are good. We're done," Jon said, already annoyed. He was ready to go. James and Kyle were not. Jon was out here every few days, but James had only been here once and wanted to see more of the BZ's world. Swinging arms of electrically charged mesh passed over the land, pushing a boulder out of sight. The violence of the movement was hidden by the invisible lines of electricity.

"Two more minutes, Jon," James said, transfixed on the activity of their enemy.

"Yeah, we don't get outside much," Kyle added, handing the binoculars to James who accepted them gladly.

"Two minutes. I'm timing it. That's protocol,"

James and Kyle stayed silent, choosing to spend their limited time watching the action rather than argue with an aggravated friend.

James focused on the farthest of the three turbines working next to one of the mountains. BZ tech did not make matter simply disappear. Pulverized rock debris extracted from the mountains was shuffled around to different parts of their worksite. Piles of the stone filled dirt ended up all around the worksite, disappearing at random when a new project was undertaken. They used all parts of the earth.

He zoomed in with the enhanced binoculars to get a better look inside the caves. Cement openings like the ones he and Kyle had escaped through in the jungle served as entrances. Darkness enveloped the doorways, much to everyone's annoyance. But the caves remained as active as ever. Ships delivering troops filtered into the sloped pathways. Sentinels used as construction workers continually entered and exited. Their limitless strength and ability to work in extreme conditions made them ideal for operating the turbines or fixing problems.

The deadly humanoid machines floated eerily in the cold stillness even when the terraformers were not running. They were unperturbed by the mesh netting that passed over them regularly and walked through the charged curtains without hesitation.

Shimmering light from the nets reflected off the Sentinel containers' dull metal surfaces and refracted back into the partially frozen pools of liquid splashing over the banks of the swift rivers. It was something to behold. The sun's twinkling yellow light played across the scene, dancing from one surface to another. *What would that do to us?* James wondered, thinking about the trillions of charged particles zooming through the air.

"Time to move." Kyle tapped James's shoulder. He pointed at the base of the mountain where a stone wall shifted ever so slightly. James watched as the solid rockface opened, spilling darkness.

His stomach seized as the hulking forms of larger-than-normal Sentinels emerged from the opening, their translucent skin difficult to distinguish in the bright morning sunlight. They lumbered onto the field, their arms and bodies swinging, human-made giants.

"Come on, time to move," Jon said. "They released the workers, and they'll expand their Sentinel field in a few minutes. The cameras are set, so let's leave," The iciness in the air added to Jon's biting tone, and James reluctantly turned away from the scene.

"Back to HQ," James said, as he walked nimbly down the rock-strewn hill.

"About goddamn time. I hate it here," Jon said, leading the way.

Looking back one last time, James could swear he heard the giants working on the other side of the hill. Their electricity-bound limbs carrying thousands of pounds of iron across the tundra's plains, moving the terraformers from one position to the next and reshaping the world to fit their needs. The increasingly familiar wave of anxiety rippled through James's thoughts, and he followed Kyle down the hillside, praying they'd know what the BZ was up to before it was too late.

CHAPTER 16

Thinning trees and wispy grass signaled their arrival at the Gothic outpost.

Long stained-glass windows decorated the south side of the building with medieval flare greeting James, Kyle, and Jon as they approached. Late afternoon sunlight cast speckled colors on the brown grass surrounding the HQ. Gargoyles, angels, and other mythical creatures adorning the stone parapets produced long shadows across the smooth rock face. The lengthier shadows reminded James that fewer daylight hours remained, a paradox he contended with regularly in the North's quick days.

Wooden doors opened inward, and Stacie stood, blank faced, hands on hips inside the threshold watching the three of them enter.

"How you doin', Serial?" Kyle asked, picking her up and kissing her, eliciting the slightest of smiles when she pushed him away.

"Better now that you're all back. Council's starting," she said, looking in James's direction.

"I'll be there in a few," James replied. He had been mentally preparing himself for hours of boredom in another meeting with Dolly, Stacie, Teresa, and Liam. He hated the council meetings. It was always planning and strategy. He wanted to be in the field, gathering information and running operations, not sitting at a desk calculating supply needs for the outpost or developing exit strategies.

"Get there quick."

"I will. Why do you need me there anyway, Stace? You're the logistics expert."

"You're needed for a lot more than your input on organizing details, James," Stacie replied, sighing and shaking her head.

"What the hell does that mean?"

"It means you have valuable experience with the BZ. You also happen to be our group's leader, so you better hurry and be ready to sit your ass down at that meeting in ten minutes."

Annoyed, Stacie turned with tightness in her movements as she marched down the hall.

Kyle nodded at the two of them as he followed Stacie, turning around to roll his eyes at James shrugging.

"What's with her?" Jon asked, sitting in a chair along the wall and flipping up a HOLO screen.

"Been a long month," James said, brushing off the interaction. *No point in reading into it*, James thought preferring to save his last strands of energy for their upcoming conversation with the council. "What are you doing?" he asked. Five different screens had appeared since Jon arrived, floating in mid-air illuminating the masonry in the hall with an eerie glow. The techie manipulated the images, his fingers twitching at lightning speed across the holographic controls while his eyes flickered unblinking following his work.

"Post-work," Jon said. The bite in his tone told James that Jon would prefer to be left alone.

"Well, I'm gonna go," James said, walking away awkwardly, hoping Jon would be a little more bearable soon.

James strolled towards the basement where the council meetings took place. He did not understand why they were held underground instead in one of the rooms overlooking the estate, but didn't care enough to argue. Lights turned on as he descended the stairs. As he walked, his feet clicked on the marble floors and the ever-present smell of smoke tinged the air. *Impossible to escape,* he thought brushing his hands in front of his face. He wished Clint could divert energy from the solar arrays spanning the roof to heat their residence rather than use the stoves, but Jon and Rhia insisted they needed all the solar power to keep their HOLOs, the roaches, and the other recon equipment running. *Small price to pay for an eye on the enemy,* James thought rounding the corner to their meeting room.

The hallway was empty, but lit. *Someone must be here,* he thought. Walking into the noiseless cold space though, he decided he was alone.

"So much for hurrying up," James mumbled, annoyed at Stacie's insistence on his immediate presence when she had yet to arrive.

He sat in the semi-circle of chairs facing the HOLO emitters used to communicate with Dolly in NOLA and waited for the others. He leaned back on the hind legs of the chair and stared at the ceiling trying to balance in that position without falling.

"You're going to hurt yourself," said a voice, startling James. The chair came down with a clatter on all four legs. He turned to meet Rhia's gaze. The slender woman sitting at the back of the room met his eyes, then disappeared behind her screen.

"Sorry, I didn't know anyone was in here," James said.

Silence engulfed the room as James struggled for words. *Why didn't she say anything?* he wondered. An uncomfortable pallor hung in the air and James squirmed internally determining what to do. He realized he knew nothing about Rhia beyond her connection with NOLA and her initial opposition to teaming up to do recon. During their first meeting at the base, Teresa indicated Rhia had connections to Deerfield and the Northern Assault, but only in vague detail. Worried she might think he was trying to avoid conversation, he cleared his throat.

"So, how long have you been here?" he asked, awkwardness filled the air

"We don't have to talk, you know," The woman's eyes remained fixed on her screen.

"No. I...I realized I have no clue who you are, other than being the only person Jon has ever complimented for their technical abilities. So, I do want to know some more," James replied, pushing forward.

"Three years. Came here a little after the Northern Assault. I planned to go north until I reached nothing but ice. Ice and polar bears. I ran into Teresa's team who had moved into the area. She offered me a room while I got ready for the journey. I stayed." Rhia shrugged.

"You guys have done a lot in three years."

"It's a dump, but it will do."

"It could be nice," James rebuffed. He had been taken by the building with the scent of old wax hanging in the air and the aged wooden doorways. It may be a relic, but its past beauty was undeniable. Ornate, but chipped doorway frames, rusted iron windows, lattice gates in need of a dose of paint. The estate instilled a lost sense of architecture as if he was living inside a forgotten world.

"It's a dump. Was before the war, too."

James was surprised, he had no idea anyone knew what the fort had been prior to the war.

"Before the war?"

"Boarding school. My mother attended as a child. My family came here when we were kids, and my mom would point out her childhood memories. It was abandoned for years before the invasion. I figured I'd be safe here while I worked out my route north."

That makes sense, James thought putting the pieces of the building's history together—a gothic building with large shower areas, industrial kitchens, and dormitory-style beds.

"Where are they now?" James asked, easing into the conversation, A coil sprang from the back of his mind, remembering Rhia's comments about her family during the first meeting. *Shit*, James cursed to himself, searching his brain for the right words to say.

Acidic silence engulfed the room, and a new level of discomfort washed over James when his eyes caught sight of the HOLO screens at the front of the room.

Rolling past were images of the Northern Assault. People had been powerless against the BZ's Sentinel forces. Ionic weaponry had not been fully developed and getting any charged devices mass-produced took Dolly even longer. Before the assault, the impetus for these defenses had not existed. No one with knowledge of the BZ military, including James and his team, ever thought their enemy was capable of something so horrific. The power to execute a Sentinel attack on that scale was something James previously thought impossible. They had all been wrong.

Cement and steel buildings torn apart by Sentinels as if made of sand. Husks of burned bodies covered the charred roads and stretches of concrete. The scenes of pure destruction took James back to those moments. Hearing of the assault, the team had raced north, trailed by every NOLA operator available. James had believed his father was still alive at the time, but in all likelihood he had probably died during the earliest stages of the attack.

The images kept filtering across the screen. James's eyes were glued to the display when it came to the final picture. In it a young family with slender bodies and wide smiles watched him from their still frame. James scanned the faces, resting on the shortest figure in the middle with long frizzy hair and a tooth gapped grin stretched so tightly it looked painful.

Rhia's grown up fast, James thought, turning around to compare the little girl's face to the hard nose coder sitting a few rows behind him. Rhia focused on her controls and James turned back to the images

"Rhia, I don't... I'm sorry. I shouldn't have..." James's words stuck in his throat as he tried to apologize for his misstep.

"They only live in here now," Rhia said and a tapped a finger to her temple.

Before James could respond the door flew open with a *swoosh*, and Liam entered followed by Teresa and Stacie.

Glancing at the monitors James saw they had changed to display the NOLA seal. He looked back at Rhia whose blank face was buried in her HOLO. James pushed the memory of the Assault out of his head.

"James! How'd the trip to the BZ go?" Liam asked, pulling out a chair and sitting heavily. The wooden legs screeched against the floor as his weight caused the chair to move back across the tile.

"Great, I think we got everything we need. Those terraformers…" James shook his head.

"They're something, huh?"

"That's one way to put it," James replied, as his mind still raced north, chasing an army of ghosts.

"Hey, everybody!" Dolly's voice filled the room as a 3D image of her face stared down from her HOLO emitter. "We all here?"

"Looks like it," Liam replied as Stacie walked into the room with a blank look on her face. James knew the pony-tailed strategist better than most and could tell she was pissed. James tried but couldn't force eye contact with her as she sat and opened a HOLO.

Have to learn what's going on there, James noted to himself, wondering about ways to approach Stacie or Kyle without getting anyone more upset.

"Am I late?"

Heather's head popped in the door, and James's stomach jumped at the sight of her. They rarely had guests at the councils. Nobody else wanted to attend. James was happy she was there though. He was always happy to see her. Since their arrival, they had worked long hours together manipulating images of the BZ's terraformers and matching them to the satellite images to review in meetings like these. Heather was one of the most capable people James had met, and he always relaxed in her presence.

"What are you doing here?" James asked, instantly regretting his words. *Why so judgy?* he thought, kicking himself.

"Wow, Mr. Exclusive," Heather replied, pulling the chair next to him. "Teresa asked me to come."

"You two have been doing all the analysis together, and she has more local experience than anyone else. Thought she'd be a good addition to the group." Teresa glanced at James, and he swore he saw Liam wink out of the corner of his eye.

What are they pulling here?

"Right, of course, I mean you should be here. I just didn't expect anyone else. So, yeah…" James stopped himself, making eye contact with Dolly whose phantom body shook its head. "Dolly, what's on the agenda?" James asked, changing topics.

"Most recent images from the BZ, Exil, and supply chain updates. Any other notes to add, T?" Dolly replied as Rhia whipped a slideshow of images across the various HOLOs floating in the room.

"Nothing from me." The stocky leader leaned back in her chair looking at James with a knowing grin.

"Great, Liam, let's hear it. What's the word from Oz and co?" Dolly shifted her transparent upper body towards the couple.

"Oz leaves tomorrow. We're low on ammunition, but only because of the latest NOLA guidelines regarding supply needs," Liam said, looking at Dolly.

Dolly nodded in return. "We increased recommendations based on the problems with Exils. They may become a nuisance for more than the Northeast sooner than we think. Better to be prepared."

"Fair enough," Liam said, shrugging. "We also need to replace a few HOLO emitters and get more solar arrays. Then the normal stuff TP, rice, MREs, the works."

"When does Oz take off?" Rhia asked from the back of the room.

"0600," Teresa jumped in, turning around to address the techie.

A satellite image of the area appeared on screen followed seconds later by an overlay spread across the map outlining a list of pathways leading to and from their location.

"These are the latest trails I have. Tell Oz to come see me before he heads out. We can get him going in the right direction based on our estimates of the Exil's and BZ's latest movements."

"Thanks, Rhi!" Liam said, reaching to fist-bump the woman who resolutely ignored him, instead, bobbing her head and continuing to work.

Liam turned back around and shrugged at James with a grin while Dolly continued, "Now that we have supply issues out of the way, I understand there's another update from the team?"

"That's right." Heather's voice broke into the conversation.

Heather walked to the front of the room and a different set of satellite images appeared. They were the same ones Rhia had shown already, but these were overlayed with a different set of patterns and movements. Swaths of gray swirled in clouds with a legend indicating that each gray patch represented a potential Sentinel camp.

James watched the screens while Heather spoke. "The BZ has pulled most of their land operation to the North. Despite our sensors and running a constant ionic pulse from our solar arrays, they've consolidated their entire force on the newly terraformed land. This overlay is of all the Sentinel camp movements during the last three weeks. Only a few remain in the surrounding areas. We think that's why the Exils have been more active. Without the threat of the BZ, the power balance has shifted in their favor, and they're going to exploit it."

"What does this mean for us?" James asked.

"It means we need to uncover what the hell the BZ are doing there. The clock is ticking. Every day they build their fortress they get closer to attacking. Where, when, how, with what? All great questions. We have zero answers."

"What do you suggest?" Stacie asked, her eyes flicked across the screens absorbing and parsing the information in a manner James envied.

"Send in a team and steal their plans."

The room was quiet. James looked evenly at the woman standing at the front of the room. Her breath was shallow and even, her eyes calm as they searched the faces in the room.

"Steal their plans?" Stacie asked, chewing on the words.

"That's right. We need to get inside. There's no other way. We don't have to enter the actual fortress. Close enough for Rhia to establish a direct connection and download whatever plans she can find. Then we get out."

James analyzed the room's reactions. Stacie's brow furrowed as she looked at the ground, Liam eyed his wife, and Dolly tapped her fingers on her desk.

"I don't need to be all that close, but far closer than our stationary cameras and sensors. It will be risky. It'll take me about ten minutes to get into their system and another ten to download everything I can."

"Ten minutes to break into their system?" Stacie asked doubtfully.

"You did the groundwork for it with your initial hack," Rhia said, her voice cool.

"What?" Stacie's eyebrows raised in confusion.

"Jon told me all about it. The data packet, ionic mapping, all that jazz," Rhia replied, waving off Stacie's surprise.

"That's class—" Stacie started to say, but Dolly cut her off.

"Nothing's classified anymore Stace."

Frustration and annoyance read plainly on Stacie's face, but she composed herself and continued, "Okay, so ten minutes in. Ten minutes to get what we need, and we're out. Small team, there and back with no stops. Everything should be prepped." James saw the gears in her head working as she arranged the pieces of the mission.

"I'm guessing you'll guide?" she asked, looking at Heather.

"That's right."

"I'll be joining the party, too," Liam said, raising his hand. "Won the coin toss with this one." He shoved Teresa's shoulder, getting a punch in return.

"Who's running the connection and hack?" Stacie asked, glancing at the woman still engrossed in her screen.

"You're looking at her," Rhia said, without looking up.

Stacie's eyes shifted from person to person, "Sounds like it's already been discussed."

"It's the best shot we have, Stace," Dolly said, her eyes watching the strategist with care.

"I guess so." Stacie sat back in her chair and everyone else waited engaged in their own thoughts. She scowled at the ground as she spoke again, "You should bring Deck."

"Me too," James spoke, not expecting to hear his own voice.

"James…" Dolly said, her voice trailing.

"You want the best scout in the field, and that's Deck. You want someone with the best knowledge of the BZ in the field, and that's me. I'm going."

Dolly opened her mouth to speak but closed her lips without a word. Silent agreement filled the room, and Stacie gave him a stiff nod.

What the hell am I signing up for? James asked himself.

"Great, we'll leave in two days," Heather said, looking at James.

"Anything else on the agenda?" Liam asked, already halfway out of his chair.

"Yes. I want to tr—" Stacie started.

"Stacie! We'll talk about this later," Dolly said with an edge in her voice, her eyes gleaming with an intensity James had never seen on the NOLA chief.

The two women stared at each other; tension filled the space. James made eye contact with Teresa who shrugged. *No one else knows what's going on either,* James realized.

After thirty seconds of awkward glaring Stacie stood and walked briskly from the room.

Dolly sighed, glancing at her watch. "Quick meeting, council adjourned. Let me know if I can help with preparations in any way."

"Yes, ma'am," Heather replied.

"Oh god, please don't call me ma'am," Dolly whined pitifully, getting a chuckle out of James before her HOLO evaporated and the wall her figure had blocked reappeared.

Chair legs scraped against hard tile flooring and echoed off the walls as the group exited. James stretched his arms overhead, purposefully avoiding another conversation with Rhia. A tap on his shoulder forced him to turn around. It was Heather.

"Wanna eat?" she asked, pointing to the door.

"I'm starving, yes," James said, his stomach growling as he spoke.

"You two want to join?" Heather asked Teresa and Liam who stood by the door in quiet conversation, their faces tense.

"We're good right now. Thanks, though," Liam said, with mock cheerfulness as Teresa's stony features brushed past them and out the door.

Liam smiled and jogged to catch up with his wife.

"What's going on there?" James asked pointing a thumb in the direction of the couple.

"Teresa hates losing. I'm sure they're still arguing over whose leaving with us."

"Sounded like a done deal in the meeting."

"We'll see," Heather said with a knowing grin. "Enough of them. Enough of everyone. Too many abrupt exits today. Kevin's been cooking something in the kitchen since yesterday."

"He has a way of bringing people together like that."

"Best thing that's happened to us in a long time is Kevin's cooking."

"I'm glad we could help." James said, following Heather through the door and up the stairs.

"I mean it. Before him, it was MREs, water, protein powder, crap."

"Not horrible, better than our training food."

"I thought Teresa said it was pretty good. Ours was good out West that's for sure."

"In basic it ruled. The next stage though it seemed like literal crap." They reached the top of the stairs and James opened the courtyard door for Heather. The building's storage areas had changed drastically with the arrival of James's team. To make room for the overflow supplies, surplus gear that could withstand the cold had been moved into the courtyard. Waterproof boxes with ammunition, hardened HOLO emitters, ion shields, and other field supplies sat in well-organized corners beneath the menacing gargoyle heads topping the walls.

James and Heather meandered across the empty grounds to the other door. The enclosed area protected them from the harsh effects of the wind outside, but enough cold air swirled in to make James pull his jacket tight against his body. Meanwhile, Heather walked without a care, brazenly defiant of the temperature.

She's adapted, James reasoned, envious of her cold impervious nature.

Opening the heavy wooden door on the other side of the courtyard a rush of thick steamy air, heavy with scents of cooked onion, tomato, and spices crashed into their faces. James's stomach lurched at the thought of food, bringing on a wave of hunger-induced nausea.

"God, that smells good," Heather said, sniffing the air. The door closed, trapping them in a stew of humidity from the food prep. A sheen of sweat formed on James's forehead, and he wiped the moisture away with the back of his hand. Ordinarily, the air in the building was arid and James was constantly drinking water to keep any sort of liquid in his body, but around mealtimes the kitchens heated the rest of the rooms, sending wafts of scented warm air throughout the attached corridors.

"Let's get there before everyone else does. Deck's a bottomless pit and doesn't believe in waiting for others," James said, starting into a light jog, following the practically visible aroma in the desert air.

Heather followed his lead, and they entered a familiar scene. Nearly the entire HQ population sat in the dining room looking at them with wry smiles, letting them know they were in the right spot, but not early enough.

"Dammit." Both Heather and James cursed, and he searched the other hungry faces for the answer to his question: *when would Kevin be done?*

"Thought you'd get the step on us?" James heard Deck's voice and turned to find him in the corner next to the entrance. Deck smiled coyly at James with his hands draped over his knees. Meanwhile, Bob and Clint hunched over a HOLO emitter that cast a lifelike body across the stone floor. Clint used a specialized pen with haptic sensors that fashioned itself after whatever instrument was needed during a surgical procedure. Bob cautioned him in a low steady voice.

"You want to cut just above the place the bullet entered in this scenario." Bob pointed a finger to where the tip of Clint's pen-scalpel hovered. "Right there. What's under that?"

"The liver," Clint replied.

"Good," Bob said, and he swiped his other hand across the HOLO control on his wrist. The body's skin turned translucent as Bob manipulated the X-ray capability until the organs appeared behind a faint outline of the skeletal system.

"Cut as shallow as you can, too low you hit the liver, too high you miss the wound and cause a lot of bleeding."

Clint nodded as he dipped the knife under the surface of the fake skin and extracted the very realistic bullet from the wound. As he pulled it out though, the tip of the metal projectile tore against the side of the exit wound. In an instant, blood poured into the cut.

"Goddammit," Clint said, his calm face tightening in a frown.

"Relax, get some gauze, and clear the blood. Might still be able to—" As Bob spoke, the HOLO's pulse dipped and flat lined.

"Fuck!" Clint threw the pen at the wall as Deck fist-pumped.

"Sucker!"

"I pulled it one second too fast."

"You had it," Bob said, grinning and blowing away the mini-operating room. "So close."

"I'm too good, Clint," Deck bragged. "Now give me your ticket."

"Sonofabitch," Clint growled, throwing a piece of paper at Deck.

"What's that about?" James asked, sitting next to Bob and motioning for Heather to sit beside him.

"Tickets. Kevin started doing them today because some people have been confrontational with line-cutting," Clint said, glancing in Deck's direction.

"Kyle should have said savesies, fives, anything! I did it by the book." Deck declared as he held his ticket in the air. "Now I win again and get front of the line, baby!"

"Why'd you bet with him?" James asked Clint, confused as to why the mechanic would opt to move farther back in line.

"Deck was going to give me his whole helping."

"That's some balls," Heather said. "Props to Deck."

"Thank you, Heather. For that I will allow you an early bite of my food," Deck said, giving a slight bow. "You two should head there to get your spots. Kevin said no one eats unless they have a slip." Deck held his square piece of paper in the air. His fingers clasped his winnings tightly. "Don't want this one to go to waste."

"What's he making?"

"Short ribs and polenta. Don't ask where he got any of it. He doesn't disclose sources, but I can't wait."

"I'll get ours," James said to Heather as another wave of smells hit him in the face. A thin piece of drool fell from his lips to the floor, and James wiped his mouth hoping no one saw.

"Probably a good idea. Don't need you making puddles all over the ground here," Heather said, grinning, and James gave her the finger as he hopped to his feet and walked over to the metal table separating the chef's plating window from the rest of the dining room.

James nodded at the groups waiting hungrily along the walls. They watched James warily, analyzing him as he walked by subconsciously looking at the slips of paper each one held and remembering the new system.

Fierce competition, James thought as he rapped his knuckles on the metal table.

"Kev! Heard you're cooking a feast," James said with exaggerated joviality in his voice.

"Get a ticket, James." Kevin did not look at his new guest.

"What? Oh, right, they told me you were doing something different. I'm beat is all. Back from a field tour and ready for some of my buddy's cooking." James was well aware he was pandering, but the smell of the spices and ribs forced his mind to a desperate place.

"Ticket," Kevin said, pointing at the stack of Post-It notes on the table.

"What about a taste, Kev?"

"Can't all be special, James."

"Well, what about just me?" James asked, trying the unabashed approach.

"Ticket."

"Dammit," James swore under his breath and pulled two cards off the top of the pile. Turning around, he ran into a stout body that knocked him into the table. James's hand flew back to support himself before he toppled over, hoping no one noticed. *Everyone always notices*, he grumbled to himself as he turned back to the room.

"Didn't see you there, my man," a deep voice and a free hand guided him upright.

"I'm good," James said, checking to make sure his meal tickets were still in hand, "How's it going, Oz?" James asked, recognizing the bearded man's bass tone.

"Not bad. Head out again tomorrow morning."

"I heard something about that," James replied, nodding, never sure how much he was allowed to reveal. "Anymore camps yet?" The odious scent from the tents resonated in his nostrils whenever he passed clearings in the forest, haunting his memory.

"Nothing yet. I'll tell you if we find more though. Hope we can keep those Exils off our asses. They've been a royal pain the last few times out. Acting strange, too. Ever since we met you all on the bridge. Then the camps. Weird bunch." Oz pulled two Post-Its off the counter. "More aggressive and direct. Not like they used to be. They're intentional now."

"What do you mean?" James asked, interested.

"They're setting traps on the way out of camp. That would've never happened. In the past, it's only been risky on the way back. Now, they're trying to hit us before we even have our supply load."

"Any reason why?"

"Who knows?" Oz said, shrugging. "Desperation makes people do odd stuff sometimes." The risk-inclined man was unperturbed about the Exils' behavior, but it made James rethink what was happening. *What are the Exils doing attacking empty supply runs?* James decided to worry about it another time. He could talk about it with Stacie later.

"Right," James replied. "Enjoy the meal."

"Thanks. Hope there's some left."

"There's plenty, Oz, but you come up when I call the first batch of numbers. I'll give you an early helping," Kevin said, interjecting into their conversation.

"Thanks, man!" Oz said. He grinned and headed into the crowd, handing his tickets off to the stragglers walking to the table.

"What the hell, Kev?!"

Kevin looked at James. "He's leaving. You're not." With that, the oversized chef refocused on the food preparations and James left, grumbling and headed back to the rest of the group where Bob was suturing a compound fracture.

"Remember, reset it and don't move the limb when you're done. You don't want a free piece of bone poking through the stitches while you're working. Patient won't like it either," Bob said, finishing his explanation with a careful cross-stitch.

"I'll say," Deck said, shivering at the sight of a life-like bone disappearing under the skin.

"He let you cut?" Heather asked James.

"Only if we're leaving with Oz tomorrow."

"Oz always gets the luck," Heather said, looking at her number with a frown. "Hopefully there's enough at the end."

"Yeah, sure," James said absently. He couldn't help but think about Oz's Exil comment. *Why are they acting differently? What are we missing?* The BZ's odd behavior of consolidating its forces for the first time in years, torture camps, uncharacteristic Exils' activities, and Sentinels recalled from the field. Something was connected there, but James could not see the whole picture yet.

"Hey!" Heather yelled, and James startled as she grinned at him. "Stuck in the clouds?"

"Yeah, something Oz said," James replied.

"The great and powerful Oz?" Heather asked with a smirk on her lips.

"Yes, the great and powerful Oz." James grinned in reply. "Talking about the Exils, camps, the BZ, all of it. Somehow it's related. Don't know how yet."

Heather nodded. Her face had taken on a more serious expression. "Let's get our food and head upstairs."

"Sure, wh—" James asked, but Heather held a hand up.

"Upstairs." He met her eyes and nodded. There was something more.

What does she know?

"Food's up!" The shout came from the front of the room and heads whipped to its owner.

"Numbers one through seven, including Oz and any smugglers leaving tomorrow, you're up!" Kevin's voice bounced off the stone, rebounding throughout the room.

James and the rest of the room watched as the lucky first eaters made their way to the serving table, led in their self-satisfied parade by a cocky and boastful Deck.

"Sometimes you want to trip him. Ya know?" Clint said as Deck got his food.

"You'll get your revenge," James said, patting the mechanic's bulging shoulder.

"Yeah, wait 'til I'm driving him again. Not enough buckets in the world."

James grinned and felt a pang of nausea, imagining sloshing puke buckets and Clint's reckless driving.

"Remind me to skip that trip." James said as the next set of numbers got called and Deck returned with a plate piled high with steaming short ribs and a maniacal look in his eyes.

Thirty minutes later James sat with an empty dish and full belly in front of two plate glass windows looking across the inky black grounds. Heather and he ate with their food on their laps, saying little between mouthfuls of roasted vegetables, short ribs, and polenta. The sky was a blanket of stars with the moon yet to make an appearance. James enjoyed the vastness of the woods and grounds at night. Everything surrounding the castle blended together, creating a swirl of unknown dangers and wonders James's couldn't see. It was cold on the roof, but as full as he was, James didn't mind sitting in a cool room while he recovered from the feast.

"Weird eating in a castle tower, huh?" Heather asked, putting her tin plate on the ground with a clatter and taking a deep swig of water from her glass.

"Not where I thought I would be ten years ago. None of this is though," James replied, easing back in his chair.

"That makes two of us," Heather said. Quiet engulfed the room, and James realized how calm everything was when they were away from the HOLOs, the solar batteries, thermal generators, people. A moment of silence in a castle tower was a rare treat.

"So, what'd Oz say about the Exils?" Heather asked, breaking the spell of peace.

"They're acting different is all. Attacking when teams go out for supply runs. Chasing us across the bridge. Diving into attacks for the sake of them rather than from necessity like they used to."

"What do you think?" Heather asked, revealing very little with her monotone voice.

"I think I don't know enough about the Exils here to tell the difference. They've always been more aggressive. Right?"

"They have, but this is out of character. These are former Feds, James. They're trying to survive is all. They're not known to attack for the sake of it, like Oz says. This strays from their MO." In the darkness James could make out the shadowy lines of concentration etched in Heather's brow. Her mind worked like his, delving into a problem with such determination until it was pounded to dust in his brain before he could let it slip into the world.

"Any theories?" James asked, sipping his water.

"A million. But only one makes sense, and it would be heinous," Heather replied.

"And?"

Heather kept quiet. James glanced and saw the same furrow appear as if gauging how to respond. James was about to withdraw his question as she started to speak.

"I think the BZ got to them. We know they have ways of threatening people. We know they have continents of people under their command. What's to say that's by choice? Who's to say they couldn't have replicated their practices with the Exils?

"They're the perfect victims, Exils. Unaffiliated warriors with knowledge of the Federation and the local area. I don't know how they're doing any of it, but it makes sense to me. How did the BZ convince an entire set of continents to go to war? What are they doing?"

James turned the idea over in his head, remembering the way Raspin pitched the BZ to him during his incarceration. A world run in perfect unity needs to be broken first. Rearranging a shattered society was easier if people started with a blank slate. Raspin would have no problem toeing the line of forced control over people. He had proven his intentions with James and Kyle. The idea of Exils being somehow controlled by the BZ. That terrified James to no end. If it was true, it meant the BZ was ahead of them once again. It meant they were working against more than James realized, and by this point, James thought that was impossible.

"Well, I hope you're wrong."

"So do I," Heather replied. She took a final sip of her water, and her face brightened. The curves of her nose, lips, and mouth became visible. Above the grounds a brilliant white light cast from a nearly full moon popped its head over the edge of the forest releasing its glow through the tower, casting Heather and James's shadows against the wall.

Heather looked back at James, and the two made eye contact. The moonlight lit her in a way James had never seen, and his voice caught in his throat. He coughed into his hand, breaking the moment.

"Let's keep an eye out for this. Maybe there'll be something in the files we get from Rhia."

"I hope not," Heather said, looking away from James and picking their plates up off the floor. "I'd rather be wrong."

Chapter 17

Sightless eyes followed James as he ran.

Vines, shrubs, thorns, burrs, and roots blocked his path. The vicious implements of nature tore at his skin and ripped apart his feet. Blood pounded in his ears and sweat mingled with the tears pouring from his eyes. He was being chased. Smoke swirled and stung his retinas as the gray fugue that was his path revealed only more twists and turns through a forest of constant fear.

Shapeless bodies glided on either side, pulling in closer to James. He seized in panic and overcorrected himself, running off the trail and into a tree.

He fell to his knees, scraping off skin, and leaving it stuck to the root poking from the ground.

Whispers touched his ears, and the rank odor of death filled his nose. A phantom breath left a patch of wet skin on the nape of his neck.

Terror blinded him as he tried to stand, but the faceless people blocked him, tightening their circle.

Ash fell from the sky, and the translucent bodies of HOLOs hovered in the background of the faceless people.

A loud thumping tore through the space and the trees swayed in the clearing as the circle drew tighter.

He hugged the sides of his body, making himself as small as he could, pressing himself into a stone of panic.

A whispered scream echoed around the circle. "James…"

The faceless repeated the word. "James."

Soon it turned into a crescendo, building with each breath, pushing him further and further into a state of uncontrollable terror. He covered his head and body with his arms as tears streamed down his face. "James. James. James."

"James!"

A shove jostled James from his nightmare and he sat up in bed, his hand clasping the boot knife he kept next to his pillow.

"Whoa there, easy killer!" Liam's friendly voice put James at ease. "Time to get ready."

James took a deep breath, shaking his head to push the nightmare back into his subconscious.

"I'm up." The fear receded as James smiled, struggling to control his heartbeat while Liam walked out the door.

The rest of the team waited as he skipped down the stairs, zipping the top of his combat suit.

"Nice of you to join us, pal," Deck said as he pushed off the wall he had been leaning against.

"Yeah, yeah, everyone else ready?" James replied, hoping he wasn't the only reason they all sat around waiting.

"Have been for minutes," Deck said sarcastically.

"Sorry to keep you waiting."

"Enough banter. You two can sit on a front porch and drink some iced tea and talk all you want when we're back. We've got to leave, now," Heather said, her face stern. She had something to prove here, and James did not want to throw off her moment.

"On you, commander," James said as Deck curtsied.

Heather led the way out the door, followed by Rhia and James, then Deck and Liam.

"Loved your display of fealty back there," Liam said to Deck.

"Thanks, man. It's really all in the knee bend."

"You'll have to teach me."

"First thing when we get back."

"Deal."

James shook his head. Deck and Liam turned out to be very similar, and James wondered if Teresa thought the same. *Maybe Deck wasn't so far off his assumptions about her.* James shook his head at the two of them in a warning when he saw the tightness in Heather's shoulders. Deck and Liam responded by placing fingers to their lips and tiptoeing across the grounds.

Heather's going to hate part of this trip.

They kept a strong pace making it to the BZ in under three hours. When they arrived, the sun was still below the horizon. The approach had been faster than normal because they ran scans of the area on the fly with Rhia floating a couple of HOLO screens while Deck and Liam stood on either side of the tech expert to keep her from wandering.

They arrived at their regular spot on the side of the mountain next to one of the ground sensors and crawled to the top of the ridge overlooking the flat expanse. It had been less than a week, but the progress the BZ had made in such a short time was something James could barely believe.

One long waterway cut through the center of the tundra. Rivers, streams, and pools of water marking the landscape had been combined into the single waterway. A torrent of glacial water flowed smoothly in its carved pathway. The BZ had recreated the environment into an organized stretch of land built to suit their needs. The looms spread across the ground sweeping their ionic blankets over the land. Their positions had changed in the past few days, but their continuous motion, knitting the world to meet their designs never ended. A dull light emanated from the charged particles flowing through the earth, pushing around masses of rock and dirt.

"Rhia, anything on the scans?" Heather asked. James kept his eyes glued to the scene, watching for signs of Sentinels in the approaching dawn.

"Hold on a sec. Finishing now… Aaand we're good. Nothing on the monitors. I can't get into those mountain passages, but we should be okay."

"Can we keep that running while you do your magic out there?"

"We'll see."

"Guess that'll have to do. Everyone ready?"

Heather glanced at the three men huddled behind her. James was unused to being asked the question. His place was usually the one commanding, not accepting orders and it felt strange giving over a part of his role to her care. He nodded.

"Ready," James said, eager to get started.

"On me."

Heather took a deep breath and plunged into the unknown. Liam followed, then Rhia. Deck pointed at James. "I've got rear."

James hopped over the ridge. He half expected a surge of energy to rip through his body stopping his heart on impact, but when he was halfway down the hillside he realized he was fine.

He waited at the bottom with the other three until Deck's lanky frame came off the hill with a thumbs-up.

Heather nodded again at the group, and they took off under the brightening sky. James hunched over as they moved across the terraformed plain. He kept an eye on Rhia's HOLO watching for signs of a signal. He did not know what he was looking for, but it gave him comfort knowing Rhia did.

They kept moving, low and fast. James swiveled his head to the side as they approached one of the loom's turbines. Though far away from its deadly curtains, the size of the machine took James by surprise. It was massive. From their position on the hill it looked like any other construction tool, but up close, it towered above them. An impressive display of technology both in stature and function.

The BZ knows how to build shit, James thought, watching the spokes at the top of the obelisk crank with their perpetual force.

Rhia stopped and Heather's head whipped around.

The slender woman looked from her HOLO, searching the grounds, then put her head back down pointing to the left and Heather took off without question.

Must be getting close.

James kept pace behind the group's leaders who halted every so often to correct their path until finally, Rhia stopped for good. Heather's eyes were frosty. He knew from his own experiences that she was counting down their allotted seconds in her mind.

"Here," Rhia said. She plopped on the ground and started her work in earnest. Three HOLO screens surrounded her as she typed, swiped, and interacted with her monitors.

"Defensive positions. Don't deploy ionic charges yet," Heather said, bending to her knee.

"We're hitting daylight in minutes here, Heather," Liam said. He eyed the mountain entrances warily.

"I know. We'll be all right"

James chewed his bottom lip. Even though the Sentinels could function at any time, they seemed to emerge in daylight. It could have been when they operated best or perhaps it was easier for their human controllers to verify the work they accomplished during the day. Either way, daylight complicated things for the team. The sky brightened as James scanned his defensive quarter, hoping the BZ kept its schedule.

A sliver of light escaped over the edge of the mountains. The nets, already illuminated by their own glow, lit in a display of sparkles, waving their welcome to the first touch of day. A cloudless sky revealed a pale blue backdrop while the stars disappeared for the next part of the earth's daily cycle. Blues, whites, and silvers twinkled in neon brilliance while the sun rose higher every second leaving a spectral vision of nature and humanity mixed in the world of ice and rock.

Amidst the beauty and wonder of the moment, James's stomach dropped. They needed to hurry.

As if she felt the same pang of anxiety Heather spoke, "What's going on, Rhia?"

"Almost done."

"We've got two minutes."

Rhia did not respond. Her eyes were trancelike, her fingers a blur, as they swept across the HOLOs at speeds unnatural to James.

"We've got movement," Deck said. James turned to look at his friend's quarter. Deck faced the mountain farthest to the left directly behind James. From the awkward angle, he could pick out the Sentinel discs floating their way into the early morning. Matte gunmetal gray cast a dangerous reflection off the floating discs. The BZ was awake.

"Rhia…" Heather's voice trailed with urgency.

The woman in the center of the group did not respond.

"Rhia, thirty seconds. I'm calling it."

"One minute."

Heather's cheek bulged as she clenched her jaw, and James could practically hear her molars grinding.

James watched as Sentinels emerged from the mountain he was facing. He thought he could already see the transparent bodies of their HOLOs appearing around the edges of the openings.

James flipped the safety off his ionic pulse charge and waited. He couldn't turn it on. The charges acted as a sort of beacon and the second he did the entire BZ army would crash down on them. Odd that the Sentinels were attracted to the very things that killed them the fastest. *Mosquitos*, James thought remembering the bug zappers his Dad had used in the summer on their back porch to keep the pests away.

"Rhia."

"One…done." Rhia snapped out of her daze as her HOLO's disappeared. Without waiting, Liam took off, followed by Heather. James lifted Rhia off the ground and pushed her ahead of them. Deck filed in behind. James heard the footsteps of their scout padding rhythmically along the dusty earth.

"The big boys are out." Deck alerted the crew in a whispered shout, and James turned to witness the massive head of a giant HOLO surface from beneath the mountain. Like the looms, the monstrous size of the HOLOs up close sent James into a state of awe. He watched for a second as it trundled towards the nearest turbine lumbering with long fluid steps over the rock-strewn dirt.

Snap.

"Agghh!"

James swung to the side to avoid stepping on Rhia. The slender woman sat on the ground clutching her knee.

"Fuck, fuck, fuck," Rhia mumbled under her breath as she held her leg in agony.

James did not hesitate. "I've got her."

Deck nodded and helped James lift her onto his back in a fireman carry. His legs braced against the added weight, and he looked at the ridge ahead calculating the distance they still had to close. He grimaced, they had at least a thousand yards to the ridge with the ascent over the top of the hillside after that.

"You got it?" Heather asked jogging back to them.

"Yep, keep us moving."

Heather evaluated the situation nervously and took off again leading the way.

"Sorry." Rhia's voice was strained in pain. "I shouldn't have looked."

"It happens. We'll get you back," James said. He kept his response short to conserve his breath, "I've carried a lot more much farther."

"I'll take that as a compliment," Rhia replied in her wry tone.

James grunted his response as Heather picked up the pace.

"Only giants so far, but more Sentinels at the mouths of the caves. Rounds about to start." Deck yelled from the rear.

"Let's pick it up. You still okay, James?" Heather asked, glancing back.

James nodded and dug his toes into the ground. He needed his breath when they hit the hillside.

They finally reached the bottom of the incline. James took a deep breath and plowed ahead, worried if he stopped for a break his legs would seize in cramps.

They were halfway up the hill when Deck spoke up. "Four Sentinels coming this way. We need to move."

James gritted his teeth. His eyes stung, and he tasted salt as the sweat dripped from his forehead. These were the moments he worked for. Times when the world dropped from beneath him and all he could do was churn his legs. Every breath he took stung.

Every footstep sent waves of pain up his calves and thighs. Every jostle of Rhia on his shoulders sent muscle spasms down his back. But he had to keep going.

"Two hundred yards and closing."

"Get to the top and drop over," Heather yelled. James kept moving. His vision blurred as they neared the precipice. He wanted to throw up.

"Hundred yards," Deck called out.

Keep fucking going, James's voice yelled inside his head, throwing everything he had into each step until Liam disappeared. Then Heather fell from view. Finally, James hit the rim of the hill, and he pulled Rhia from his shoulders.

Rhia's face was pale, her body going into shock. Her knee swelled beneath the combat suit.

Deck was over the side a second after him, and they looked at each other.

"She can't go down," Deck said.

"I'll stay here with her."

"Glory hog," Deck said as he threw Rhia's HOLO bag as far as he could. "Get on the ground and hope those fuckers don't see us."

James fell to the ground next to Deck covering Rhia with his arm and slowing his breathing and heartbeat as best he could.

The seconds ticked by in James's head. Each one a beat of his heart. Another moment of life. Dread seeped into his bones as the eyes of an unnatural predator broke the plane of the hillside.

He held his breath, hoping Rhia was conscious, and waited for their world to explode.

Time dragged on, stretching to infinity. James's face burrowed further into the sharp frozen earth. His hand clutched his ionic knife with his finger poised over the pulse on his suit.

Not going easy, he thought, ready to get up swinging when a tap on his shoulder made him peek out from his blind shell.

Heather's eyes met his and a smile broke across her face. "I owe you a beer."

Chapter 18

Low-hanging clouds reflected gray light but no sun. James and the recon team traveled under branches stripped naked for winter. Their trip was slow, mired by Rhia's worsening leg injury, but the mood was more of relief than concern. Happy to be alive.

"That's a tear. Yep, seen it a dozen times." Deck said, squatting by the techie's leg.

"Thanks, Deck. The wealth of experience you have gained by practicing fake sutures on holographic cadavers puts me so at ease." Rhia rolled her eyes and gritted her teeth sucking in a breath through her clenched jaw. James wondered if the sarcasm was worth the pain it caused her. "No one has *any* painkillers?"

"Sorry," James said shaking his head. Their medical kits were meant for immediate triage and their limited drug supplies, used strictly for serious injuries, were held in HQ. *Ironic planning, I guess,* James thought, looking at the woman balling her fists, fighting the pain, cold, and shock battling her central nervous system.

"Bob will need to reset that and repair anything else if necessary," Heather said. Worry tinged her voice, but her face remained a mask of resolve.

"Let's get moving. Liam, your turn," James said. He and Deck positioned their hands on Rhia's back and under her armpits. Liam bent and braced himself.

"Up you go, my lady. One, two…" Liam counted as James and Deck hoisted Rhia onto his back, "Three."

Standing upright, Liam grunted as the weight settled on his shoulders. Rhia groaned in pain and her knee hung loosely by his hip. Deck tied the injured appendage to Liam the best he could, but the tendon was gone. Her lower leg hung like a shoelace from her thigh.

"That'll have to do. How're you feeling?" Heather asked, wiping a bead of sweat off Rhia's cold skin.

Rhia's head lolled as she summoned the strength to nod.

James glanced at Heather whose eyes betrayed the apprehension her body language hid from the rest of the world.

"We've got distance to make. Come on."

"I'll join you," James said, and he walked to the front accompanied by Heather.

A gray backdrop illuminated the dense layer of leaves covering the forest floor sprinkled with broken branches from past storms or rot. Popple trees, both dead and alive, clumped in tighter groves as the group continued their trek. James contorted his body into awkward positions to make it through the denser spots before cutting them back for Liam and Rhia. It was not the first time he wished they could take the main trail.

"We've got at least another twenty miles," Heather said, her voice dropping low enough so only James could hear. "With Rhia's injury that's going to take us another four or five hours. I don't know how much more damage this hike is doing to that knee, and she's developing a fever."

"What do you want to do?" James asked. He knew the pressure Heather was under. Having been in similar situations, acting as a sounding board was the best thing he could do.

"I'm thinking of sending Deck ahead."

"Makes sense. He's the fastest. What's the hesitation?"

"Exils, BZ, wolves, everything. If we decide to wait it out, and she loses her leg…or worse…" Heather chewed the inside of her lip.

James clasped her shoulder. "You've got this." Heather looked him in the eye, releasing a slight smile before scrunching her face back into its concentrated scowl.

"Deck!" she shouted.

"Yes, oh, great one!" Deck replied.

"Get up here," Heather said, turning to meet the scout.

"What? What's happening? What'd I do?" Deck asked, looking between Heather and James's faces for an answer.

"We can't safely get Rhia back to camp without the right meds. We're twenty miles out. I need you to go ahead of us. We'll follow more slowly on the trail. Tell Teresa to send a truck for us. If not, maybe a stretcher and reinforcements." Heather spoke quickly, outlining her plan. James could tell she had been coming up with it for hours. It was solid. Now that they were close enough, Deck would make better time on his own. With even a little luck they were looking at shaving an hour off their trip.

"In the meantime, the rest of us will keep moving," Heather said, addressing everyone. "Good thing is we can try to avoid any serious damage by going slower."

"I'll be fine," Rhia grumbled semi-coherently into her chest.

Heather ignored the comment and glanced between Liam and James. "You two good with the plan?"

"A stroll through the woods with you three sounds like a dream," Liam said, taking a swig of water from his canteen.

"Couldn't be happier," James replied.

"Good. Deck, use the trail but get off if anything happens. Understand?" Heather's eyes were stone when she gave the orders. James knew what she was thinking. If Deck got caught, they'd all be dead. *Good thing Deck doesn't get caught*, James thought, watching the scout adjust the straps and weapons on his body.

"Righto, boss. Let me get some water, and I'll be on my way." Deck turned to go, but stopped short. "Anyone else hear that?"

"Hear what?" James asked, straining to hear any new sound..

"That. The creaking. *Eeeeeee...*" Deck dropped his voice and let out the "*e*" in a high-pitched shudder. "Hear it?"

"No...." James said, continuing to concentrate. Swooshing leaves held most of his attention. He dug deeper into the ecosystem's sound. Birds on branches, rustling insects and mammals, tree limbs scraping against one another. It was all where it should be.

"I don't hear" A breeze hit the group, brushing across their faces followed seconds later by the sound.

Eeeeeee…

What is that? James's mind raced through possibilities as his eyes searched the dense forest. Young saplings dotted every space in the wooded area. James needed to find a creak in the pile of dry tree branches.

"Hey." Liam caught their attention with a loud whisper. His bearded face concentrated on a grove of trees. With Rhia still on his back, Liam lifted the rifle hanging across his chest and brought it to his chin.

"Deck, get on the other side of Liam," Heather spoke with a calm sense of urgency. "James, approach on the right with me."

"On you," James said, affirming her directive. He spread out to capture more space between the two of them. They tread parallel towards the sound. James's heartrate drove into a battle-ready state.

The gray skies gave nothing away. Swaying trees were followed by the noise and James glanced at Heather as she stepped over a log, her eyes maintaining their focus on the sound's origin.

A breeze. *Eeeeeeeeeeee…*

An unnatural stutter followed.

Eeeeeeeeeeeeeeeeee…

"James." Heather's eyes remained fixed straight ahead, but the fear on her face caused James's muscles to bunch. He followed her gaze five feet above the ground. Another breeze swept through the woods.

Eeeeeeeeeeeeeeee…

When the breeze subsided, James's eyes traced a line from the pointed toes of the boots dangling in the air to the pale gray blue face of Oz. His neck tilted as if in question as the rope used to hang his corpse dug into his skin, etching a line of raw blood over waxy skin. Glassy residue covered his bulging eyes, and his mouth opened in an unending question: how?

"What the…?" Heather's voice trailed as the world shrunk.

"Walk backward," James said in a whisper.

Heather nodded, probing with the nose of her rifle around the area, fishing for something unknown.

James's heart hammered as another long *eeeee* reverberated through the woods followed seconds later by its stuttering twin. His eyes met another pair of feet, this time only one boot remained on the corpse suspended off the ground. Coagulated blood had turned the toes purple with black skin marring the tips as they pointed at the leafy earth.

"Fuck, fuck, fuck," Heather cursed under her breath. Both their eyes absorbed every detail of the scene.

"Heather, we need to—" James was cut short by a rustle in the forest. Too loud to be a squirrel, too conspicuous to be a larger animal.

James's eye went to his rifle sight as he scanned the area. His heart pulsed in a steady rhythm, and he evened his breath to slow its pounding. Earthy scents wafted under his nose as the breeze was followed by another tightening of rope fibers. *Eeeeeeeeee…*

Something lurked, hidden by the forest. He tasted a salty bead of sweat that dripped from his forehead.

"James." Deck's whispered yell prompted James to look away from the dormant forest. His friend nodded in the direction of a pine grove.

James narrowed his eyes, focusing on the trees. *What does he see?*

The trunks from the full pines cast shadows on the ground and James probed deeper. He took a step towards the tree line.

A blur of wood, pine, and leafy ground created a spectral of yellow, green, and brown. James took another step and noticed it. An arm. An elbow jutting from the pines.

They're still here. James pretended not to notice the limb as he thought of how to warn Heather.

He turned to the mission lead and made eye contact. He nodded in the direction of the grove and pointed at his elbow.

She looked at him questioningly, not understanding, when a shadow appeared above her head falling rapidly. It took a second for James to recognize the descending body. He whipped his rifle up and fired three shots, blasting the stillness of the grove into a frenzy of echoes.

Heather shot the would-be attacker lying on the ground in front of her in the head before looking back at James. "Exils."

Wind surrounding his head stirred from a bullet ripping through the air and he dove for cover. *Where are they coming from?* James searched wildly, trying to determine the direction of the attack, but it was pointless. They were everywhere.

A host of featureless bodies fired shots from the grove where James had seen the elbow minutes earlier and he let off a salvo of bullets at the tree line. Splinters erupted as two of the figures fell to the ground. Two more disappeared and James turned his attention in Deck's direction where he stood back-to-back with Liam firing desperately into the woods.

While continuing to shoot, James worked his way over to the pair to help them clear the area. Rhia's body curled inward on the ground between them as the seasoned warriors expertly stepped around her, maintaining their defensive assault.

A wide tree stump gave James the cover he needed to reload.

"Motherfucker!" Heather shouted through the cold dry air and James popped his head up from his cover. He watched as she coolly pulled her knife from the neck of an attacker and grabbed her shoulder, squeezing as blood seeped through her fingers.

James hopped over the stump and took a position in front of her.

"Get to the tree over there." He gestured at a wide tree blocking the path to another patch of dense popples.

Heather nodded and grabbed her rifle with the bad arm, holding her wound closed with the other. James fired into the woods covering her escape before he followed, diving behind the tree.

The two crashed through the whip-like branches of the saplings and James felt blood tickle his cheek.

Heather fell against a tree clenching her jaw. She held her flapping skin between her fingers as blood poured from the cut, soaking her combat suit in the red liquid.

"Wish we had full armor suits on now," she said. James unzipped his top and ripped strips of cloth from his undershirt, tying it around her upper arm.

"Can't think about it now. You okay?" he asked. He tied off the wound splitting his brain in two directions trying to listen for the consistent one-two punch of Deck and Liam's rifles.

"I'm good," Heather replied. Her face had gone pale, and her eyes glassed over. It would have to do. James shoved the rifle back into her chest.

"I'll be back," he said.

James studied their position. Deck and Liam spun around one another, shooting at encroaching Exils. The circle grew tighter, and the shots were closer every second. Deck's upper arm had been hit with something, but otherwise, the pair were remarkably unscathed.

James hopped from behind the trunk that blocked the grove. He ran counter to his friends' position, hoping to flank the Exils. He let off a burst of gunfire every time he spotted an Exil. The shots from Deck and Liam had slowed and James cautiously moved towards the pair of soldiers.

"Deck!" James shouted over the gunfire, and Deck glanced at him. James signed:

I'll cover. Heather's behind the trees to your right.

Deck nodded his understanding and patted Liam on the shoulder. Liam reached down and picked up Rhia.

Even amongst the explosions and chaos, James could hear her scream as Liam lifted her onto his back. Deck covered his movements while James walked in their direction keeping up a steady stream of bullets to cover their move to safer ground.

The tide of the battle was tipping in their favor.

Ooomph!

An explosion sent James flying headfirst and sprawling onto his back, skidding against the edge of the pine grove. He flipped over in time to catch the barrel of a rifle from cracking his skull in half. He pulled his attacker closer, grabbed him by the ear and smashed the person's head into a tree. Motionless fingertips let James know he was safe for the moment.

Ooomph!

Another explosion rocked the area, followed by smoke and dried soil falling from the air.

What happened? James looked at the area, reawakened with furious rounds of Exil fire. Neither Deck nor Rhia were anywhere to be seen, but James saw a body lying on the ground. His heart stopped as he recognized the dense beard. Liam.

James gritted his teeth and pushed to his knees. He had lost his rifle in the blast and picked up his attacker's gun. He chambered a bullet and fired through the trees at the faceless bodies. The Exils, confused by the sudden onslaught of bullets, realized they were being attacked and returned their attention to James.

James dove into the pines. A bullet ripped through the back of his calf. He tasted the blood in his mouth as he bit his lip to stop from screaming. An Exil's body was propped against a large pine, and he used it as a step and pulled himself into the tree's canopy. Warm liquid soaked his toes as he climbed higher, pushing the pain from his mind.

He reached a branch strong enough to support his weight, stopped, and listened.

Silence filled the void that the bullets and violence had left in their wake. A breeze swung the hanging bodies letting off a chorus of eerie creaks. Adrenaline shooting through James's veins amplified the noise.

Footsteps padded. Four heads walked below taking careful steps across the ground. James counted his breaths as he waited for them to leave the area. If they kept walking through the grove, he could make it over to his friends.

He held his breath. Hope filled his chest as the last of the soldiers disappeared.

"AHHHHHH!" A scream of pain echoed through the trees followed by shots.

The soldiers returned.

James pulled the boot knife from his waistband and dropped onto the first one, driving his blade through the top of the soldier's skull.

Surprise gave him the upper hand as he twisted and sliced the second's throat.

The wind was knocked from his body as an Exil tackled him. James flew face first into the needle-covered ground. His eye barely missed a root poking from the frozen earth. James swung around and got a hand under the jaw of his tackler. He clutched the man's head and pushed with all his strength to dislodge the man from his back. Once clear, James grabbed the man's hair and pounded his face into the sharpened root point, welcoming the squelching *crunch* that followed until a boot smashed into his side.

James rolled onto his back reeling from his pulped ribs. A faceless body hurtled through the air diving at him with an axe. James shifted in time for the blade to bury itself next to his shoulder. He rolled over two more times stumbling to his feet, but his attacker was waiting. James spun to avoid the steel pointed head of the weapon swinging through the air.

The two moved in an awkward dance back and forth. James winced every time he put weight on his right leg as the axe sang through the air. Finally, James felt a large rock under his back foot. He dodged to one side avoiding a strike, positioned his foot on the rock, and lunged at his attacker. The surprise on the Exil's face was clear as James buried his knife in the man's arm.

Before the Exil could recover James grabbed the axe haft and tripped his attacker. With the man face down spread-eagle on the ground, James lifted the axe above his head and drove it through the middle of the man's spine spraying James's face with blood.

Warm liquid dripped down James's face and neck. Heaving for breath he wiped a hand across his mouth and dropped the axe on the ground. Noise was non-existent. A void of violence filled with death.

"James!" Deck's voice bounced off the trees absorbed by the needles on the ground. "James, dammit, I need help!"

James took off in the direction of Deck's voice. Shock overtook his system and his hands grew cold. The pain in his leg ebbed to a dull throb, and he concentrated on the location of his friend's cries.

He came upon the tree blocking the grove from the path and looked for Liam, but the bearded man's body was nowhere to be seen.

"James!"

"I'm coming!"

James, dragging his leg, rounded the massive tree trunk. The bodies of two Exils lay on the ground. Their blood pooled in thick red globs of liquid on the surface of the frozen earth.

"About goddamn time," Deck said, glancing from his work. His hands were covered in blood, his sleeves rolled past his elbows. Liam's pale face lay still under Deck's hands. James followed the bushy beard to a point near the left eye where part of his face was simply missing. In its place was an empty hole filled with gore and a jagged piece of bone surrounding an opening to the brain.

"We need to cover this up," Deck said his voice distant and concentrated as he pulled supplies from the medical kit.

"What do you need me to do?" James asked, kneeling next to his friend and rolling up his sleeves.

"Pass me gauze as I ask for it."

"Gotcha." James accepted the roll of gauze from his friend, careful to keep his own blood off the fresh bandaging.

"I'm going to stop some of the bleeding with quickclot, but I can't promise anything," said Deck with concern in his eyes, seeming unsure of what to do with his hands. It was the only time James had ever seen his friend uneasy.

"Clean it first," a faint voice whispered. James glanced around as the scout picked up his cleaning fluids. Heather leaned against the tree. Her face sunk into itself. A combination of the loss of blood, shock, and the cold was hitting her hard.

"How're you feeling?" he asked, but Heather only had the strength to nod in response.

"I'm fine, too," Rhia's voice came from behind James, and he turned to see a sarcastic smile tainted by pain stretched across a disturbingly white face.

"Good to see that," James said, nodding at the slender woman. She bobbed her head in response peering at the sky.

"Heather's having a rough go. Bullet nicked an artery. I fixed what I could, but we need Bob. Or someone who knows what the hell they're doing," Deck spoke low so Heather would not hear the anxiety bubbling in his voice. James grabbed his wrist.

"Pull it together. Remember what Bob taught."

Deck nodded and bit his lip.

"All right, cleaning."

James watched the procedure. Removing the gore revealed the extent of the damage that the Exil's explosion had wrought on his friend's face. A third of his facial skull was completely gone. James was not sure what kind of man they would find on the other side of surgery, but at least he'd be alive. When Deck finished with the last touches of gauze, he noticed James's leg.

"The fuck? Let me look at that."

"No time, bud." James shook his head. "We need you to get help ASAP. Tell Teresa what happened. She'll send the cavalry."

"James, let me…" Deck's voice trailed off when James looked him in the eye.

Deck stood and checked his rifle. He grabbed an extra magazine off Liam's vest. "I'll be back in three hours. Stay alive."

"Plan on it," James replied.

Deck examined the area, a ball of muscle formed in his jaw before he took off into the woods.

"I hope he's as fast as he looks," Rhia said, shuddering from cold and pain.

"He is. Hold on a little longer," James said. The techie dug her nails into the earth.

Rhia nodded and pointed her pale face back at the sky.

James leaned against a tree. He lowered his back on the knotted wood, careful to protect his ribs. As his shock wore off, the pain in his leg increased. Dried blood coated his pants. Frozen and dried liquid had created a stiff shield along his calf and James cut the fabric to avoid aggravating the injury.

He inspected the entry and exit wounds. Lucky for him the bleeding had stopped, but the areas still needed to be cleaned and bandaged. A wave of fatigue rippled across his vision sending streaks of blotted light through his eyes. He realized how tired he was and lowered his eyelids. *Just a second,* he thought. A wind cut through the grove of trees followed by the tightening fibers from the ropes holding the smugglers' bodies. James's eyes whipped open. There was no taking a break. James had to get to work if they were going to survive from freezing while severely injured. Night would come fast. *Easy to freeze to death if your body is already fighting to stay alive*, James thought, grimly reviewing their options.

He glanced at the still body of Liam, Heather's cold vacant stare, and Rhia shuddering as she watched the clouds. James pulled the med kit from his pack. He poured biocleaner into the bullet's entrance hole on his leg first. After nearly a decade at war, he had plenty of experience caring for his injuries. The sensation of the metal fragments vaporizing was familiar, and he watched mist flow out of both wounds. When the smoking subsided, he applied quickclot and put on a bandage that attached itself tightly around the wound, adhering seamlessly to his body.

Bizarre stuff, James thought examining the imperceptible edges of the bandage. After certain levels of James's healing enzymes were no longer present it would dissolve naturally. James had no idea how it all worked but was glad NOLA gave Bob plenty of resources to understand it for him.

Finished with his self-care, James rechecked Liam's eye, Heather's arm and head, and finally Rhia's leg. Like Heather, the slender techie had drifted into a semi-conscious state, twitching whenever James grazed anywhere near her leg. He could not imagine the pain.

Warmth was the next order of business. Lifting Heather in his arms, he placed her next to Rhia and wrapped two heat blankets around the women's shoulders. He covered Liam with the last two.

Gotta keep moving, James thought, tucking the final edge under Liam's shoulders.

Under the blanket, Heather and Rhia stopped shaking. Liam's color remained its white pallor. *At least he's not blue. Small victories.*

Eeeeeeeeee…

A breeze swept through the area reminding James of his fallen friends. He got to work. Gritting his teeth through the pain, James climbed each of the hanging trees, cutting the ropes with his boot knife and lowering the bodies to the ground. All five of the smugglers lay in a line. Their necks covered in permanent circles of raw skin. Their eyes bulged from past asphyxiation.

Staring at their faces James tried to work through how everything had happened. Why were Oz and the team this far east? They must have been chased by the Exils, but that didn't explain why the Exils were so intent on getting them. James shook his head. He could not dwell on things that he did not understand. Plenty of time to do that back at HQ. He needed to stay alive.

He rubbed his hands together and started putting the Exils' bodies into a pile. Maneuvering the thirty-four stiff corpses was made more difficult in the forest's tight quarters. After what felt like hours, James sat on the ground, wiping sweat from his brow. He had one more set of bodies to move, but his vision was blurring again. Exhaustion, blood loss, thirst, hunger, and pain. Bodily effects of multiple avenues of deprivation cut into his psyche.

"Come on," James growled to himself. He pushed to his feet and swayed as he walked to the next set of bodies. As he was pulling the leg of another Exil corpse, a heavy breath stopped him.

Was that real? James spun around to the bodies splayed on the ground.

Patiently and silently he waited until it came again. A wheeze, barely audible above the quiet.

James checked the body of the man whose leg he held, but it was no more than tissue and bone.

He inspected each body, examining pulses and feeling for breath.

Believing he was hallucinating and about to give up, he came to the final woman and saw her chest move.

Her eyes flickered open and her head lolled in his direction. Gray pupils stared lazily at him, more dazed than alive. Blood trailed from the corner of her mouth. Her face maintained its languid stare as a smile perked at the corner of her split lips.

"Hello, James. It's been a while. Nice to see you. We have a lot to talk about." The woman spoke in a tone James knew, one of superiority, intelligence, and reptilian emotion. James stared in confused horror, wondering how Edgar Raspin had managed to get inside her head.

CHAPTER 19

Raspin. The name rolled across his mind.

Gray eyes gazed at him thoughtfully, matching the smirk on the woman's face.

"Didn't expect to see me. I guess not see *me* though, right? How have you been? Almost a decade since our last encounter, no?" As she spoke, the woman pushed her body to a sitting position. Her voice's cadence and body's mannerisms recreated the image of his past tormenter. Precise control with an inhuman ability to shape movements. Everything in sync. Premeditated and manipulated to a degree of prescience unnatural to most people.

"Who are you?" James asked. He wanted to confirm his worst suppositions.

"Ha!" The bark of laughter bounced off the trees, startling James. "I suppose that's an excellent question. I guess I'm whoever this"—the woman inspected her body before turning back to James and smiling—"was. But we both know exactly who *I* am."

"How? How are you this?" James pointed up and down the woman's shell of a body. The ramifications of what he was witnessing were beyond James's comprehension. His muscles remained coiled. Whatever was happening, James needed to learn more.

"*This* was my dream. When we first captured you, we were too early in beta stages for me to properly manipulate anyone in this manner. No. It was all too rough. All very messy. Controlling our soldiers is one thing; they don't require anything more than a joystick and simple directions. Their movements are indistinct and easy to design on a mass scale. What I discovered and what we have achieved for humanity, though, is breathtaking. Our ability to mold the world to our needs doesn't stop with the dirt, rock, and water." Raspin's surrogate body scraped the ground with dry fingernails. Gray eyes stared at James with a new intensity as the body sat cross-legged, clasping its hands with cracked, bloody fingertips.

James drew back. The posture from all those years ago flashed in front of his eyes. His old enemy returned, this time inheriting the body of some poor woman.

"Have you visited our base yet? No doubt you have. No way for us to know." The woman's shrug deepened James's horror at Raspin's unnatural new form. She continued to ignore James's discomfort. "We stopped all our surveillance and defenses here. Once your Federation fell, the offensive threat, even in your land, became much less of an issue."

"We're looking to change that."

"I'm sure," Raspin said with a dismissive wave. "If you have visited, you've seen the most magnificent things, James. A worldly man such as yourself would appreciate the lengths we've gone to build the earth to meet our needs. Shifting the dirt is easy. Getting it to stay there is a little harder. It's intoxicating to harness the power and construct a world in your own vision

"Back to my original story. I realized after our brief jungle encounter that I could not recreate people like those in your Federation. Our population is different. Our societal vision remains contained along an ironbound pathway that very few of us know how to properly traverse. Yes, the capabilities of our machines are stunning. I'm sure you remember the images we shared of Africa, the base we set up on the continent. I think it defines the term 'awe-inspiring.' However, it's not enough. There's more to a plan as grandiose as ours than simple military infrastructure and the ability to bend the physical world to our whim. People. We need people. *They* are critical pieces to the solution. Integral cogs in a machine that can be made to do exactly as we please."

The surrogate body stood and paced while Raspin continued his diatribe. Blood covered the woman's hands, staining her skin and wrists in an iron wash. Darkness loomed and threatened James's vision and the cold's presence grew even more obvious. James shivered while he eyed Raspin's new shape.

"If you recall, violence was our problem. Not that we could not have it. On the contrary, violence is what we *needed*. What we yearned to breed into our population. A population intended to drive the next step in human evolution. One with so many checks in place, so many guardrails it is impossible to accomplish without full submission.

"When one creates a military machine there's a certain amount of independence required. Military resources who are highly skilled to perform their duties need to be well trained, obedient, and are able to operate in any environment. They also need a certain independence. An internal mechanism that allows them to break protocol as they see fit."

Raspin paused to look at his damaged fingertips. He picked one of the broken nails, pried it off, and tossed it aside. A fresh well of blood erupted from the torn skin, but nothing registered on Raspin's face. The body kept walking, reclasping her hands behind her back.

James watched with horrified curiosity, listening to Raspin's monologue.

"There's something that you may not have realized, James. Other than what I already shared about our people, we needed ways to show them how to complete the tasks that were necessary. Not all were on board, but they don't need to be. We can take care of what we need to without their permission." A lethal grin flashed his way as the woman turned in his direction.

Realization tickled the back of James's mind.

"You controlled them?"

"You always were quick." Raspin's surrogate smiled broadly.

"The attack on Midway? The Sentinels? Everything?"

"Don't be ridiculous. *I* can't control everything. And our programs were not close to what you see today. Much more 'point and push' earlier on. This level of control is something entirely new." The body had stopped walking again and stood looking into the pine grove with its back to James.

A wind whipped across James's body and icy air penetrated any exposed parts. Raspin's surrogate did not react, robotic and unaffected by earthly elements.

"How? How are you controlling her?" James asked.

The woman's face turned around and examined its body. Raspin's ever present smirk floated on her lips. "Ahhh, the *how* of it all is something I can't get into. Your people are very good at verifying that for themselves. The *why* we already reviewed. What's next?"

James narrowed his eyes. *What's next? What's he talking about?* James ran through the questions in his mind. Raspin clearly wanted to brag to James about something, but James needed to get there first. *What's next…?* A thought formed, beginning as a kernel, mushrooming, and assuming control of his frontal lobe.

"There is no next," James said almost inaudibly

A full smile stretched across the surrogate's face.

"There's no way to separate from a controlled subject, is there?" James tried to get absolute confirmation from his former captor, but only received a smile. He continued, "You implant them with whatever control is needed, put them in your military, run them through missions, and use them until they're no longer needed. And when you do have future needs…" James's voice trailed off as he walked through the grotesque logic of it all. His mind flitted to the torture camp Oz had found. Tents erected to turn the Exils into the unwilling subjects of the BZ. James's hands tightened into fists as he refocused on his former captor.

"There are always more foot soldiers, James. When a vision requires such a stringent path to success there are sacrifices we need to make."

"Taking the minds of your people and discarding them. That's a sacrifice you're okay making?"

"Absolutely."

"Why? Why not create a way to bring them back?"

"What good would that do? A group of damaged soldiers? No. This is cleaner. We keep them in service until we're done. Then…"

James was quiet, and he turned away from his former tormenter. The black masks marching off the boats of Midway flashed across James's vision. Their lockstep movements and undeterred forward progress made way more sense now than it had all those years ago. They were not functioning under their own control. They were shells.

"So who controls them? If not you, who?" James asked. He turned to look back at Raspin, but the woman was gone.

James moved as quickly as his body would allow, but it was too late. A hard object slammed into the back of his head. Nerves exploded in his vision and an intense pain assaulted his other senses. Dirt filled his nostrils, and the ground stared at him fringed by multi-colored light.

Urgent thoughts crawled across his mind. He needed to get up. Where was the woman? Where was Raspin?

Palming the ground, he pushed himself upright, but a kick dislodged his arm and he fell onto his face. A hand gripped his shoulder and turned him onto his back. James lay staring at the face of Raspin's surrogate. The sickly disconnected smile glistened, and frothy saliva pooled at the corners of the woman's lips.

"I can't tell you everything, James. Of course not. I've worked so hard to get here. I could not believe my luck when you of all people entered the picture. The first coincidence in my career that has worked so brilliantly. Alas, that mind will officially be gone, but the influence it holds will stick around for a long time."

A HOLO's blue glow emanated from beside James, streaking across his distorted vision. *What's he doing?* The smooth edge of a knife pricked the skin behind his ear. "I apologize for the crude methods I'll need to use, this will be anything but pleasant. The mind is not meant to be torn from itself, but you won't remember anything soon. We'll work together for a long time, but you'll never really know it. Sad I guess. Goodbye, James—"

BANG

Red enveloped James's sight. He wiped a hand across his eyes to see the woman's body straddling him. Her forehead was a mash of bone and pulped brain fragments with rags of skin hanging across the gaping wound. James pushed the body off and spat, choking down a surge of vomit in his throat. With the back of his hand he wiped the red liquid staining his lips and tongue. He spat blood that was not his own, rubbing his tongue across his teeth to try and rid himself of the iron taste coating his taste buds.

His head pounded. Touching it, he felt a chunk of blood-soaked hair covering a growing bump.

"Even," said a voice.

James glanced in the direction of the voice. Heather's pale face stared at him, her neck barely supporting her head. She held her pistol in place and nodded at James before lowering the weapon and leaning gently into Rhia's shoulder.

PART III

Chapter 20

"How's that?"

A jolt of pain ripped through James's skull.

"Not great," James replied, holding a hand over his head pressing away additional pain.

"I figured that would happen," Bob said, sighing. He typed rapidly into the HOLO, facing away from James. "Keep up with the pain meds. The head might be a problem for a little longer. Your leg's healing great though."

"Good to hear," James replied, wondering why Bob insisted on poking his injury if he suspected it would hurt. Common sense told James that it was dumb to try something if you knew the outcome would be bad, but he kept quiet. *Trust in Bob.* The motto echoed in his mind for perhaps the thousandth time, recalling various horrendous injuries that their medic had fixed over the years.

"You done with him yet?" Stacie asked. She stood in the doorway of the medic's makeshift operating room with her arms folded in a display of controlled impatience. James was glad Bob was never bothered by Stacie's brashness.

"He's good to go. Take it easy for a couple of days, James," Bob said, slipping a rolled joint into James's palm. "Relax a little if you can."

"Yes, doctor," James replied, shoving his hand into his pocket.

"Come on, they're waiting for us." Stacie pushed off the wall, practically bouncing.

"Yes, ma'am," James replied. "You comin', Bob?"

"I'm gonna clean up here and check in on Rhia. I'll be down in a few."

"Want us to wait?" James hopped off the exam table, exaggerating the time it took to stand.

"James…" Stacie's tone was on edge, and James grinned.

"Can't be patient with a poor, injured soldier?"

"I'll shoot your other leg," Stacie replied, rolling her eyes as she walked briskly away from the room.

He caught up to her in the hallway and they made their way to the council meeting.

Their footsteps echoed off the hewn rock walls as they skipped down the tile stairs to the basement. Quiet had descended over the HQ since their return, and James was thrown by the eerie silence. Such a normally boisterous atmosphere was replaced by a noiseless ambiance he had never experienced in an HQ. He was used to the field, the on-ground movements where noise was predicated on the mission. The new environment revealed a type of desperation that James was unaccustomed to.

Deck had returned in time to save Liam's life who, according to Bob, would make a full physical recovery, but there was no knowing how his mind would be affected by the trauma. For the time being, he was in an induced coma, which Bob insisted would help with a speedier recovery. Teresa operated with a split brain lately, simultaneously attending to her husband and the needs of the base. James became exhausted watching her. Heather was relatively unscathed concerning any permanent injury. Exhaustion, dehydration, and minor frostbite aside, she was okay. Rhia was alive, but the fate of her leg was a different story. By the time they had returned to HQ the limb was too far gone, and Bob was forced to amputate. Because her body had been in such a state of shock and nearing total sepsis Bob had her in an induced coma, too, to help the healing process. They had yet to wake her to tell her the news.

When they entered the room, most eyes were focused on HOLOs.

Not seeing any of his team members in the room yet, James turned to Stacie. "Where do you want me?"

"Windows are good."

James sat at the front of the column on the far side of the room. He could feel eyes peeking in his direction. He looked idly out the window, preferring the view to awkward eye contact of people glancing at him surreptitiously from behind their HOLOs.

Attention was nothing new to James. For years he had dealt with looks and whispers when he walked through NOLA. He managed to ignore it, but at times he wished he could disappear, leave the unwanted fame and stay in the field until he merged with the rest of the world. He could become a part of the landscape, unbothered by those compelled to get a glimpse at the man they did not know but felt compelled to stare at.

"Okay, folks, what's happening?"

Stacie's voice cut through James's inner voice, and he turned back to the front of the room. The rest of the base's population filtered into the room as if on cue. Stacie scanned the crowd and settled her sights on their medic, walking through the door while wiping his hands on his shirt. "Bob, you first."

"Liam's in stable condition. His brain has maintained steady activity, but I want to wait another day or so before I wake him."

Teresa perched on the edge of a table with Stacie, but her face was inscrutable.

"And Rhia?"

"We can wake her whenever we want. Latest blood tests show her body has stabilized. We'll want a few friends around though."

"I'll be there," Teresa spoke with unchallenged authority, and Bob nodded.

"Other two are doing fine," Bob said, glancing in James's direction. "At least that's what they tell me. They've been known to lie though."

"Feel like a new man, Stace. I'll have to run another trip to the BZ base to feel this good again," James said, eliciting a chuckle from the room.

"I'm sure you'll get your chance. All right, where are we with the autopsies?"

"They're complicated, but it looks as if the brain stem was altered in the woman Raspin manipulated," Bob replied. "Given some of the markings on the other Exil bodies, I assume this is the group that lost all that blood in the camp you found."

"Any way to prove that?" Stacie asked.

"I've started running the tests.

"Good. What are we looking at here?"

"These are images of the implants we found in the Exil groups brain. This one specifically shows the woman who woke back up to talk with James."

The HOLOs showed images of a human brain, and Bob continued explaining his findings.

"This little device was implanted in her. There's nothing running in it now though. Looks like it used its host's energy to power itself. Ingenious really. The only way for it to turn off is if the host dies, and it self-destructs. BZ are ruthless.

James had listened to enough medical talk for the day, and his eyes drifted around the room. He noticed the rest of the team had joined, but spread through the crowd. Kevin and Kyle sat in the back focused on the presentation at the front. Meanwhile, Clint and Jon's faces were buried in HOLOs, and their fingers flickered every moment or so manipulating their screens.

Movement came from the doorway and Deck's face appeared. Poking his head in cautiously, he snuck around the back of the audience and took a seat behind James. He clapped a hand on James's shoulder in hello and leaned back in his chair.

For the first time in his life, Deck was getting attention he did not want. The entire base saw him as a hero. Yes, he had run twenty miles from an active battle scene and led a group back in the freezing cold to save four people clinging to life, but he knew how lucky he had been and getting attention for something he did not believe he deserved bothered him. Deck wanted none of it.

"How late am I?" Deck whispered in James's ear.

"Right on time, buddy. We just started."

"Good."

"Thanks, Bob. Clint, you're up," Stacie spoke. She glanced in James and Deck's direction with narrow eyes and the two put their hands up apologetically.

"Geez, she's tough," Deck muttered as Clint started his part.

"We did a full rundown of the cars we found near the battle site," Clint started. Images from his HOLO sprang onto the screens. An aerial view of the forest marked the locations where the Exil vehicles had been left.

"All of these were standard Federation. Pickups with some minor alterations for the most part, solar arrays in the beds, and enhancements to the armoring on the doors and windows, but nothing too special. The engines are a different story. Brand-new battery installs for cold resistance, fuel injectors to combat freezing, and even extra heating rods connected to their external solar panels to avoid stalling in bad weather. High level of winter proofing so these guys were planning on being outside for a while without taking much of a break. In this environment, that's nothing new. I didn't recognize some of the parts, but the Federation's a big place, could be something I'm unaware of."

"Which parts?" Teresa asked.

"The solar panel connections. They had a different hookup than we use."

"Huh," Teresa said. She left that as her reply and returned her focus to the screens.

James tried to recall a single instance where Clint had been stumped or unaware of an engine part in the Federation.

Clint stopped as the images scrolled through the various shots of the engine and flipped to the car's dashboard.

"The weird part was the car's interior. Jon?"

Jon walked to the front of the room replacing Clint while the rest of the screens changed to the vehicle's interior.

"This is what the truck looked like to the naked eye. Pretty standard dashboard, deck, analog radio hookup, charging ports, solar array controls, comms equipment, the works. Even has a slot for HOLO emitters. Anyone see anything different?" Jon looked around the room.

James examined the picture closely. *What's he getting at?*

Everything appeared normal. The room was silent while everyone struggled to find what they were missing.

"Anyone?" Jon asked again. He loved the suspense and James waited for him to loftily explain what no one else knew or understood, a favorite of his techie.

"The emitter's different." Teresa's voice broke through the air, and the cocky smile that had been growing on Jon's lips disappeared.

"Umm, well, yes. That's exactly correct. The hookup is wrong for Federation emitters. As we suspected, these trucks aren't Exil or Federation at all. Or not anymore. These are BZ-altered trucks. This means without a doubt these Exils were controlled by the BZ. If not for this one very small detail we never would have known it."

"That, the camp we found, and the fact that one of them tried to bash James's skull in with a rock talking to him as our old friend," Deck added sarcastically shaking his head.

James looked at the picture, unable to ignore the difference in the HOLO hook installed in the dashboard.

"Question I have is why would the BZ take over groups of Exils?" Deck's voice piped up from behind him. James nodded, wondering the same things. *What's the point in that?*

"We're supposed to hear more from NOLA on that any minute now," Teresa replied. "Anyone else presenting?"

Quiet greeted the question.

"In that case, let's give it five for NOLA to join us. Everyone stay put." Teresa leaned against the table and returned her gaze to the floor.

James watched her from his seat and decided to join her.

He stood next to the stocky commander and folded his arms. "How you holding up?"

"I've been a hell of a lot better, James, but thanks for asking," Teresa replied, taking a deep breath.

"If there's anything we can do…" James voice faltered. He never knew how to approach these situations except to offer support. He wanted to do more, fix the situation, but the world had a different plan and he was a bystander, watching as the future unfolded.

"James, without you and Deck, we would not be talking right now." Teresa looked up from the floor and at James. Her eyes revealed exhaustion, fear, and determination. James took an odd solace from her gritty personality.

"Without you two, Rhia would have lost more than a leg, Heather would have frozen to death, and Liam… Well, we all know about Liam."

James nodded. "Still, anything at all."

"I appreciate it. Speaking of Heather, where is she?"

James followed Teresa's gaze, searching the room for their friend, but she was not in the audience.

"I'm sure she's just taking a rest," James said, disappointed by her absence.

"She deserves it."

The center HOLO screen crackled to life and Dolly's face loomed as a ghostly apparition.

"Can everyone see me?" Dolly asked, struggling with her video feed.

"Hard to ignore a floating head in a packed room, Dolly," Deck quipped from his seat.

"Thanks, Deck," Dolly replied, ignoring the sarcasm. "Is everyone there?"

"As good as it's going to get," Stacie answered, multiplying the NOLA leader's face to the other screens. James walked back to his seat as the rest of the room quieted and Dolly started to speak.

"Well, I know it's been a busy couple of days for everyone there, but we're working as quickly as we can to get answers. Stacie, can I drive?"

"Be my guest," Stacie said. She swiped up on her HOLO giving Dolly control over the room's optics.

Dolly wasted no time diving in. "We finally managed to correct our satellite orbits, and they are now stationed above the BZ base. These are the first images we've seen of the area. They confirm everything you've told us. Shifted river pathways, altered mountain ranges, flattened hillsides, retrenched watersheds, the works. They're reconstructing the tundra, creating a new glacial face for the Arctic."

The satellite images gave a time-lapse view of the changes the BZ had made to date ending on the massive waterway cutting through a perfectly flat piece of earth protected from the elements by a manipulated mountain range. The scope of the change was incredible, and James's mouth parted in awe as he stared at the altered landscape.

"When you initially told us what was going on, we thought they were designing a new operating base, similar to the southern jungles or the West Coast—a place to set up shop and deploy their Sentinel troops, bleed us from the inside. Until today."

A new image appeared at the center of the combined HOLOs. A mothership loomed over the rock-strewn earth casting a monstrous shadow across the land. Its hull fit perfectly within the confines of the waterway, acting as a cradle for the monstrous ship.

"Holy shit," Deck muttered under his breath.

A new voice spoke, and James recognized his sister's crisp tone. "We believe the BZ is trying to create a northern passage. After clearing most of the far north, they have a straight shot across the country, right to the heart of the Federation military's operation." The screens zoomed out and the waterway where the titanic ship sat turned into a faint line intersected by denser color tracing its way across the North. "They can't come in from the Southeast and they already have control of the West Coast.

NOLA's too strong for them to attack, but they do have one target in mind for sure." The route stopped as it crossed Lake Michigan and ended abruptly.

"Chicago. They're creating a path to hit the Federation at the heart of the country. Once they have the center of our landmass, anything's possible."

Silence engulfed the room. James broke it down in his mind step by step. Looms shifted the earth and water to create a passage that had never existed. Altering the ice and rock of the Arctic and paving the way to the last remaining stronghold and the heart of the former Federation onto which they could unleash one of their greatest weapons.

It makes too much sense, James thought, wondering how no one had realized it before.

"They've got a lot of land to cover to get there," Kevin said, his deep voice filling the room.

Dolly's face disappeared replaced by Caitlin's analytical gaze. "Not as much as you may think. The BZ has already set up dozens of similar sites across the north. The only reason we're not able to watch them from our defensive satellite positions is because we can't access them without sacrificing the safety of other NOLA strongholds.

"We think they're almost halfway done with the project. Granted, they need to make some major connections to their primary pathway, but we're behind them. Again." Caitlin finished her sentence grinding her teeth in frustration. James felt the same annoyance and dug his nails into his palms. This always happened. The BZ was ahead of them every time. The motherships, the looms, the Sentinels. If it wasn't one thing, it was another. Now they were taking over Exil soldiers and sending them on attacks against NOLA personnel. *What else could they do now*, James thought, his mind overloaded with the constant flow of horrific futures spinning across his mind's eye.

"So what's next?" Stacie was already in planning mode, and her eyes twitched across the screens, soaking up information.

"We wait." Dolly's face replaced Caitlin's again. The firm set of her jawline matched the tone of her voice. Her word was final.

"Dolly, Caitlin said it herself, we're already behind. You want us to wa—" Dolly held up her hand cutting off Stacie.

"I get it, Stace. I do. But we need time. Give me eighteen hours, not even a day, and if I don't have a plan for you, you call the shots. Deal?"

The audience held its collective breath for the ten eternal seconds it took for Stacie to make up her mind.

"Deal." Stacie nodded, and Dolly returned her gesture with a nod as a sort of virtual handshake.

"Okay, that's all. Teresa and James, could you two stick around? Also, Heather if she's there," Dolly said, running a hand across her face.

Chairs scraped the floor, and people left the room in quiet order. The apprehension was tangible. Waiting was not easy for a group of people used to taking matters into their own hands.

"I'll catch up with you guys later," Deck said as he followed Kevin and Kyle into the hall as they manually guided Jon, Clint, and Stacie, whose faces were buried in HOLOs.

"Where's Heather?" Dolly asked, searching behind James and Teresa.

"Didn't come today," James replied.

"No big deal," Dolly said, shrugging and relaxing into her chair. "How's Liam?"

"He's getting better. I think. I haven't heard him speak yet. He lost his eye, but hopefully that's all," Teresa answered. Her eyes looked through the HOLO and her voice remained distant as she spoke.

Dolly nodded, her face displaying honest concern. "I'm sure he'll speak, T, and we've done a lot of eye replacements. NOLA's R&D team is something else."

"Yeah." Teresa stopped speaking and glanced at the exit. "Hey, I've gotta check on defenses for the night." She was trying to escape, and Dolly nodded in understanding.

"Of course."

James and Dolly waited for the stout woman to exit before turning back to each other.

"And you? Healing okay?"

"As well as can be expected I guess," James said, shrugging. "Head still hurts, but Bob says my leg is doing okay."

"Good. Heather the same?"

"I think so. Haven't seen her a ton since we got back."

"Fair. And Rhia?"

"Bob said we can wake her whenever."

"When you do, let me know how things go. We may be able to help her with some bionics. They're in testing phase now, but who knows?" Dolly was going through the motions, but James sensed there was a different reason she had asked him to stick around.

"Right. What's up, Dolly?" James asked. He crossed his arms and leaned against the desk facing the HOLO screen.

"I'm that obvious, huh?"

"I'm that good," James replied, grinning. "What've you got for me?"

"That Exil. We can't figure it out."

"What do you mean?"

"Why the hell was Raspin there? How did he stumble upon you? Weird thing is…we think it was dumb luck."

"It's never dumb luck with him," James said, shaking his head, annoyance tickling the back of his mind.

"I hear you, but think about it like this. Raspin is building the most significant canal in history through glacially altered land, thousands of years in the making. They're throwing all their resources into the project. Raspin can't spare his soldiers in the field, and the Sentinels are too valuable to send out on defense missions. Plus, the amount of energy they'd suck up that far away from camp would be unsustainable. Also, if a bunch of BZ soldiers started popping up in the North, I'd have hundreds if not thousands of requests from NOLA teams looking to head there. He doesn't want that."

James nodded along. "You think he's covering old tracks?"

"Bingo. You know better than anyone the way they run their Sentinel programs. Large rooms with operators plugged in all over the place. During your recent conversation with him, Raspin made it clear their tech is not sophisticated when it comes to controlling humans. He's probably running teams to take out anyone they deem a threat in the North and masking it with Exils as dupes. It's genius really. And then you happened to run into him, and he couldn't resist."

James found himself back underground, staring at the pods of blank-faced BZ operators. He reviewed the idea in his head and let the pieces click together. She made a lot of sense, and this played into Raspin's MO without question, but he couldn't shake the fact that they were missing something.

"I see that, but there's something else to it, Dolly. There's gotta be."

"I'm sure you're right, but that's the next part. Now we have the *what* and a part of the *why,* right?"

James nodded. "Yeah, sure."

"I know. Not the answer you wanted." Dolly let out a long breath and threaded her long fingers together resting her head on them. "This was always easier when the general ran shit."

James was surprised. Dolly rarely mentioned their old commander.

"He always had a knack for this part. Getting into people's heads. He was involved in a lot back in the day, too."

What is she talking about? James stayed quiet while Dolly continued.

"International relations, clandestine meetings, political and battle strategy, thinking as the enemy." Dolly chuckled and looked away thoughtfully. "He's an enigma.

"Sounds a lot like Stacie."

Dolly snorted. "Hate to tell you, all of you have pieces of him in you."

"I doubt that."

"It might not be a bad thing."

Where did this come from? James wondered, trying to decide if he should ask about her casual drop of Croyton's past associations, but decided to play it cool. He'd do his own fact finding.

"Dolly, I'm not sure what…"

"Nothing, nothing. Sorry. Listen, get some rest, and don't let Stacie do anything…Stacie-ish for the next eighteen hours," Dolly said, rolling her eyes.

"You got it," James replied. "Talk to you tomorrow."

"Good night, James."

James waved as the screen went blank and he sat in the empty room thrown back to the days under his old commander, training in grueling conditions.

Exhaustion and pain. The daily emotions under Croyton's tutelage forever internalized.

"Get it out of your head," James said aloud to himself. He shook his head to physically dislodge his thoughts.

He left the room, his brain stuck on a loop bouncing between Croyton and Raspin trying to come up with more constructive thoughts.

That night James lay in bed staring at the white painted ceiling. Humid summers and cold winters had done their damage to the blank space. James traced the spiderwebs of cracks from corner to corner hoping his brain would turn off, just for a second.

He desperately wanted—*needed*—to sleep, but thinking about it produced the opposite result leaving him frustrated and angrier at himself by the second.

"Goddammit," James mumbled under his breath. He threw off his covers and placed his bare feet on the icy tiles of his bedroom floor.

The moon's light filled the room, and James found his clothes.

He poked his head out the door, hoping someone on the team would be working and could distract him. He was out of luck though. Snores from Kevin's room were the sole signs of his team's presence.

"Lucky," James grumbled as he made his way down the hall.

Rarely was James afforded the opportunity to explore the grounds uninterrupted. There was plenty of space, but with only two wings of the building receiving proper heat from the geothermal generators, room got tight. Even now in the hours between morning and midnight, a few people strolled the halls.

There's gotta be a place where I can be alone. James scoured his brain trying to think of somewhere to go when it clicked. The tower.

He stopped and closed his eyes, recalling the directions to the tower where he and Heather had eaten dinner. Satisfied he knew the way, he opened his eyes and started walking. In such a confusing building, James knew he had limited options to get upstairs.

While he walked, James thought back to that night with Heather. The moonlight had been similar to this night's, albeit much earlier in the evening, but as powerful and probing. It shocked him to think that had been fewer than eight days ago. So much had happened in such a short period of time it scared James to think of what could happen next. In barely over a week, Rhia had lost a leg, Liam an eye, Raspin had reappeared, the satellites had realigned, and they had the first part of the BZ's plan.

What a week, James thought, realizing it was no wonder he could not sleep.

He arrived at a heavy wooden door and pushed it open. He was rewarded by a set of cobblestone steps winding up to the tower.

Moments later he stepped into the circular room. Vibrant moonlight illuminated every corner and for a second James was so spellbound by the moment he did not notice the other person standing at the far window.

Heather's back was to him, and she leaned against the cut stone windowsill looking onto the manor's grounds.

James coughed into his hand.

Heather turned around and smiled. "Sleepless night for you, too?"

"Like you wouldn't believe," James said, walking into the room. "I can leave if you want privacy. I don't want to—"

Heather waved him off. "No. Company sounds nice."

She turned back to the wide-frame window, and James stood next to her.

They looked across the estate. The moon was so bright it cast shadows of the trees across the grounds giving the impression of a brilliantly sunny day if the sun were a halogen flashlight. Twisted trunks and leafless branches appeared as gnarled stretches of silver reflecting the moon's aura with a strange kind of magic.

"So what's your thing? Too much coffee tonight? Leg keeping you up?" Heather asked, her eyes still glued to the outside.

"Brain won't shut off."

"Damn brains," Heather said, shaking her head. "They get us in trouble sometimes."

"They do. Bob's usually got some medication to help," James said.

Heather grinned. "He's some doctor huh?"

"The best. What about you? What brings Heather to the moon tower so late at night?" James asked. He felt at ease talking with her, and his muscles relaxed as he leaned his elbows on the windowsill.

Heather was quiet. James glanced at her, but could not read her expression.

Well, that was a mistake I guess, James thought, wondering how he had gone from comfortable to tense with just a question.

"I guess the same. Brain won't shut off. Brain never shuts off. I always wonder…" Heather stopped. She sounded like she wanted to keep going.

"Wondering's not bad," James said, probing after an extended silence.

"I wonder how the hell I got here. Training, deployment out west, traveling across the country, working for NOLA, meeting T, meeting Liam, following them here, scoping out the BZ, the Exils, the thing that used to be an Exil. It all…"

"Never ends," James said, reading her next thoughts.

"Exactly! And we always find ourselves on our heels. We're always catching up. Wondering what the BZ's up to, how can we get ahead of them….I keep thinking about that, and I go to sleep, and the dreams come, and…"

Heather stopped herself. Her knuckles had gone white. Even in the pale moonlight, the stress lines carved into her face were abundantly clear. James reached out a hand and placed it over hers.

"The dreams suck."

Heather turned his way and looked him in the eye. She was the first person to ever acknowledge something amiss within herself.

The two stood staring at each other for a second. James reached his hand up without knowing what he was doing and cupped her cheek. Her eyes shut slowly as James brought his lips towards hers brushing against the soft skin.

A hint of her honey lip balm coated his tongue, and Heather's hands wrapped around the back of his neck pulling him in deeper.

The two fumbled with each other's clothes grabbing aimlessly, realizing how much they needed one another. How much they needed comfort beyond simple words. James focused all the pain in his mind and body on a different facet of his being and found himself in a new world. A place only they could find.

Something was different.

Something was here to last.

Finally.

CHAPTER 21

James slept. When he awoke the reflective ceiling paint did not punish him for daring to do so.

So this is what rest feels like.

It was a sensation of defiance and relief. His brain had shut down, meandering through stretches of nothing. Dreams had come and gone, leaving his subconscious state without lodging in his memory. Demons had let him be for the night, and when he awoke, he only had to brush against the bare shoulder next to him to recall the reason for his sudden release from anxiety.

He remembered sitting on the floor of the tower the previous night. Talking quietly with Heather during breaks from flurried activity. Sneaking with one another downstairs, hugging the shadows and dodging unwitting soldiers.

They were hardly the first people in the base to hook up, but a relationship felt more illicit when James was the one involved.

A deep breath and shifting of sheets sent a waft of warm air carrying their mingled scent from the depths of the bed and Heather's sleep-creased face turned to him.

Her eyes cracked to slits and she smiled. "Morning."

"Morning," James said, still pondering how he had ended up here.

"How're you doing?" Heather asked. The question could have been loaded, but James sensed it wasn't.

"Best sleep I've ever gotten."

"Same. It's been forever, too."

James nodded.

"Any idea what time it is?" she asked settling on her back and joining James as he stared at the ceiling.

"Nope. Not sure I want to look at my HOLO, but I have a feeling we'll be getting a knock on that door any second now. No one's used to me sleeping even to the faintest of sunlight, let alone full-blown dawn."

"Think they have a search party out?"

"Deck's probably halfway to the BZ base by now."

Heather chuckled. "Dedicated man."

"He's always got his friends' backs. That's for sure."

"I can tell. So, how do we do this?" Heather turned her head to the middle of the bed, and James returned her gaze.

Her eyes were such a strange hazel, and James found himself stuck trying to decipher their color.

She asked you something, idiot, James thought, chastising himself for his loss of concentration.

"We have two options. Casually have you walk out of the room and freak Deck out, or we try to hide it. Either way, Deck's out there right now."

Heather thought for a second, biting her lip. She nodded with finality and a touch of mischief cast in her gaze.

"Casual walkout."

"Whatever you say, my lady." James grinned and was rewarded by her smile.

He pulled her in for a final kiss before they rolled out of bed and donned their clothes.

Heather left first and James followed, closing the door, his back to the hallway. When he turned, Heather was seated on the bench on the opposite wall next to a barely contained Deck whose eyes shifted between the two of them. His expression matched that of an overexcited and frustrated toddler.

"Morning, Deck," James said coolly.

Deck studied the two in disbelief as James offered Heather a hand. "Breakfast?"

"Lead the way," Heather said, standing.

They walked down the hall with Deck's eyes boring holes into the backs of their heads until they turned the corner.

James looked at Heather and smiled. "This is killing him."

"What is happening?!" Deck exclaimed.

Heather chuckled. "No kidding."

Three days later James and Clint sat at one of the long tables. Dolly had gotten back in touch with them, but the news had been less than stellar: wait.

It seemed that's how things tended to tip for them. James thought Stacie was going to lose her mind when Dolly stared her down and told her not to do anything stupid. They were all glad Kyle was there to absorb Stacie's wrath.

James was fine waiting. Free time was a gift for him at this point, what with his and Heather's budding relationship. Three days and they had been joined at the proverbial hip, while still maintaining their privacy. Neither wanted a lot of questions from even the most ardent well-wishers. Even through the secrecy, they always managed to end the day locked away together in one of their rooms. *Or any room for that matter*. James thought fondly back to the moon bathing their skin in silver light.

A buzz alerted him, and he pulled up his HOLO. Heather's key popped up:

Tower tonight?

James grinned typing his response:

Be there.

The smiley face from Heather confirmed his plans, and James blew away his screen trying to do his best to think of something other than the tower.

"What's with you?" Clint asked, eyeing him with suspicion.

"Nothing. Happy to be here, I guess." James regretted his words instantly. *That was a dead hint something's up.*

"What? What the hell are you talking about? How much of Bob's pot did you smoke this morning?" Clint was staring at him with legitimate concern.

"No. No, I didn't smoke anything. I guess I'm coming around to this place," James said, trying to dissuade his bulky friend from continuing his questions.

"James. I don't believe that's possible."

"I'm fine. Am I that much of a downer that I can't be happy at all?"

"Yes. At least here, yes."

James was surprised. "I guess I need to change my attitude a bit."

"Don't. It's freaky." Clint kept watching him as he scooped another spoonful of oatmeal, "Whatever, I'm probably more on edge than normal. This is the fifth feeding in a row of straight fucking oatmeal. When the hell is NOLA gonna make up its goddamn mind?"

"Who knows, man," James said, shrugging into his bowl. "Change of pace."

"No pace," Clint grumbled while dripping a spoonful of oatmeal back into his bowl.

"Hello, gentleman." Deck's voice came from behind, loftier than usual for an entrance. The scout slid onto the bench beside Clint making far too much eye contact with James, but the mechanic was too preoccupied with his hatred of oatmeal to notice.

"How is everyone this afternoon?" Deck overemphasized every word, but James ignored it focusing on his meal.

"Fine, Deck. How're you doing?" James responded calmly.

"Good, I guess," Deck replied, sounding light and airy while he pretended to inspect the ceilings.

"What the hell is that supposed to mean?" Clint asked, not picking up on Deck's behavior.

"I haven't slept well lately."

"I'll say, you've been on the fucking phone with Cristina every night this week." Kevin plopped into the seat next to James. Kyle and Stacie took the remaining seats.

"That's not why," Deck said, glowering and thrown off his game. "It's another reason."

"Stop being weird, and spit it out," Stacie said, rolling her eyes while trying to get an eye on the food line.

"The walls are thin around here, Deck. Stop calling your damn wife in the middle of the night and you'll sleep better," Kevin continued.

The chef's elbow nudged his ribs, and James grinned. Kevin always knew when to cover for a friend.

"It's been months since we've seen each other. And they're not that thin. You've gotta listen pretty hard—" Deck tried to continue, but Stacie interjected.

"We get it. You're lonely. But if you're sleeping poorly, try not calling Cristina all the time and listen to Kevin."

Deck's lips pursed, his frustration at not being able to blurt out what he wanted killed him. James watched as his friend's inability to keep a secret tore at him, his face reddening. *I really shouldn't dig into this.* James knew Deck was trying, but he couldn't help himself.

"I think you should listen to their advice, Deck," James spoke solemnly as he pushed his empty bowl to the middle of the table.

"You can sleep with me if you want company. This one's in the operations room all night anyway," Kyle said, pointing at Stacie, her face buried in a HOLO, apparently having had enough of the conversation.

"This is so…" Deck spoke shaking his head.

"Tiring?" Kevin interrupted, maintaining a straight face while Deck's eyes flared with anger before regaining his calm.

"All right, fine. Just fine."

"Enough of this. James, you going to see Rhia?" Stacie asked, brushing Deck aside.

"Shit, I knew I had to do something. You coming, Deck?" James asked. He stood in a hurry and threw his bowl in the wash basin at the far end of the table.

"Yeah, I'm coming," Deck said, standing, "And for everyone's information, I sleep damn fine."

"Stop talking about it so much." Kevin was too quick for Deck, and all he could do was walk away dejected at his failure to steer people towards James's relationship.

When they were in the hall, James quickened the pace and headed in the direction of the med bay.

"When are you telling everyone?" Deck asked, keeping stride with James.

"What? Deck it's been three days," James replied.

"So, I told you about Cristina that quick."

"I never asked you."

"I know. That's how good of a friend I am. I mean, James, I'm starting to think you wouldn't have said anything about it to me unless I brought it up."

"Good instincts, bud."

"Well, of all the people, James Coffey, I never thought you would keep secrets from me."

"Truth hurts."

The door to the med bay was ajar, and James walked in as he heard his friend mimic *truth hurts* in a mocking tone.

Bob, Teresa, and Liam stood around the bed. Liam wore a brown leather eye patch that covered most of the ruined flesh where his eye had been only a week earlier. Bob had offered to try a bionic, but Liam was adamant. He'd wait until NOLA. He said he didn't want Bob making him Frankenstein's monster using a squirrel's eye instead of a human's as a placeholder.

James took a spot next to the head of the bed alongside Bob.

"We doing this today, Bob?" Deck asked, leaning against the foot of the makeshift hospital bed.

"No time like the present," Bob replied. "Anyone else coming?"

"Heather's on the way, but you can start," Teresa answered. Her eyes were glued to the comatose woman's face.

"Remember, she's going to be groggy. I asked you all to be here, so she's not confused when she wakes up, but she won't know what's going on. Keep things slow and answer her questions as simply as you can. We can fill in details soon enough." Bob glanced around, prepping them for the next moment.

"What if she…?" Deck didn't finish his sentence, but Bob understood.

"We wait."

James held his breath as Bob's finger flickered across the screen. IV tubes, innocuous seconds earlier, came alive and a new batch of life-giving fluids accompanied by drugs intended to break her coma poured into Rhia's body.

A hand slipped into his and he glanced over to find Heather's face framed by her brunette hair, staring at her friend. James squeezed her fingers, and they waited.

Rhia's breath quickened. A deep controlled inhale sparked life on her face as her eyelids fluttered revealing hazy, but awake dark brown eyes.

The atmosphere in the room was pure elation as the pressure of losing a friend lifted off everyone's shoulders.

"Nice work, Bob," Teresa muttered, as the stoic woman wiped a tear from her eye.

"Rhia. Rhia. Rhia, can you hear me?" Bob's voice was low, but firm as he spoke.

The slender woman turned her face towards his. She stared without recognition for a second and nodded.

"Made it back."

"You did."

Rhia kept nodding, then, with a confused look on her face, lifted her sheet and gazed at her new limbless appendage.

"Rhia, I'm sorry. I had to remove the leg when you got back here. The damage to your knee was beyond repair. There are tons of bionic options now. I've already go—" Bob was stopped by Rhia's hand.

The blanket fluttered onto the bed, and James's heart ached as the woman processed her reality.

"I'm back. That's what matters right now. Thank you, Bob."

Bob nodded and stepped away from the bed, his face reddening from the compliment.

"Everyone else made it I see. Liam, love the new look," Rhia said, nodding at the bearded soldier.

"It's all the rage right now. I told T I want a telescope put in here," he replied, pointing at his patch.

"Great idea. And, Deck, nice to see you, too."

"Glad your back. Jon's been unbearable without someone smarter to shut his ass up."

"I'll be happy to oblige," Rhia said turning to James and Heather. "And you two, when'd you start hooking up?"

What did she say?

James's heart hammered in his chest.

"Wow, that coma must have been pretty powerful huh?" James said, uncomfortable and deciding to go with an inappropriate joke.

"You're holding hands," Rhia said with a casual nod at their interwoven fingers.

James glanced at Heather and then at his hand.

"Well…" James said, fidgeting and trying to determine how to explain everything away.

"Three days," Heather said, the confidence in her voice attracting James to her more than ever.

"Good for you guys. Nice couple," Rhia said. She reached out to her bedside table and picked up a water bag, "Now who wants to fill me in on everything else that's happened during my slumber?"

"That's it?!" Deck said incredulously. "That's how everyone finds out?! And you were trying to get me to shut up about everything?"

"I never said you couldn't tell anyone," James said calmly. He winked at Rhia who grinned into her straw.

"Unbelievable. I mean…" Deck shook his head with his hands on his hips and stared at the two of them, "You two owe me a reveal."

With that, Deck strode from the room grumbling to himself about never keeping a secret again.

"He's going to drive himself crazy one day," Rhia said, watching him go.

"Afraid he already has," James replied. He pulled out a HOLO and placed it on her lap. "We've got a full rundown here for you."

"Right on. Dolly see this shit? She has to know they're creating a pathway through the tundra," Rhia said, flipping through the screen.

"How'd you know that?" James asked, surprised. That had been a major revelation to them a few days earlier only uncovered by the satellite images from Dolly's team.

"The loom. Haven't you looked at my HOLO data?" Rhia asked, her face turned up in confusion.

"We were locked out."

The techie grinned. "Jon couldn't get my algorithm, huh? Dummy. Here give me that." She snatched Teresa's HOLO screen with energy unexpected for a recent coma patient. After a flurry of keystrokes, she displayed a map of the BZ base, but it looked odd. The key in the corner had a different set of icons depicting the various landmarks.

"Here. Those looms were connected to the base's network. I ran a backdoor from the loom's interface and, voila, we have their plans."

An architectural diagram was followed by a set of 3D maps stretching from their BZ base through the tundra and onto Lake Michigan. Another set of diagrams showed similar activity on the other coast.

"They're forming a pincer." Teresa's voice lowered as they stared at the plans with a shared sense of dread.

"We've gotta warn the Federation," Liam said.

"Get Dolly right now. She needs to get in touch with them," Teresa said.

"On it," Heather said, pulling up her HOLO screen.

"James, we need to find Stacie and come up with a series of plans ASAP."

"Agreed".

Direct attack lines headed to the heart of the Federation. James was stunned by the enormity of the BZ's mission. *How do we stop this?*

The question floated through his brain as he stared at the screen. Hopelessness consumed his mind, spinning around the future defying movement of their enemy.

"Hey." Clint's voice punctured the air, and James turned to the mechanic standing in the doorway. His calm demeanor was replaced by an uncommon urgency. "We need you here."

"What's up?" James asked.

"You need to come with us."

James glanced at Heather who nodded.

"Can I come?" Rhia asked.

"Hop in the chair," Bob said.

James lost the rest of the conversation as he rounded the corner tailing a fast-moving Clint through the halls.

No one else was around, and James eyed the stillness warily.

"Where the hell is everyone, Clint?" James asked, but Clint shook his head.

"You'll see."

James was frustrated by the sense of secrecy, but he bit his lip and complied. Clint navigated to a wide stairway leading to a hallway of plate glass windows overlooking the north lawn.

Dozens if not all one hundred of the base's personnel were crammed in the hallway staring out the window. James's eyes narrowed and he walked to Kyle who stepped aside.

James's heart fluttered for a second and the breath left his lungs.

A hovering crowd of thousands of Sentinels hung silently. Time stopped as James stared at the horde of gunmetal gray discs. They packed every square inch of air cutting off the view of the ground under the trees and reaching so far back into the forest it was impossible to estimate their number.

"When did this happen?" James asked, his voice steady through some effort.

"They just…showed up," Kyle replied. The athletic soldier's hand was holding Stacie's shoulder as the floating mass of dull metal death waited hundreds of yards away.

James reached out and squeezed Heather's hand as she and Teresa joined them.

Silence ruled the air as James went through flashbacks of the Northern Assault, Sentinel camp hunts, battles out west, and more. This was nothing like he had ever seen.

"What do…?" Stacie's voice trailed as one by one, the Sentinels formed their humanoid creations and transparent limbs took shape.

The base watched in awe as an army of wispy gray ghosts appeared.

The BZ had decided to act.

CHAPTER 22

James's stomach muscles clenched. The discs coating the ground released their humanoid figures. James's gaze traveled deeper into the forest following the crowd of ghostly apparitions..

There're too many, James thought. He considered their options, his mind racing through the box of ionic ammo he saved under his bed while staring at the shroud of death waiting on their doorstep.

"Goddammit," Rhia's voice broke through the silence. "Wake from a medically induced coma without a leg and things get worse. Can't happen often."

"You're probably the only one this has ever happened to, if that helps," Jon said, holding the back of her wheelchair.

"Whoopee," Rhia replied in a withering voice.

"What are our options?" James asked.

"We have the pulse pillars," Kevin offered. His laconic voice somehow put James at immediate ease.

"Those are spread around the base. They'd have to be moved to be of any use," Heather replied.

"We might be able to run them through a single pillar. It'll take some network reconfiguring, but I think I can do it." Rhia grabbed the HOLO emitter Bob held in his hands. "Give me five minutes." Her face was cast in the screen's blue glow and her eyes glazed over, a familiar feature of the woman's intense concentration.

"That won't be enough. I'll work on rerouting our geothermal and solar battery stores to add extra juice," Jon said. The competitive edge in his voice was obvious and James was happy his friend's petty one-upmanship was paying off.

"You two work on that. T, what do we have for close combat? Close *Sentinel* combat," James asked, correcting himself.

"I've got two pallets of ionic ammo and another filled with knives and batons. We should start shelling those woods now though, take as many as we can."

"That'd take too long. They're close enough to strike right now," Stacie said, the muscle in her jaw jumping with battle anticipation.

"She's right. We need to get out front now. My team can take care of moving the weapons. Teresa, get your people where you need them. Stacie, you, Kyle, and Clint organize a ground force with T. Deck and Kevin, help me get the gear from downstairs. Bob, stick with these two, make sure they get the hell out of the way. When everyone's in position, meet me in front." James was already walking away as the team split in different directions.

"We're not helpless, you know," Jon said. His eyes were buried in his HOLO, and Bob steered him out of the way as two of Teresa's people ran down the hall nearly trampling him in their haste.

"Yeah, sure, you're not. I've got them," Bob said, giving James a reassuring wave while he pushed Rhia's chair closer to the side. "I'll swing by the med bay to pick up triage gear."

James nodded at his medic and followed Deck, skipping down the stairs.

The basement was cold but humid. James flipped on his HOLO's flashlight to get a better look at the layout.

Crates of gear stood in piles organized with the familiar Federation symbology adopted by NOLA.

James searched. *Maps, explosives, MREs, tactical suits, everything we would normally need... Where are the ionics?* His light probed farther into the low ceiling space.

"Back left," Deck said, pointing to a darkened corner.

James flipped his light back, illuminating a set of pallets with electric shock icons marked on them. *Bingo.*

The ionic pulses were one of the few symbols that had been created entirely by and for NOLA, and they were hardly uniform. Without a single source of manufacturing and design for NOLA's military industry, each lightning bolt and electrical sign was different which could make tracking difficult. Luckily, Teresa had gone through the supplies, making his job a little easier.

James held the light for Kevin who pried the top off the wooden crate. Inside was a row of ionic batons and knives.

"That'll work," James said, counting the boxed items and mentally distributing them to everyone on base. It would be tight but would have to do.

"Kevin, keep opening everything. Deck and I will run gear upstairs." Anticipatory cramps crept into James's legs while he thought about the trips up and down the stone steps.

"We've got that." Liam's voice entered the room before he did. The bearded, one-eyed man walked in followed by a dozen soldiers. "Tell us where to go. We'll make sure we get there."

James breathed a silent sigh of relief as he started directing the troops. "Take these. Find Stacie and her crew." He put the open-topped crate in the hands of the soldier nearest to him as Deck did the same to the next in line.

"Take these to Teresa," Deck said.

James and Deck followed Kevin around the room while he tore the tops off the weapons' crates. After five minutes, the boxes were open, and soldiers dispersed to all corners of the building carrying the lifesaving munitions along with them.

James grabbed a set of ionic pulse grenades. "I'm taking these out front."

"We're with you. Liam will know what to do with everything else here," Deck said, grabbing a box. He was followed by a wordless Kevin who picked up two more crates in his gargantuan arms and lumbered his way up steps barely large enough for his feet.

James passed hurried soldiers as he made his way outside. Their grim faces and determined jawlines gave him the push he needed to move. Nearly fifteen minutes had already passed since the Sentinels had started releasing their weaponized creations.

James had no idea how long until the attack. He only knew it would come.

He flipped on his HOLO comms to the team's channel. "Jon, where are we with the pillars?"

Empty airwaves responded, and James repeated his question, "Jon, what's going on?"

Nothing came again. James eyed Kevin and Deck out of the corner of his eye and tried a third time, "Jon, what—"

"James, I can't fucking work if you're going to keep asking me questions. When I'm done, I'm done!" The sheer frustration and annoyance in Jon's voice was enough to tip James off that things were not going as planned.

"How long do you need?" Kevin asked, his measured tone diffusing any tension.

"At least five more minutes." Jon's reply came ten seconds later with a hint of personal shame.

"You hear that, Stace?"

"I got it," Stacie replied. "Sentinels are still…never mind. We've got movement."

The usual stone dropped to the pit of James's stomach, and his heart rate quickened. He controlled his breath and mentally directed the rush of adrenaline towards his arteries. His body readied itself.

James flipped to the base channel. "Everyone out front. Attack imminent."

Without waiting for a response, James turned down the hall and sprinted to the front of the building. Soldiers were already streaming through the door grabbing whatever ionic weaponry they could from the open boxes near the exit.

James dropped his box, taking a baton along with a couple of pulse grenades from a separate container. He clipped the grenades onto his belt and fell in with the crowd. He made his way through the surge of bodies to the front line where Stacie pointed in every direction, organizing soldiers for their defense.

The backdrop was one of terror and confusion. A horde of empty bodies bore down on the castle. James did his best to keep emotions from showing on his face as they picked up speed. No one needed to see the fear bubbling in his gut.

"Ready?" Heather's voice relieved some of James's stress as he glanced at her, her eyes concentrating on the approaching swarm of electrokinetic bodies.

"Not really," James replied.

"Inspiring," Heather replied, grinning at him.

James returned her smile before facing the crowd of approaching Sentinels. He flipped his comms to the public channel and spoke with as much calm and patience as his body would allow.

"Use your charged weapons. Stick to quick movements and avoid getting any part of your body caught in their grip. Even the smallest ones are strong enough to rip off a human limb. Stay in your spot. We're not advancing but listen for directions. If we can catch them in a line, we can move forward as a unit."

As he spoke more Sentinels were released, their discs hidden by the bulk of bodies multiplying and moving forward en masse. The sheer awe of witnessing the emergence of giant Sentinels thundering towards them was enough to send more adrenaline than he thought possible flooding his body. His vision buzzed and a tingling sensation in his fingertips spread along his skin, moving in a web pattern through his body.

"When engaging, keep your head up. And remember, do not stop moving. Good luck." James finished his speech as the horde reached a hundred and fifty yards from them.

He glanced at the building. One of the ionic pillars at the northeast corner of the building pulsed a deep purple.

Never seen that, James thought hoping that whatever Jon and Rhia were setting up would be done soon. Their force would not last long against the army of non-human soldiers roaring in their direction.

"Grenades!" Stacie's order came over his headset and through the open air. James pressed the release on his ionic grenade and tossed it. His missile was joined with dozens of others arcing lazily across the purple sky. Streaks of iridescent blue created stripes in the citrus-tinged sunset creating a paradoxical beauty James did not expect.

The silence of the moment was starkly different from any other battle James had known. The grenades crackled as they erupted in the pack of false human bodies running towards them without the familiar grunting and heaving of breath. Absent were the fear-induced cries of pain and anguish. Those were of a different world. Instead, the earth stood still and the sound of electricity buzzing in a cloud created a new dimension of tense warfare. One where humans fought machines controlled by humans. Regardless, this was war.

Hurry up, Jon was the last thought that went through his head as the first wave of Sentinels crashed into the line.

James whipped his baton into the head of a Sentinel grasping for him, and the hands around his throat vanished. He slashed wildly, careful to avoid hitting the other soldiers standing nearby, but it would have been impossible to tell. It was fighting in fog, against the fog. The baton flew across his limited vision snagging onto the electro-webbed flesh of the Sentinels, creating fresh space where their bodies had been.

Heads and necks were the name of the game for James as he swung his weapon with cruel ease, whistling through an air of crackling static.

"James!" He turned at the sound of Heather's voice and saw her pointing over the crowd. A group of giants lumbered their way to the line.

James acted quickly and pulled the ionic blade from his belt.

He sprinted towards the behemoth creations, dodging, slicing, and swiping at the creatures filling his pathway.

A setting devoid of form and sound created a wind tunnel interrupted by muted grunts of pain. The noises were uttered and forgotten, swallowed by the electric storm attacking from every angle.

At every turn, James confronted a new eyeless creation swinging at his head or reaching for him. James moved with ferocity, ripping through the sea of gray. If one of those hands made contact, or worse, managed to grip him, his life was over.

He ducked under the sweeping arc of a translucent fist and stabbed with his ionic blade. The Sentinel disappeared, replaced by the spectacle of one of Teresa's men getting clocked in the side of the head by a humanoid form that had joined its arms to create a club.

A sickening crunch of the man's neck echoed in James's ears as he spun and jabbed at the killer, hopping deftly over a trio of mutilated bodies as he churned through enemy combatants.

Each step was through a new bath of horror. Twisted human remains rendered the floor a wash of blood, liquid pouring from limbs wrenched from their original owners. Faces backwards on their torsos, shoulders torn in positions more fit for a toddler's toy… James's stomach churned, and he suppressed the nausea that clutched his gut as he pushed through the mayhem.

By the time he reached the massive creatures, his team was there.

Kyle was already working on the first of the monstrous ghosts. In a scene out of *The Iliad*, Kyle stepped from side to side, dodging the bodies trying to rip his limbs apart. He found the thinnest of chasms to move within and, planting his foot on the ground, launched into the air.

In physics defying movement, Kyle twisted and embedded his ionic knife under the jaw of the beast. The space its disappearance left sent Kyle tumbling to the ground. But in the time it took to blink, the athletic warrior was on his feet again, parrying and thrusting.

Showoff, James thought as he swirled from the grip of an unusually small Sentinel, whipping it across the head with his baton and watching the static dissipate in thin air.

James fought his way to the other giants who were swinging their massive arms over the ground. Kevin appeared, swinging a baton and running at the backs of a giant who had torn another one of Teresa's people in half, spraying gore and intestines through the air with casual ease.

Without warning, it disappeared and an ionic knife dropped to the ground. Deck sprinted from nowhere and grabbed it, spun around without missing a beat, and whipped it at the neck of a second giant. Static erupted and the giant vanished. Kevin ran to another giant terrorizing its next victim while Deck followed close with two knives held loosely in his grip.

A massive hand gripped the back of his neck, and James flipped around, smashing the forearm with his baton before landing a crushing blow to the face of his attacker. He was rewarded with another silent disappearance.

A scream pierced the air. James whipped his head to see a man fall sideways with his arms torn off at the shoulder. The ghoul that had inflicted the carnage held the limbs in both hands only to disappear seconds later as Stacie's baton rocked the side of its head. Mind-shattering howls of pain ruptured the air, bouncing through the cold space incessantly. Pained shrieks increased with every moment, and the smell of iron hung heavy, even in the dry winter air.

There were too many. The battlefield crawled with the BZ's monsters.

He glanced at the pillars. Their color had changed. They pulsed a deep electric blue. With some concentration, he could hear a buzz under the sensation of pain and terror.

A spray of blood from the eviscerated neck of another soldier blocked his eyesight. With his eyes closed, he heard a woman yell and, fearing it was Heather, turned around, blindly lashing out with his baton when all noise ceased.

He was lifted from his feet and stuck in midair, still for a second, then flying over the ground. At first, he thought he was caught in a game of catch between two Sentinels, but when he opened his eyes the wave of translucent bodies was gone, replaced by an odd aura of white light that left a haze of residue on everything it touched.

His skin prickled and the hair on his body stood as waves of electricity coursed across the ground until he dropped and rolled over the frozen earth.

Broken blades of grass stuck to the side of his mouth. He tasted blood, salt, and earth. Cold and horrified relief welled inside of him while a thought ran through his brain. *They did it*.

CHAPTER 23

Butane lamps and candles lit the stone passageways of the ancient building casting dancing shadows on the walls.

James hunched over one of the fires in the courtyard. He huddled under a shared blanket with Heather who shivered from the cold.

"At least there's no wind here," James mumbled, rubbing his hands together.

"Stop looking for a bright side," Heather grumbled. The scowl on her face was evident even in the darkness, and James grinned at her insistence on the negative. *Her turn to be there*, he thought, reminiscing about the team's early trips hunting Sentinel camps in the southeast during the summer. Endless humidity and constant mishaps, miscommunications, and outright failures in those days had turned James into a ball of anxiety and disappointment. He preferred optimism in the cold over misery and anger in the heat.

"Anything working there?" James asked Rhia over the fire. The slender woman toyed with an old radio, splicing wires and reconnecting nodes inside the device trying to spark some life into the retro tech.

"If there was, you'd know," Rhia said. The snap in her voice was normal, but the frustration was new. She wasn't used to struggling with technology.

"Anyone hungry? Cold biscuits and powder MREs for dinner," Kevin said, walking around holding two bags filled with dinner's contents.

James picked a roll from one bag and an MRE from the other. *Soup* was stamped in bold letters on the side of the foil MRE packaging.

"You couldn't figure this out?" James asked, holding the soup to Kevin.

"You want me to cook a meal of individual packets? Come on, man, grab a damn tin," Kevin said, shaking his head and lumbering away.

Exhausted, Heather and James stared at the biscuits. James glanced at the woman sharing his blanket. Her glassy eyes told him everything he needed to know.

"I'll grab the soup stuff," he said, pushing to his feet.

Heather nodded and took a listless bite of her biscuit, chewing on the fibrous dough. "You're a saint."

James stepped around the other fires sprinkled in the courtyard, surrounded by the tired and huddled masses.

He entered the mansion. The building had suffered no structural damage from the battle or the blast. Everything appeared as it should. The combined pillars had projected their concentrated electrokinetic pulses directly at the battlefield. Their merged strength had left the ionic pillars in tatters along with the generators, but their shelter was sound. The uncontained energy of the blast and its immense concentration of power traveling at such a high velocity shredded any electrical implements in the area. All their equipment completely wiped with the push of a button. HOLOs, comms pieces, ionic weaponry. Even the vehicles were useless.

As Deck put it, they had EMP'd themselves.

While he walked, a window fluttered open, nudged ajar by the winds buffeting the outside of their fortress. James slammed it shut and shoved the lock down making sure it would stay closed. They needed the castle to retain as much heat as possible.

He reached their newly established sick ward, previously their mess hall and kitchen. Given the excessive number of casualties and lack of artificial light, they thought it best to keep everyone on the first floor.

When he turned the corner, his heart sank. In a few short hours, the number of cots with sheets pulled over bodies had tripled. Candles and lanterns did their best to combat the darkness, but they fought a losing battle.

Odors of iron, rubbing alcohol, bile, and human decay filled the visible mist hanging in the air. Humidity saturated the room from steam rising from the bodies cramped inside the tight space.

"Hold there." Bob's calm but firm voice rang off the walls. James made his way towards the kitchen where he spotted the shadow of Bob's face as the medic intricately stitched the leg of a woman. Her head lolled from side to side in delirious pain. Deck's fingertips were white with exertion from holding the torn shards of skin Bob was attempting to reconnect.

"Almost…done," Bob finished and examined his work. The disappointment and distress on his face was clear. There was no winning.

The woman gurgled, and her ashen face fell to the side. Her eyes were dull. James knew she would not be there in the morning.

"Let's move her to triage, Deck."

"On it." Deck's voice was reserved as he stood and pushed the woman's cot to the side of the room where she joined a set of other injured soldiers waiting to die.

"How you doing, Bob?" James asked, approaching his friend.

Bob glanced at him. His eyes were wells of exhaustion and sadness.

"Not good. I've got no light. No heat. No way of knowing when we'll get either, and bodies keep piling up." Bob shook his head and glanced at the walls of his operating room. "I can't get ahead."

"You need a break, man," Deck said. He returned to redress the bed and dropped their used tools in a bucket of disinfectant overflowing with soiled surgical implements.

Bob shook his head. "There are more. When we're done with the worst of it, I'll take a break. T and her folks can do the stitching and post-op care." The medic cracked his back. "Let's bring in the next one, Deck."

Deck nodded and walked to the waiting room.

"You want any help?" James asked, nervous to jump in, but guilt would have found him.

"You're fine, man. Water for soup I'm guessing?" Bob asked.

James nodded, feeling stupid for needing something as insignificant as water.

"Sink on the right is still kicking. Keep the drip going. The other two are gone."

James nodded and left, eager to get out as quickly as he could.

He filled his bowl and canteen, careful to leave the drip on. They would need that water, no matter what happened in the ER.

When he reentered the operating room, Bob was seated at the head of the table. A woman lay on her back with half her neck torn down the side, flayed, exposing glistening tendons and bone. Blood had stopped flowing and the injured site was covered with dried liquid, appearing dark in the shadows, providing a stark contrast to the rest of her mutilated flesh.

Bob's fingers worked meticulously with a scalpel removing dead skin and scabs.

The woman's chest rose and fell laboring methodically. Deck held a finger to her wrist. A shudder rippled through the woman's rib cage.

A second passed. Bob placed his scalpel on the table. He glanced at Deck who concentrated deeply before he looked at the medic and shook his head.

Bob's shoulders drooped, and he pulled a sheet from under his chair. He draped it over the woman's damaged body, pushing her to the wall to join the rest of the covered corpses.

James left without saying goodbye.

By the time he made it back, Stacie, Kyle, and Clint had joined Rhia at their fire.

"He's inside?" Kyle asked, prodding the fire with an ionic baton rendered useless by their Sentinel defense. "Where?"

"Don't know. He said he needed to think," Clint replied.

"Can't think out here?"

"You know how he gets."

"Our Jon is a particular one." Kyle quit poking the embers and stood for a stretch. He nodded as James entered the circle of light. "How is it in there?"

"Bad," James replied. He sat and let the light from the fire sear his retinas, wishing the scenes of hopelessness would burn away with the flames. The stink of blood and ruined flesh stuck to the insides of his nostrils. He hoped the smoke would eliminate that soon. He handed the water flask to Heather who took it wordlessly.

She squeezed his elbow. "You need to eat."

James shook his head, the images of the triage room lingered, but she was right. Increased hunger would do nothing for his mental state.

"Every single vehicle we have is completely fried. Gonna take me at least a week to fix it all," Clint said, sitting back on his elbows and staring at the sky. "Really hope the BZ doesn't try anything."

As the poorly mixed powdered soup hit his lips, the raw anxiety boiling in his gut rushed to the surface. Something he had pushed into the back of his conscience for hours. They were more vulnerable than ever. A quarter of their forces had been wiped by the Sentinels, another half injured, and most of those would not be able to get up again. There were no working comms equipment or weaponry, and, according to the best engineer he knew, no way to escape except on their legs. If Raspin decided to attack now, it was all over. Poof.

"If they were going to, they would have already." Stacie's monotone voice caught James off guard. Their normally pessimistic strategist would have been all over his thoughts before, but she seemed oddly calm.

What's she got up her sleeve? James eyed her from across the fire, as she stared into it.

"*You* think they won't?" Clint asked, incredulity in his tone.

"They would have by now," Stacie spoke briskly, glancing at the tower. James followed her gaze to a flickering candle reflecting through the mottled glass windows. Jon, working on comms. Stacie's hope.

"If Stacie's not worried, we're good." Clint rolled out a sleeping bag and ensconced himself in it. "Wake me for my watch."

James grinned along with the rest of the group and took another mouthful of soup, but unease disturbed his appetite.

"Clint's got the right idea. We should head to bed," Kyle said, hopping to his feet, shaking his arms as he did. "My dear." He reached a hand for Stacie who waved him off. "I'll take first shift." Kyle glanced at James and back to Stacie before nodding and walking inside.

"I'm gonna crash, too." Heather kissed James on the cheek and followed Kyle.

Clint's heavy breathing from his unnatural ability to fall asleep so quickly and Rhia's silent slumber were all that kept James and Stacie company.

The two sat lost in their thoughts for a moment. James drifted to the worst possibilities that could happen at that moment. A Sentinel's dull metal reflected the flames of the courtyard back at them. Instant death would be the only hope at that point. He'd rather that than suffer the fate of the soldiers in the triage area who had been torn apart. He shut his eyes, working to block the visions of the trauma center as the odor of death flooded his senses. He spit his mouthful of soup on the frozen earth and stared at the darkness. His appetite was gone. He chose to concentrate on the fresh night air and stars instead.

"How do you think Raspin got those Exils?" Stacie asked, looking at the sky.

"No clue. Haven't had a ton of time to dwell on it honestly," James answered, only now realizing that between thinking of Heather and the implications of the attack, he had not done a full deep dive into the Exils.

"I think he grabbed them. Maybe not him, but a team of his. Sentinels probably. But how do you think he did it? He couldn't have lured them into the camp. They're too smart for that, no one operating here would fall for something so stupid. And how did he get inside her? You know, the woman. Did he remove a part of her brain? Implant something? What was it?" Stacie shook her head, conversing more with herself than James.

"I don't know, but he was…in there."

"What do you mean?" Stacie asked. Her eyes were shrewdly focused on James, a characteristic he had come to know over the years.

"Like she was not inside her own skin. As if the being that controlled her was trying to break out of her body. Her bones didn't fit anymore." James flashed back to the awkward movements. He recalled how the woman's arms shuddered and how each joint appeared at odd angles with the rest of her body. More marionette than person.

"Think there're more?" Stacie asked, "Of course there are. That camp. He's done that before?"

"Undoubtedly."

The two let the thought sink in. James realized his lack of understanding about the BZ's latest reveal worried him to no end.

"I wo…" Stacie stopped. Her ear perked up, and she held a hand up to James, signaling silence.

He watched their analytical mastermind tilt her head closer to the sky. Her eyes were shut tight as she attempted to block out the world.

"Stacie?" James whispered, but Stacie's response was a single finger telling him quiet.

That's a little uncalled for, he thought, feeling he was being treated like a toddler.

Stacie glanced at the tower, and James did the same. Jon's shadowed head was turned towards the night sky. He had heard something, too.

"Stacie, what is it?"

"Listen," Stacie replied impatiently.

James, frustrated by her response, closed his eyes and concentrated. He blocked the world around him and focused on what he couldn't hear. Then it came.

An alien sound caught by the wind. His eyes flickered towards the sky. The beat was followed by another and more. They merged into a constant drone echoing across the stone courtyard.

Four massive helicopters flew overhead accompanied by their gunship counterparts. James glanced at Stacie. He hoped she had noticed the Federation insignias too. He walked out of the courtyard followed by Stacie to the front door where he hauled the heavy wooden slabs open.

The gunships circled and their lights cast dark shadows against the half moon, creating pitch-black space intersected by cones of brilliant white light.

The hatch of the first ship opened and out stepped a single figure. His arms were held loosely against his sides. Light and dark intersected his pathway, but James knew by the gait. A confident step, with no swagger or frill about it. A defined unbending stroll that would not be deterred. One name echoed in the back of his mind.

Croyton.

CHAPTER 24

Figures clad in the guise of night disembarked from the helicopters, ducking their heads as cold wind whipped from the rotors.

Their leader stepped into the stone hallway. James's eyes were unflinching as his former commander pulled back his hood. Croyton's gray crew cut stood in sharp contrast to the mismatched uniforms, beards, and shoulder-length hair of those who filled the halls. Croyton drew a HOLO emitter from his jacket and in seconds was engrossed with the screen, his eyes twitching while his fingers pecked at the light-based keyboard.

Four people followed him from the choppers. Their identities were revealed one by one as they entered the light. The first was Martin, who glanced around with a look somewhere between disgust and admiration. James did not know the next two, but a soft spot formed in James's heart as the last person came into view penetrating the distrust swirling in his gut.

Riley Brandt stood observantly behind her father. Her eyes roamed the stone hallway searching faces in turn. She finished her probe of the room, nodding at James with a slight smile and settling her gaze back on her father.

At least she's in the loop.

Croyton, finished with his HOLO perusal, snapped the screen shut. The air left the room, and James released the breath he had been holding since they entered.

"Who's in charge?" Croyton asked with a pent-up fury in his voice that resounded in the echo-inducing chamber. He glanced at everyone in turn, settling on James for a heartbeat before moving past without engaging his former pupil.

What the hell was that? James thought, unsure of how to react.

The rest of the room eyed James. The familiar weight of expectation hovered over his body pressing him to speak. James held his tongue.

"Right here." Teresa's voice sounded from one of the archways surrounding the room. She glanced at James who caught her eye before she approached Croyton.

"Are all your comms completely broken?" he asked, brushing past introductions.

"Must not be if you're here," Teresa replied.

"I'll assume yes," Croyton replied, irritation creeping into his voice, "Take me to your meeting room. We need to conference in NOLA. I have emitters and portable generators we can use."

He waited impatiently for Teresa to get the hint. She looked at Stacie and James. Stacie's nod registered in James's peripheral vision.

Glad she can keep her head about her, James thought.

"We'll use the auditorium. Might get some moonlight to help us." Teresa turned and left, followed by Croyton and his team.

The rest of the HQ trailed the visiting party. Their intrigue overruled their suspicion of the Federation's presence in their home.

James was stuck. Croyton's previous treatment of the team and the sadistic training to break them hung in the back of his mind. His dreams were occupied by visions of his time in the compound, haunting the corners of his subconscious. Extreme fatigue and impossible expectations were carved into his mental state.

"You all right?" Stacie asked. Concern etched on her face and James nodded.

"I'll be good. Been a while since that airplane ride," James replied, thinking back to his last conversation with their commander.

"Remember, James, he's helped us since then."

"Yeah. Also got the chance to take out a front line base of the BZ. It was a win for him," James said, allowing negativity to permeate his every thought.

"I get it. Believe me, I do. Be smart about this though."

"Stacie—"

"James. *You* are our commander. We don't owe nor want anything of him. You say the word. We follow you."

James turned to his second-in-command, humbled by her steadfast friendship and loyalty. She meant every word. James was their leader; Croyton didn't matter. They did. That was all.

James bobbed his head. He clenched his jaw and counted his heartbeats.

"Let's get this over with," James said, and he led the way followed by Stacie. He felt her eye him warily as he walked through the hallways. James was not sure if she could see the mounting confidence that grew with each echoing step.

Flames from the candles created a mystical aura in the room reflecting off the red velvet cushions lining the inclined rows of collapsable chairs.

James beelined for his team's row on the far side of the room. He focused on his path. He did not need to see the faces in the room to know they watched him.

Kevin and Clint were perched in their spots, gawking at their former commander with confusion and contempt.

"What the…?" Kevin's voice trailed off as he shook his head.

"Not sure yet," James said.

"Gotta be Dolly," Stacie chimed in, taking the seat next to Kevin.

"Ahh, yeah, that tracks," Clint said nodding.

"Makes sense. Good to know we've got a bigger team forming up."

Clint shrugged, and Kevin looked at him with a blank expression.

"What? They're in the same boat as we are, man," Clint said, settling back in his chair. "Wish she had told us, but it doesn't matter now. He's here."

Kyle hopped up the steps moments later and took the seat next to Stacie. The athlete leaned over the back of James's chair and glared at Croyton.

"You good, man?" he asked. His tone and body language leveled an obvious threat towards Croyton.

"Easy, guy," Jon said, clapping Kyle on the shoulder. The techie stepped over James to get farther into the row. "But if you do need us to do anything…" Jon's voice trailed off. His implication was shared through a chorus of nods from the rest of the team.

Without warning, the HOLO screens flashed white, and silence reigned. Croyton's straight posture ruled the dais as he paced.

Flashbacks to injury-riddled sessions in their armory rifled through James's mind. Sitting on metal chairs as blood pooled in his mouth, too much to swallow, too gross to spit out. Burns and cuts kept in check by gritted teeth and tightly clasped hands covering the wounded areas until Croyton deemed the team ready to administer their own medical treatment. Terrified, emaciated hostages and bodies of the soldiers in the jungle. It all flooded James's mind along with the decade at war that had sharpened him into the man he had become.

"In another moment we'll have NOLA and Deerfield on our comms. There's a lot going on, but we'll get everyone on board. Understood?" Croyton turned back to his HOLO emitter and conferred with his tech team while the rest of the room sat in silence.

Tension and apprehension rose amongst the soldiers in the crowd. An undercurrent of mumbling stirred the room. James and the team remained silent. Teresa, Liam, and Heather hovered casually on the far side of the stage. Heather grinned at him from her spot, and James smiled back. It helped to have her there.

Increased noise always brought out Croyton's ire. He whipped around to the crowd as the animal James remembered emerged.

"Anyone have something to say?" Croyton's steely voice let off steam, sending a ripple of anxiety through the room. The fire in his eyes remained as the aged commander returned to his team as they finalized their network connections.

James's mind boiled. He had not fought his way this far to end up under Croyton's command again.

The screens flickered, and Dolly's face appeared. She was surrounded by NOLA operatives, including Caitlin. They stood in a room looking at their HOLO. Dolly's face remained passive, but her tone was friendly as she spoke with her former commander.

"How're you doing, General?"

"Cold as hell, Dolly. You?"

"Better now that we know T and her group are all good," Dolly replied, crossing her arms. "You bring Martin with you?"

"Right here, Dolly," Martin replied, waving at the screen.

"Good to see you Martin. Is Arthur joining?"

"Patching him in riiiiight…" Riley's voice trailed off as Arthur's thin face graced the screen.

"Good evening, everyone." Arthur nodded politely at the assembled crowd.

"Evening, sir," Martin bowed his head towards the Deerfield leader, and nausea rippled through James. "I think we have everyone now. That right, General?"

"That's right," Croyton said. His eyes bounced from screen to screen as images sprang to the HOLOs running across the room. "You'll want to expand your views, Dolly. We've got a lot to review."

"Will do. Hey, where's the team?" Dolly asked. Her eyes scoured the screen on her side, looking for them in the camera view.

"I'm here," Croyton said, his tone indicating more than a statement of fact. It was an order. It cut off anyone or anything from assuming where he stood in the line of command. He was the line.

Dolly stopped her search and the tension in the room grew. James stomached it.

Not yet.

Images of the motherships popped up on dedicated screens while the main HOLO displayed a map identifying three different spots in the world: one in the North Atlantic, one off the western coast of the Southern Federation, and a final one near the entrance to the Mediterranean Sea.

James examined the images as Croyton spoke.

"More than forty years ago, an event broke the world. It broke the fundamental nature of what it meant to be a human. Our hemispheres stopped interacting. We gave into our basest of instincts, fueled by beliefs mounted on egos unable to understand that complete control was impossible to exert across all levels of society. For centuries we had worked together, and, with the advent of technologies beyond our wildest, collective imagination we broke in half. We turned into two warring factions determined to prove each of our ways right."

Croyton paused. Ensuring he had captured his audience, he continued, "A decade ago an attack occurred that had been in the making since that event four decades earlier. An attack predetermined by the fates of time. Our country was ripped apart from within by forces driven by photons. Our cities were decimated by contained nuclear energy, capable of razing buildings in the blink of an eye. We lost the basic structure of our society.

"Now we are at the beginning of something different. For ten years the BlankZone has tortured our land and slaughtered us at will, but we've learned. We've built ourselves a way to fight back and we've reached a point where we must strike.

The screens shifted and the map in the center focused on the ship hovering off the Southern Federation's coastline. Lines with markers and directional arrows painted a historic view of the ship's pathway.

"Since the attack on Midway, we've watched the rotation of their ships. We know how long they spend on tour, their attack routes, common time in port, and engineering needs. Given this surveillance information, we know how long they can spend at sea, the number of troops per ship at any given time, the resupply chain, power requirements, defense mechanisms, attack tendencies, and dump sites. If those ships have done it, we've witnessed it. After all our data gathering, one thing is clear: we will not win this war if they have those ships."

James listened, doing his best to keep his emotions out of his thoughts, but the general was only repeating common knowledge. What did he have to tell them?

"Understood, General, but where is this going? We're all up to speed on the importance of those ships." Dolly's question validated James's thoughts.

"I agree with the woman from NOLA," Arthur chimed in. His tone was condescending even as a compliment. "We know all of this. We've *lived* this. My people and I are content behind our walls and protecting ourselves from Sentinels and any other BZ troops. Your protégés proved the power of our defense mechanisms a few days earlier. The blast even affected some of our growth mechanisms, so we witnessed ourselves how well our protections work."

"Understood. But this war does not end until those ships are gone. Sentinels and troops are a dime a dozen as far as the enemy is concerned. Therefore, I propose we destroy this ship right here." He pointed at the ship in the North Atlantic. "It's fresh from being restocked, and if we can sink it, we've got a good shot at taking the other two."

James frowned. *That won't work.*

Croyton explained his plan while James stewed. He went through the strategy in his head, always coming back to the same conclusion. The remaining two motherships would retaliate and destroy them instantly. Raspin was a sadistic sociopath and would never underestimate an enemy twice. He proved that with his

Sentinel attacks, Exil experiments, and willingness to destroy anything to achieve his goals. Croyton's plan would never work.

Stacie's legs bounced against James's chair. It seemed like his strategy expert had other thoughts, too.

James reentered the conversation as Croyton finished outlining his idea. "We huddle in the Federation HQ, set up for the attack, and defend from a place of strength. We have enough in our arsenal to fight, and with the right timing, we can sink the remaining ships."

Croyton's dominant stare scanned the crowd, daring anyone to speak up.

Stacie's leg movements accelerated, and James dug his fingernails into his palms.

Dolly and her NOLA cohort nodded, soaking up the words. Liam, Teresa, and Heather looked on without emotion. He caught Heather's eye from across the crowded room. She nodded slightly at him and a rush of adrenaline hit his abdomen.

"Here's the de—"

"Nope."

Silence reigned. All eyes in the room shifted in his direction, and James realized it was he who had spoken.

"Excuse me?" Croyton's face scrunched into a curious mask, his eyes always lethal even when caught off guard.

Heartbeats echoed in James's palms. A grin painted the corner of Heather's lips.

No stopping now. James steeled himself and continued, "That will get us all killed."

Croyton's face tightened as the ball of muscle in his jawline protruded.

"Explain," Croyton growled.

"If we destroy one of their ships and leave two, we're dead. The amount of firepower on each ship is enough to level a small nation, let alone a city. We need two of those ships destroyed. Then we can lure a third one to its fate. If we don't hit two out of the three, we should give up now."

Croyton glared at him over the crowd. "So you want us to fight our way through enemy-occupied territory to take out one of their most prized possessions?"

"No, I suggest a different way. We go after the North Atlantic ship, no doubt about that. We have too much information not to. Otherwise, it's negligence."

James stopped himself, as he quickly reviewed the next part of his idea one final time. There was no taking his next words back.

"And…what? There are still two, James," Arthur said, whiny impatience coating his words.

"We take a team to the BZ and knock out the one in their harbor."

"Go to the BZ?" Arthur's eyes showed amusement at the suggestion. "What kind of plan is that?"

James caught Martin's smirk. He looked Deerfield's commander in the eye and replied, "Those Sentinels we destroyed are the tip of the iceberg. The general's right—Raspin doesn't care how many of those Sentinel shells he loses. If he had wanted, he could have sent waves of them until we had nothing left. To him, they're just metal and photons. To us, they're a living nightmare. If we don't take the fight to them, we're bound to lose."

"Our defenses are strong enough to hold them," Martin broke in, dismissing James's assumption.

"For one wave, maybe even a few, but the BZ can send countless waves." James kept his focus and channeled his inner Stacie as he spoke. "You already said you absorbed some of the effects from our defensive measures. It ruined every piece of our electronic equipment. What do you think will happen to your grow operation after sustained Sentinel attacks? How do crops fair without any support in freezing temperatures? How well do your platforms float with nothing to power them? I thought you would have put the pieces together yourselves. Glad to do it for you though."

A snort echoed across the space. Deck held a hand over his mouth, and he waved for James to continue. Meanwhile, Bob stood next to him trying to crawl under the floor as eyes floated to the back of the room.

"All right, we get what you're saying. But enter the BZ?" Dolly asked, motioning for the embarrassed Deerfield leadership to stop talking.

"We sneak into the BZ and destroy the final ship in their harbor. It's the only way."

More chuckles followed as Deck left the room. An embarrassed Bob tried to move away from the giggling scout as everyone else processed James's suggestion.

Stacie's legs had stopped convulsing, and Croyton's face, normally a ball of rage, was pensive.

"That's ridiculous. How would we even start—" Arthur started, but Croyton cut him off.

"He's right. We need to hit their home. What's your plan?" Croyton turned back to James, and the pressure of expectation landed on his shoulders.

A room and an entire society's survival rested on the next words James was going to utter, and he let himself absorb the blow. He caught Heather's grin across the room, and smiling, answered, "Leave Stacie in charge of operations here. She'll be able to run something this large far better than anyone. Give me a team and a means of getting over there. I'll take them out."

Betrayal sunk into his bones. He had never torn the team apart for so long.

Croyton chewed the thought silently and the rest of the former Federation waited.

"Let's do it."

CHAPTER 25

His family's new home was cramped. Noise bounced through the tight space echoing off the walls. The temperature rose as hot breath, food, and packed bodies heated the former shipping container.

James glanced at his mother talking off to the side with Jon, Rich, and Bob. She smiled and laughed as Jon told a story, gesturing animatedly with his hands. James had not seen his mother that happy in a long time.

Haven't seen her in a long time, he reasoned, remembering the gaps between his visits.

He scanned the rest of the group, all bunched together chatting, laughing, and relaxing.

A hand squeezed his bicep, and he turned to find Heather looking at the crowd with him.

"Weird, huh?"

"Weird is right," James said. "My dad would have loved this."

He meant it, too. His father was always one for a gathering. Strangers, friends, or soon to be friends, it did not matter. He loved it all.

"Well, look who it is!" Deck's voice rose above the din and heads turned.

A draft of cool air wafted through the space replacing the heat for a second.

Riley ushered a group of kids into the balmy house. James studied them, smiling at the awkward pre-teen movements of the Brandt children. George, Shannon, and Danny entered with heads slumped staring at everyone and no one at once. They conveyed the classic look of boredom, trying to be inconspicuous and appear uninterested in their surroundings. In the years since he had seen them, the Brandt kids had turned from hellions into mirrors of their parents, each taking on various physical traits in some way or another. But it was clear, they were Luke and Riley's kids through and through.

Following right behind was a younger woman with piercing hazel eyes. James had not seen his sister Mar in years, and he grinned at her through the packed bodies.

"What the hell?" Michael interrupted the arrivals, hopping into the entryway and lifting his older sister in the air.

"Put me down, son of bitch!" Mar yelled, and her decidedly larger younger brother plopped her on the ground with a goofy smile painted on his face.

"How you doin', sis?" Michael asked, folding his arms across his chest. The room resumed its conversation as the family convened around the welcome mat.

Tears flowed freely down James's mother's face as she hugged her youngest daughter on the threshold of her newly adopted home.

"I know, Mom." Mar patted her mom's back gently as Michael pried her away. James hugged his sister, ignoring the question bouncing through his mind yet again about how long it had been since he had seen someone.

"You look great, Mar."

"You too. I hear about you though. Your crew is in a lot of bar stories around the Federation HQ."

"It's not all true," James replied, waving her off.

"The good parts are though," Deck interjected as he walked from the kitchen balancing a plate of Kevin's mini tacos. "Hi, I'm Deck. Pleasure to meet you." The scout held the plate out to Mar. "Mini taco?"

"Hi, Deck. And I'm sure they are," Mar said with a grin, plucking one of Kevin's creations from the plate.

"Whatever," James said, stepping back alongside Heather. "I'll tell you the truth some other time. In other news, this is Heather. Heather, this is my Federation faithful sister Mar."

The two shook hands as Mar winked at James. "Oh, I've heard about Heather. Nice to meet you. Welcome to the party."

"You too," Heather replied, grinning.

"You need more food." James's mom took her daughter by the shoulders and ushered her through the bodies in the tight space.

A tap on the shoulder interrupted James's thoughts, and he turned to find one of Croyton's nameless emissaries waiting by the door.

"The general would like to speak." Without waiting, the soldier left the room.

"I'll be back," James said, popping the cap off his beer.

"Don't agree to anything stupid."

Frigid air shocked James as he walked away from the wind barrier created by his mother's home.

Shadows grew longer and a deep orange sunset reflected off icy patches of snow covering the barren earth. A lone figure in a flak jacket watched as a litany of colors danced around Deerfield's mirrored surfaces.

James approached his old commander and admired the sun sparkling off the arena in its last act of the day.

"Last time I was here, that stadium was a wreck. Craters all over from our explosives trying to take out the Sentinel discs, smoke everywhere, bodies… It was a different scene." Croyton spoke with an air of tragedy, lost in history.

James had not known his former commander was there that day, but was unsurprised by the revelation. "I remember it well," James said, almost smelling the smoke as he took a sip from his beer, wishing he had chosen a warmer beverage.

"I'm sorry about your father."

"Thank you." James tread with care, not knowing what to expect. The commander he had known all those years ago would have already jumped to the point and would be walking away by now. This was new territory for them.

"I have a ship and crew that can get you across the sea. When you make landfall, wherever that is, you'll need to make it to Marrakesh most likely. It's one of the last free cities. If you can call it a city anymore," Croyton added, frustration and mystery underpinning his words. "Either way. My contacts will meet you. They'll get you into the BZ. Then it's up to you."

"Make it there?" James but held his tongue, suppressing the frustration mounting under the surface.

"It's a different world, James. The BZ has made sure of that. They've created borders in more ways than one. Those looms can do a lot, and they've been busy since their attack. Waterways are nearly impassable between our landmasses. The ship I'm putting you on is run by the only people in the world to make it through those waters, outside of the BZ's motherships. They'll get you there one way or another." Croyton's lack of clarity was common, and James filed his words away for later.

"Can we know who your contacts are?"

Croyton nodded slowly. "In time, yes. I want you all on that ship before I give anything over."

"Why's that? Don't explain the borders. We'll have to find our way to a city that may or may not still stand… Hell, it may not even be the city we need to find. Now we can't even know *who* we're meeting? Can't you give me a goddamn break?" James asked. His annoyance had overtaken his quest for inner patience. Croyton's reticence, a standard of their old relationship, had reared its ugly head and James had taken the bait.

"What can you tell me about those camps we found?" Croyton ignored his pleas for clarity entirely, and James shook his head.

"Come on. You're delaying the point. What do I need to know? I'm the one who's going into the storm. Give me something to work with." James glared at his old commander. His chest heaved from his outburst, and the mental scars from his training hung in the back of his mind.

Fear tinted the corners of Croyton's stoic gaze when he looked at James. He spoke with an earnest voice James had never heard before. "James, whatever Raspin was able to do with those

Exils is terrifying. I don't know how long those people had been controlled. I don't know if anyone else is being controlled by him right now.

"Corralling humans into groups of livestock is on target for a commander like Raspin. When we worked together in the past…" Croyton paused, and James hid his surprise. "Maybe things could have been different. I don't know. What I do know is if I can get you on a boat and across the ocean, you're probably safe. He wouldn't let you get that close to him otherwise. Until then, you'll have to trust me. I've known Edgar Raspin for a very long time and his ambition is boundless. His motivation is driven by winning this war. There are no limits to his actions."

"Deal." James nodded, and the aggravation mounting seconds earlier dissipated. James knew, in Raspin's eyes, that humanity was a monstrosity that needed fixing.

The two were quiet. Spices and hot cooking oil wafted through the air accompanied by the aroma of grilled meat. James's stomach growled. *I need to eat*, he thought, looking for the easiest way to leave.

"Anything else?" James asked, taking a step back in the direction of his mother's house.

"Everything lies on this James. You're the guy. Always have been. Stacie will take care of things here, but trust your instincts." Croyton looked him in the eye. "And kill Raspin if you get the chance. That's an order."

"Yessir," James replied.

Croyton held his hand out, and James shook the General's strong grip.

"Good luck."

With a curt nod and smooth flip of his heel, Croyton left James standing in the cold as his former commander left amidst a purple backdrop and darkness took over the day.

When he reentered the room, more people had joined. Caitlin sat talking with Mar and their mother walking back through the tunnel of time. Heather, Cristina, Bob, and Rich watched as Jon and Deck argued with one another about nonsense. Meanwhile, Kyle and Stacie flowed in and out of the room carrying trays of food from the steam-laden kitchen.

Someone bumped into James's back as more people filed in after him.

"My bad, James. It's a little tight in here I guess," Clint said, squeezing inside, followed closely by Dolly.

"James." Dolly nodded at him as he looked them over.

Their interaction was different, more conscious of each other and connected on a deeper level.

"Had stuff to take care of?" James asked with an amused grin on his lips.

"You could say that," Dolly said, elbowing James.

James bobbed his head in understanding. "Say no more."

"James! We were looking for you," Deck shouted from across the room, freezing all conversation and ending the argument he was having with Jon.

"Well, thanks, Deck. I'm right here," James said, embarrassed by the attention.

"We saw you talking to Croyton." Kevin's voice carried over the room and settled across the crowd. Eyes, originally dismissing Deck, turned to James, interested.

"What's the word?" Stacie asked. An empty tray hung at her side as the room waited for him to answer.

"Umm. I wasn't ready to… Well, I guess I…" James's heart beat quicker. He searched the room, his eyes landing on Heather who, as she had a few days prior, nodded with a slight grin.

"I'm not great at this sort of thing. Talking to groups, especially impromptu and all, but since this will be one of our last times together for a long time…" James finished his beer and placed the empty bottle on the coffee table. "The other day Croyton recounted the history of the war. Did a nice job of it actually, and it's important because it involved all of you. Ten years ago, everyone in this room lived through the biggest change in world history.

"For the better part of a decade, we've been fighting, reacting to the horrors thrown at us. We have watched the people we know and love fall to save the lives of their families." James glanced at Riley and his mother in turn, pulling on the strength hammered into their features. "We've watched innocence desecrated and witnessed the fall of civilization. Our fight has been about holding what we have. Striving to make it another day without losing what is ours.

"Now, we have a different fight. A new fight we've never waged before. One where we get to be the first to draw blood. To those who are joining me, we'll do our job in isolation and come home ready to finish things off on our turf. Stacie's got the fight handled here, supported by the best goddamn soldiers ever to walk the face of the Earth.

"But that all happens tomorrow." Cold glass connected with his palm. Danny Brandt disappeared into the crowd and popped up next to Deck who gave him a high five as the teenager took his place with his mother. "So, while we still have today and while we're all together in one, place let's enjoy the moment. Because tomorrow, we start the fight."

CHAPTER 26

"That's a different view, huh?"

James hung his elbows over the iron railing and stared at the open expanse of ocean. A constant wind blew a spray of mist matting his face with a dull sheen of sticky residue. He wiped his brow tasting the salt building on his lips from the air's natural film of open seawater.

"Very different." James nodded. He was still adjusting to their new situation and pushed from his mind thoughts of their friends waving goodbye from NOLA's docks a few days prior. "Beautiful though."

"Certainly is. I always wanted to go on a cruise, too. Not one of those big ones, but a more classy and cute bespoke ship. A yacht, if you will, and, well…" Deck turned back towards the steel monstrosity sitting on the water and shrugged. "This is not what I had in mind at all. But still, we're cruising!"

James grinned at his friend's ability to spin a situation in his favor, envying Deck's views.

"I'm glad you're enjoying yourself. How're you feeling, by the way? Motion has never been your friend."

"I'm an ocean person now, James. I am doing great." Deck spoke with ironclad confidence.

"Good to hear." James thought back to the buckets on their bus trip in the Chameleon when they headed to the southern federation. He hoped they would not be treated to another repeat on the high seas.

"What's going on here?" Heather materialized next to James along with Bob and Clint on the other side of Deck.

"Enjoying a brisk afternoon on the water. Feeling the freedom is all." Deck's voice grew solemn and pompous.

"Not puking in a bucket yet?" Clint asked, winking across at James.

"I'm better than that, thank you," Deck said as his back stiffened. "I'm more dignified on the open sea."

"Certainly aren't in the back of a bus…" Clint said.

Bob stifled a chuckle as Deck cast a side eye at their engineer, "If someone had been a bit more careful in their driving, some other people may ha—"

"All right, all right, we get it. Glad your tummy's okay, Deck," Heather said, grinning. "Any sign of these BZ protections yet?"

"No clue." James shrugged, and Heather leaned over the railing with him. A sense of perfect contentment washed over him as he stood at the railing of the ship with three of his best friends, a woman who changed the way he appreciated the world, and the rest of a new team.

"Hmm," Heather said, shading her eyes and looking into the distance. "I can't see anything either."

"It's probably all bullshit," Deck said, waving it off.

"It's not."

A shadow cast over the group, and James tipped his head against the sun to find the captain of their vessel standing on the upper deck.

Rough features and thick cords of hair pulled into a bun of fibrous strands defined the man who commanded their boat. His eyes were dark brown, and his hands had more scar tissue than skin. He pointed to the horizon at a spot James could not discern.

"The wind will start in a half hour. The waves come after that. Then, storms and any other surprises the BZ wants to throw our way."

The gruff, but sure nature of his voice demanded respect from the group, and Deck, in one of his rare silent moments, nodded. "Well, you would know best."

"I've crossed the channel twenty-six times. Never made it through with my whole crew intact."

Without another word, the captain turned and left.

James and the rest of the team eyed his exit, Janus left them with an acute awareness of their vulnerability on the water.

"He's quite the downer, huh?" Clint said as the team stood quietly.

"I was about to say," Deck replied.

The rest of the afternoon was spent talking about the ocean, the BZ, former training experiences, past missions, and the time before the fall of the Federation.

James's sense of contentment returned. His mind drifted to his father's letter and the woven turtle he kept in his rucksack, reminders of what he fought for and the warm feeling in his stomach that everything would turn out well blossomed again. It had been years since anything akin to positivity had graced his consciousness.

"Watch it!" Deck shouted. James glanced at the scout who was leaning over the edge of the boat spitting into the ocean.

"My bad," Bob said sheepishly, turning his back to the wind to avoid more of his weed from flying out of the bowl he was packing.

"That's lethal right there. A little more wind and that could have gotten into my eyes, Bob. We need these beauties, ya know," Deck said, scraping his tongue with his fingernails.

"Getting kinda rough," Clint said. The bulky mechanic angled his body against the drop of the deck, and James noticed that Clint's position in relation to the horizontal surface had changed.

Winds and waves start it all, James thought, remembering the captain's words.

The sea crested alongside the gate, barring them from falling in and a spray of mist dampened James's face as the boat's bow crashed into the wall of water.

James soaked in everything as the ship awoke.

Across the deck, crewmembers stirred into action. Sinewy arms bulged under toasted skin as their owners moved across the expanse of the boat with steady deliberation. Each donned a breathing apparatus consisting of tubes from their masks running down the back of their necks to tanks on the sides of their bodies. *We should get our hands on those*, James thought, making a note for later.

Looking around, James noticed how much the crew had accomplished in such a short amount of time. He had thought the deck was clear when they left the harbor, but now it was desolate. Anything not welded to the boat had been removed. Normally, the bridge was a grand spot in the middle of the ship with windows boasting three-hundred-sixty-degree views from which the pilot steered the ship. Now, iron curtains covered the glass, and the doors were bolted shut with steel girders.

"They take these storms seriously," Bob mentioned, surveying the activity through glassy eyes.

"I'll say. Glad I didn't put my drink down," Deck replied, taking a sip of his water. The scout tipped the water into his mouth as a rogue wave struck the ship, sending liquid splashing on his front. Deck grabbed the railing to steady himself and errant water dripped down his face. He looked ruefully at the water below, shaking his head. "I hate the ocean."

Another breaker sent James grasping for the rails as the ship reared, traveling up a steep mountain of seawater. At once the enormous wave blocked the sun from view, but just as suddenly came back in full radiance when they crested the top.

At this height James witnessed the ferocity of the ocean boiling beneath the surface. A valley of waves greeted his sight, ending in a dark torrent of clouds appearing as a blip in the distance. Even from across the sea, James detected patches of lightning illuminating the water with dangerous glints reflecting off the tops of waves higher than James's current station at the apex of the ocean.

"HOLD!" A shout alerted the team to grab onto the railing. The front of the ship tipped over the edge of the world and James's stomach flipped into a freefall. Water sped past his face, and the ship tunneled down the side of the water mountain gathering momentum as it fell. His feet struggled to keep their place on the deck

A sensation of pure freedom flooded James's veins. *This is flying,* he thought as his feet left the deck, suspended above the floor.

He glanced at his friends to find Clint enjoying the ride as much as he was. Deck's eyes were closed, and Bob seemed more amused than enthralled by the experience.

Heather poked James's side and pointed at the approaching ocean surface. "How the hell are we going to stop?"

James's stomach dropped back to earth, and the fleeting moment of happiness from flying down the wave evaporated as their imminent crash approached.

They were forty yards from the surface of the ocean. *They have to do something,* James thought glancing at the crew frantically.

Appearing calm as the torrent of wind rushed past their faces, their eyes mere slits, the deckhands hung onto holds buried along the walls of the boat's surface.

"Look!"

Clint pointed to the outer side of the ship. James dared to bend over the railing and saw a pair of short fins sticking out from the steel walls.

As the surface rapidly approached, the fins positioned themselves farther towards the front of the ship. At about ten yards from the surface, they sprung from the side, exploding in size, angling into the descent and slicing through the air. The ship caught itself on its newly sprouted wings and floated gracefully into the valley, rolling through the waves and carving a path of roiling water across the unsettled ocean.

"Now that was cool," Clint said, his eyes wide.

"It really was," Bob said, impressed.

Heather's calm smile impressed James as he checked on the fifth in their group who was uncharacteristically quiet.

"I hate the ocean," Deck repeated. His head hung between his arms, and his face was pale. He turned towards the center of the deck and, unable to stand, crawled to the entrance, lifted a weak hand, and knocked on the metal door.

The hold swung open to admit him and he slunk over the edge of the doorway. Teresa, her hair flowing wildly behind her shoulders, stepped over their seasick friend and into the open air. Liam followed along with Rhia, who was testing her bionic leg on the uneven deck.

"What's with him?" Teresa asked, pointing at Deck's feet disappearing inside the hold.

"Tummy hurts," James said with a grin that confused the stocky woman.

"Sucks for him. Lots more of that from what the captain told us," Teresa said. She took Deck's place on the railing as Liam and Rhia filled the space on the other side of Heather.

"He mentioned something to us, too. No specifics though. Just that he's never made it across with a crew intact."

"He told us something similar."

"Well, we'll need to be careful," James said, making a note to ask about those breathing devices sooner rather than later.

"So, what's the plan when we get there James? I mean, I know Croyton has contacts for us and all, but how do we find them?" Teresa kept her eyes trained on the fast-flowing ocean beneath them as she spoke.

"I'm not sure. I don't think we're supposed to know. He seemed more concerned about us getting there than anything else. That Exil worried him. I've never seen him like that." James had only spoken about his concerns privately with Heather, but they were gnawing at him. Croyton sounded as if he knew more about Raspin's tactics than he was letting on. That made James suspicious.

"That's not very good. Either way, we'll figure it out. He give us the names of the contacts?"

"Said the captain will tell us when we get there."

"Hmmm, that's odd."

James agreed and shrugged. "Not much else I can do."

"Hopefully we can trust these guys." Teresa glanced at the salt-hardened group of sailors moving effortlessly about the deck performing one chore after another in a series of steps foreign to James.

"Don't have any other choice," Heather chimed in from James's other side, and Teresa nodded as she stared at the sea.

"Relax, T! Enjoy the ride for a second," Liam shouted at his wife, eliciting a crooked smile from the commanding woman.

A gust of wind knocked into the group, and James lost his grip on the railing. The deck pitched backwards, and James's feet gave from under him. His body hurtled towards the steel hull. As he braced for impact, two sets of gruff salt-stained hands caught him, put him on his feet, and returned him to the railing. His saviors ensured his hands were in place before releasing him from their iron grasp on his shoulders.

"Like I said, never made it through with a full crew. Keep safe out here."

The captain and his accomplice disappeared. James's heart pounded in his chest.

Heather's hand touched the top of his in a silent check, and he squeezed back in response. The wind from the speed of the ship forced oxygen into his lungs, calming him.

Lightning reflected off the dark seas across the valley of waves. James's mind wandered to the task that lay ahead, and he gritted his teeth. He thought of the team members, family, and friends they had left to attempt the impossible. His hands gripped the steel railing as he glanced into the sun, boiling the seafoam, and leaned into the rise of another massive swell carrying him closer to nature's chaos.

He grinned as they reached the top of the wave, and the boat perched itself for a moment, teetering on the edge of the world, before they plunged into swirling turmoil.

GLOSSARY

Asian Republic – otherwise known as the BlankZone (BZ). The part of the world East of Europe that stopped responding to any interaction with the rest of the world after the Melt.

Bio-Medicine – devices and remedies that utilize advanced DNA synthesis to speed up and aid in the healing process.

Combat Suit – tactical uniform that is designed for use in battlefield situations. Multiple versions of combat suits exist with the newest versions containing highly elaborate camouflaging technology.

Deerfield – an independent city-state that operates entirely in isolation.

Emitter – a device used to support the display of a HOLO.

Exil – outlaw member of society found in the Federation. While there are some larger groups of Exils in the Federation most are independent bands of former Federation soldiers who survive by any means possible.

Federation of the Americas – the continental government organization comprised of every nation state in North and South America. Formed as a response to the Melt.

Forgotten World - an independent, pseudo-terrorist organization that is believed to have taken over the BlankZone.

HOLO – an acronym standing for Highly Operable Light Object. HOLOs have a wide range of capabilities and are used in telecommunications, visual representations, and have uses far beyond their current known abilities.

Ionic Weaponry – anti-Sentinel devices used by the Federation and NOLA soldiers.

Loom – terraforming devices created by the BlankZone to reshape the world to meet their needs.

Mag Key – a device that uses magnetic fields to lock objects.

The Melt – an event of unknown origin that separated the world and created a rift between the East and the West during a heightened period of global interaction.

Midway – newly formed city after the Melt that can be found along the East Coast of the Northern Federation in the Mid-Atlantic region.

NOLA – a semi-centralized fighting force based in New Orleans. Home base for many Federation soldiers who did not want to become Exils after the fall of the Federation. Many of the former recruits with James joined up and hunt Sentinels or are rented out to independent city-states for protection from the BlankZone.

Nomad – citizen members of the Federation who travel the land rather than attach themselves to a group.

Pulse Pillar – large ionic weapons erected in most Federation cities as defensive measures against Sentinel attacks.

Republic of New World Order – The official name of the BlankZone's nation.

Río Negro – town in the Southern Federation near the BlankZone border.

Roach – a small, automated video drone used for surveillance activities.

Sentinel – a defensive tool used by the BlankZone to protect its borders.

ACKNOWLEDGEMENTS

Each time that I write a book I am reminded by the tremendous amount of effort it takes to put something like this together. However, writing the story is not the hardest part. Editing, designing, formatting, printing, and marketing are all the pieces of becoming an author that no one ever tells you about. I consider myself incredible lucky to have found what I think is the best possible team to realizing my dream of becoming a writer.

As always, I cannot thank my editors enough when it comes to helping my writing. If anyone were to read the early drafts of this book or any others that I have written they would likely worry about my ability to tie my shoes let alone write a book. They would then summarily throw that book in the roaring fire that they were planning to sit before while reading and stare into the flames for the rest of the night likely damaging their eyesight. At least that's what I imagine would happen.

Hannah and Meghan (otherwise known as my Mom) take what I write and make it readable. This story is absolutely nothing without their meticulous attention to detail and ability to refine my words into the story I want to tell. Hours upon hours are spent going over every single line of this book, and I cannot thank them enough for everything they have done.

My graphics designer Daniel once again created a cover that I have zero ability to do otherwise. I truly believe there are things that artificial intelligence does not have the ability to do and Daniel has proved that every time I work with him. He took a loose idea that I had for the cover and turned it into something that I am so proud to put on the front of my story.

Finally, my wife Alexa. I have said this hundreds of times in writing, in interviews, in person, and to anyone who will listen, I would not have chosen to become an independent author if it was not for her. Not just because she is an incredible marketing professional, but because she is the backbone of our team. It is not easy to sit down and write every night, but when you have someone in your life like her, dreams can become a reality.

I know I said finally at the beginning of the last chapter, but there are two more groups I really need to thank. First off, my parents to whom I dedicated this book. I was afforded an amazing childhood that allowed me to escape to places in my imagination and for that I am forever grateful to the two of them. I don't believe many people get that luxury in life and it has not gone unnoticed.

Second, I want to thank you. Yes, you the person reading this line, and hopefully the person who read this book and liked it so much you kept reading all the way to this point in hopes there's another part to the story. I'm sorry to say that you will have to wait until next year for part four of Crafting Humanity, but I cannot thank you enough for reading the book. Whether you loved it or hated it, I am so happy that you took the time out of your busy day to sit down and escape into my imaginary world. Your feedback and reviews online have pushed me to try and write better and better every time I sit down in front of my computer so thank you. As I said before, it is an honor to be chosen by you.